THE
HAND
THAT
FEEDS YOU

A.J. RICH

SCRIBNER

NEW YORK   LONDON   TORONTO   SYDNEY   NEW DELHI

Scribner
An Imprint of Simon & Schuster, Inc.
1230 Avenue of the Americas
New York, NY 10020

First Scribner hardcover edition July 2015

SCRIBNER and design are registered trademarks of The Gale Group, Inc.,
used under license by Simon & Schuster, Inc., the publisher of this work.

For information about special discounts for bulk purchases, please contact Simon
& Schuster Special Sales at 1-866-506-1949 or business@simonandschuster.com.

The Simon & Schuster Speakers Bureau can bring authors to your live event.
For more information or to book an event, contact the Simon & Schuster Speakers
Bureau at 1-866-248-3049 or visit our website at www.simonspeakers.com.

Interior design by Akasha Archer

Manufactured in the United States of America

10 9 8 7 6 5 4 3 2 1

Library of Congress Control Number: 2014040858

ISBN 978-1-4767-7458-9
ISBN 978-1-4767-7460-2 (ebook)

In memory of Katherine Russell Rich

*Who would not tremble to think of the ills
that may be caused by one dangerous liaison!*

—PIERRE CHODERLOS DE LACLOS,

DANGEROUS LIAISONS

THE
HAND
THAT
FEEDS YOU

Yes or no:

☐ I want everyone to be happy.

☐ I know what people need without their having to ask me.

☐ I have given blood.

☐ I would donate a kidney to save a close friend's life.

☐ I would donate a kidney to save a stranger's life.

☐ I generally appear sincere.

☐ I give more than I receive.

☐ People take advantage of me.

☐ People should generally be forgiven.

Today I would not answer any of these questions the way I did a year ago. And I'm the one who wrote the test. I was going to be the person who changed the definition of a predator by identifying what makes a victim. The test: it was part of my master's thesis in forensic psychology at John Jay College of Criminal Justice. A philosopher once said, "The threshold is the place to pause." I was on the threshold of having everything I wanted.

Here is the question I would ask today:

Can I forgive myself?

The lecture had been about victimology. Does a symbiotic quirk in the brain of the abuser also exist in the emotional makeup of the victim? The model the professor used was battered woman syndrome, a syndrome that the professor pointed out appears nowhere in the *Diagnostic and Statistical Manual of Mental Disorders* (*DSM-5*), but does appear in criminal statutes. Why? I thought I had the answer.

The morning had galvanized me; I couldn't wait to get home and back to my research. I felt a little guilty about wanting my place to myself again so I stopped at Fortunato Brothers and bought Bennett a bag of pignoli cookies.

My apartment was on the top floor of a clapboard row house in Williamsburg, Brooklyn. I didn't live with the hipsters; my block was old-world. Italian women perpetually swept their sidewalks, and retired wiseguys played chess at Fortunato's. At a headstone store a block away they also sold loaves of bread. Bennett called it Breadstone. Rumor was the man who ran it used to work for one of the big mob families. His crew, no one under eighty, sat out front on plastic chairs smoking cigars. The ice-cream truck played the theme from *The Godfather*. There was a saying: "It's not HBO, it's our neighborhood."

Sixty-eight steps spiraled to my front door. As I climbed, I smelled the ethnic potpourri: sizzling garlic on the first landing, then boiling cabbage on the second, then frying chorizo, and finally my floor, where I never cooked anything.

The door was open. Bennett must have gone out and forgotten to jiggle the broken knob as I'd asked him to. The dogs could have gotten out. I had three: Cloud, a Great Pyrenees that I called the Great White Canvas, and Chester and George, two goofy, needy pit-bull mixes that I fostered. The dogs were the only bone of contention between Bennett and me. He wanted me to stop trying to rescue every stray at the expense of my work, but I suspected he really couldn't bear dog hair on his sweaters. Bennett was always cold, even in summer. He claimed he had Raynaud's syndrome, in which the veins in one's extremities constrict, resulting in cold hands and feet. Bennett feared the advanced form in which one's fingers and toes can atrophy. But his hands were never cold on my skin. By contrast, I ran hot. I was the first to wear sandals in spring, I never wore a scarf, I never caught a chill in air-conditioning. This was not because I carried any bulk.

As I shouldered open my front door against the delirious, wagging greeting waiting for me on the other side, I noticed rose petals strewn across the foyer. Had Bennett scattered them? It seemed cheesy, unlike him. A man who remembers everything you tell him doesn't need to resort to a cliché. Bennett saw and understood me in a way I'd not known before. It wasn't just paying attention, it was that he knew before I did what I would want, whether it was on a menu or a screen or a disc. Of course, this knowledge extended into the bedroom.

I bent to pick up some of the petals and saw that they were paw prints. So: not a tired romantic gesture after all. What now appeared to be an abstract floral stencil across the hardwood floor led all the way to the bedroom. The fosters, Chester and George, had gotten into the garbage? Dogs track leftover puttanesca sauce throughout an apartment—another cliché I rejected. Chester and George were gentlemen, though Bennett was irritated by the half-chewed bones they left strewn about the apartment. His tripping over bones and squeaky toys was another reason he wanted me to find them a permanent home or give them back to the East Harlem Animal Shelter I'd rescued them from. A donation I had made to a local animal-rescue organization had apparently landed me on a mass e-mail list, and ever since I'd received near-daily photos and profiles of dogs with hours to live if I did not take action.

The pit bulls, Chester and George, had been on death row, waiting to be euthanized. In the photo they leaned in to each other and each extended a paw in greeting. It was more than I could resist. When I went to the shelter, their kennel cards identified them as "no concern." A kennel worker told me that meant the best temperament of all. They'd done nothing to anyone except give love and want it in return. I filled out the paperwork, paid two adoption fees intending only to foster, and the next day, Cloud and I picked them up in a Zipcar.

Bennett couldn't tolerate the constant chaos of three big dogs in a small apartment, and maybe he was right, the dogs *were* taking over my life. Were these rescues a form of pathological altruism? This was the basis of my research, a test to identify victims whose selflessness and hyper-empathy were so extreme that they attracted predators.

Bennett needed order to function, while I needed messy, lovable bedlam. When he visited from Montreal, he hung his oxford-cloth shirts and chinos, while I left my leggings, vegan-leather vest, and layers of tank tops crumpled on the bed. He emptied the dishwasher he had filled and run, while I left my dirty dishes in the sink. Hardest for me, he didn't like the dogs sleeping on the bed with us. He didn't like the dogs and they knew it. Dogs do. They obeyed, but Bennett gave his commands more harshly than was necessary. I had told him so more than once. How were we all going to live together?

Cloud was the first to reach me. She used her bear size to muscle out the boys. She not only failed to greet me in her normal exuberant way by putting her giant paws on my shoulders, she was clearly agitated and frightened. Her ears were flat against her head and she circled at my feet. One side of her looked as though she had leaned against a freshly painted wall. But I hadn't painted, and if I had, I would not have chosen red.

I dropped to my knees and parted the wet fur looking for puncture wounds, but no wounds were on her skin and the color didn't reach her undercoat anyway. I apologized to Chester and George for my unwarranted suspicions. Luckily I was already on my knees or I might have toppled with the first wave of vertigo. I automatically began examining Chester and George for the source of the blood. My heart was racing. And a fresh wave of vertigo came over me. They, too, had no wounds. I lowered my head to keep myself from passing out.

"Bennett?" I called. I pushed Chester off me as he licked the blood from my hands.

I saw that my new couch, a present from my older brother, Steven, for exiting my twenties and embracing adulthood, was stained. I tried to gather up the dogs, but they kept circling me, making it hard to move toward the bedroom. My apartment was a railroad design, narrow and long, each room opening off the hallway. You could shoot a bullet through and not hit a wall. I could see the bottom half of the bed from where I stood in the living room. I could see Bennett's leg.

"What happened to the dogs?" I asked.

As I walked down the hall, the red smears lengthened.

Bennett was lying on the bedroom floor facedown, while his leg remained on the bed. Then I saw that the two parts weren't connected. My first thought was to save him from drowning in his own blood, but when I fell to my knees, I could see he wasn't facedown. He was looking up, or he would have been if he still had eyes to see. For a moment, illogically, I held fast to the hope that it wasn't Bennett. Maybe an intruder had broken in and the dogs had attacked him. Even in my shock, enough of my training allowed me to know that the killer wasn't human. The blood spatter had no pattern of emotion. I had enough forensic experience to know what I was seeing. Blood-pattern analysis is more accurate than one might expect. It tells you the type of injury, the order in which the wounds were received, the type of weapon that caused the injuries, whether the victim was in motion or lying still when the injuries were inflicted. The injuries here were puncture wounds and mauling. Bennett's hands were degloved, meaning the skin was stripped off when he tried to fight back. His right leg had been torn off at the knee. The "weapon" had been an animal or animals. The wounds were jagged, not the straight lines of a blade, and whole chunks of flesh were missing. The smears of blood indicated that he had been dragged across the bedroom floor. The right foot and lower leg must have been carried onto the bed after he was attacked. Arterial spray was over the headboard and the wall behind it, probably from his carotid artery.

I could hear my dogs panting behind me, waiting to take their cue as to what we would do next. I tried to tamp down the terror. I summoned as calm a voice as I could and told the dogs to stay. I put them into a down-stay. Then I was aware of a new smell crowding out the smell of blood. It seemed to be emanating from me. I stood up slowly and moved in slow motion around the dogs. Cloud rose and would have followed me if I hadn't again given the command to stay. Chester and George's full attention was on me though they didn't move even as I continued toward the bathroom. I finally reached it and slammed the door behind me, throwing my weight against it in case they lunged after me. I heard whimpering on the other side.

I wasn't yet in shock. That would come soon enough. I was still in the nether state of tearful gratitude that I'd survived. Strangely, I felt heady, as though I had just won a big prize. And I had—my life. But that intoxication lasted only a few seconds. I rallied from this odd trance and knew I had to call an ambulance. He could not have been alive, but what if I was wrong? What if he was suffering? My cell was inside my purse, which I had left with the keys on the mantel. Then I heard the sound of paper crackling and tearing and remembered the bag of cookies. I must have dropped them, and now the dogs had found them. I slowly opened the door and bypassed the bedroom to retrieve my purse. How long would it take them to dispatch the cookies? I was all adrenaline as I checked my impulse to dart for safety; instead I grabbed my purse, never taking my eyes off the dogs. Finally I was back inside the bathroom, secured behind a locked door. I got into the empty bathtub, as if the old claw-foot iron tub would protect me, and pressed 911. It took me two times. When the operator asked what my emergency was, I couldn't answer. I couldn't even scream.

"Are you in any present danger?" It was a mature-sounding female voice.

I nodded wildly.

"I'll take your silence as an affirmative. Can you tell me where you are?"

"In the bathroom." I whispered my address.

"The police are on their way. I'll stay with you on the phone. Is there an intruder in your house?"

I could hear the dogs outside the bathroom door. The earlier whimpering had escalated. Now they were whining and pawing at the door to be let in.

I didn't respond.

"If there is an intruder in your house, tap your finger once on the mouthpiece."

I tapped three times.

"Are weapons involved? Tap once."

I tapped the receiver once.

"More than one weapon?"

I tapped again.

"Firearms?"

I shook my head no and set down the phone in the empty tub. The operator still spoke to me but she was far away. The shaking of my head—no, no, no—had given me the same comfort as being rocked.

One of the dogs howled with the approaching siren. Cloud. It used to make me laugh when she joined in the urban version of a wolf pack, as if pampered Cloud, whose teeth I brushed every week, had even a mote of beast in her. Now her howl terrified me.

"The police have arrived," said the tiny voice coming from the phone on the bottom of the tub. "Tap once if the perpetrators are still inside."

The dogs barked at the approaching footsteps, at the hand trying the front door to see if it was unlocked.

"Police! Open up!"

I tried shouting to them, but the only sound I could make was an infinitesimal moan, tinier than the voice that kept asking me if the perpetrators were inside. The only answer the police heard was barking.

"NYPD! Open the door!"

The barking continued.

"Call Animal Control!" I heard one of the policemen shout.

The next sound was the door breaking open and a single deafening shot. The whimper that followed was as mournful as a human cry. The other two dogs stopped barking.

"Good dogs, that's a good dog," one of the policemen said.

"I think this one is dead."

The footsteps approached cautiously.

"Oh, shit, oh, Jesus," the other one said.

I could hear him retch.

The bathroom door burst open and a young policeman found me cowering in the empty tub.

He squatted beside me. I could smell his sour breath from when he retched a moment ago.

"Are you hurt?"

My legs were drawn under me, my face tucked against my knees, my hands locked behind my head.

"An ambulance is on its way. Listen, we need to see if you're bleeding." He gently set his hand on my back and I screamed. "Okay, okay, no one is going to hurt you."

I remained frozen in that tucked pose, the same position that schoolchildren assumed during a drop drill to protect themselves from a nuclear blast. I would learn later that one of the symptoms of acute stress disorder was rigid immobility.

"Animal Control is here," the other cop said.

The ambulance must have arrived at the same time because a male paramedic took my pulse while a female checked me for wounds. I remained crouched in the tub.

"I don't think the blood is hers, but I can't get a visual on the abdomen," said the female. "I'll start an IV. This is going to pinch, honey."

A knitting needle jabbed my left hand. I screamed so loudly that the dogs began barking again, only two now.

"We're going to give you something to help you relax so we can check you for wounds."

A black heat began to creep up my arm, as if someone had put a warm glove on my hand. Then the blackness expanded until it was big enough for me to climb in, a merciful black bag in which to disappear.

"We need to ask her some questions. Can she talk?" asked one of the policemen.

"She's in shock."

"Is your name Morgan Prager?"

I tried to nod, but the black bag was too tight.

"Can you tell us who was in the apartment with you? We can't find any identification on the deceased."

"Can she hear us?" the other officer asked.

I was lifted onto a gurney and rolled through my apartment. I opened my eyes as we passed the bedroom. Now the scene confused rather than terrified me. "What happened?" I asked in my new, small voice.

"Don't look," said the female.

But I did look. No one was attending to Bennett. "Is he suffering?" I heard myself ask.

"No, honey, he's not suffering."

Just before I was carried downstairs, I saw Chester's body on the foyer floor. Why did they shoot him? Cloud and George were each in an Animal Control crate labeled DANGEROUS DOG.

•   •   •

The doctors found no wounds on me, nothing physical to explain my rigid immobility, my muteness, except for the occasional scream when anyone came near me. For my own safety, they issued an NY-code section 9.27: Involuntary admission on medical certification.

True or false:

☐ You have experienced or witnessed a life-threatening event that caused intense fear, helplessness, or horror.

☐ You reexperience the event in dreams.

☐ You relive the event while awake.

☐ You have thoughts of killing yourself.

☐ You have thoughts of killing others.

☐ You understand you are in a psychiatric hospital.

☐ You know why you are here.

☐ You feel responsible for the event.

I knew this well-meaning psychiatrist, who introduced herself as Cilla, was asking the time-honored questions necessary to evaluate my state of mind, but the questions I needed answered were not among them.

She was watching me with serene curiosity. "You don't have to talk to me right now, or answer these questions." She opened her desk drawer, slid the test back in, and took out some Nicorette gum. "I'm as addicted to this as I was to cigarettes." She looked to be in her early fifties with unfussy hair kept off her face with a tortoiseshell barrette. She poured herself a cup of coffee and reached for a second cup from atop the credenza. "What do you take in yours?" She took a carton of milk from the minifridge and started pouring. "Say when."

I held my hand up.

"Sugar?"

"Is what I remember true?" These were the first words I'd spoken in six days.

"What is it you remember?"

"My fiancé is dead. I found him in the bedroom. He'd been attacked by my dogs."

The psychiatrist waited for me to go on.

"I knew he was dead before I called the ambulance. I hid in the bathtub until help came. A cop shot one of my dogs." I couldn't meet her eyes. "It's my fault."

"You were in shock when you were brought in, but your memory was not impaired. Were you able to sleep last night? Are you eating?"

I said no to both questions. I would say no to any question about normalcy. I would never experience "normal" again. How could I unsee what I'd seen? What else was there to see?

"I understand that your pain is immeasurable, and I can give you something to sleep right now, but I cannot medicate against grief. Mourning is not an illness."

"Can you give me something for guilt?"

"You might feel guilty because guilt is more endurable than grief."

"What do I do?"

"You're doing it. You're talking to me. That's the first thing you can do."

"Talking won't change the facts."

"You're right, but we're not here to change the facts."

"He's dead. I want to know what happened to my dogs."

"The dogs are evidence. They're being held by the Department of Health."

"Are they going to be killed?"

"What do you think should happen to them?"

Cloud never hurt anyone. I had had her since she was eight weeks old. What could have set off the pit bulls? They had slept in my bed for two months. They even slept in the bed when Bennett visited. Though the first couple of times I had to remove Chester for resources guarding—I was the resource he was guarding. But maybe Bennett had physically threatened him? The attack on him was full-out. Bennett was unidentifiable.

"I want to know what happened to Bennett's body. Have his parents arranged a funeral?"

"The police still haven't been able to locate them."

"He said his parents live in a small village in Quebec."

"Was Bennett visiting from Quebec?"

"He lived in Montreal."

"Your brother told me he had never met Bennett."

"You talked to Steven?"

"Doesn't Steven live near you?" Cilla asked.

"We had so little time together, Bennett only wanted to see me."

"Did you ever visit him in Montreal?"

"He wanted me to, he gave me a key, but it just ended up being easier for him to come here."

"How did you meet?"

"I was doing research for my thesis in forensic psychology."

After six days of not speaking a word during our daily sessions, I still wasn't ready to tell her that I had met him while testing a theory about female victims of sexual predators online. I'd come up with five profiles for women who were at particular risk: the Pleaser, the Rebound, the Damaged, the Sitting Duck, and the Accommodator. I posted them on various dating sites. I also created a control persona—a shy, earnest, workaholic do-gooder, who could laugh at herself and liked sex—in other words: me. Bennett's first e-mail put him in the men's control group of regular guys. Unlike the other "regular guys," whose responses were more like résumés sent to a headhunter for a six-figure job, Bennett was curious about me—what books I read, what music I listened to, where I was most myself. I felt fraudulent until, our exchanges escalating, I had no choice. But when I told him what I was really doing online, instead of being angry or hurt, he was fascinated. He asked me countless questions about my work, and I was flattered by his interest, more than flattered.

His interest in my work opened up another arena in which our minds met. His enthusiasm for my ideas surpassed that of my classmates, including the hot Dominican cop I dated for a while. If anything, Bennett's interest turned a little obsessive. One afternoon I found him reading a response to my Hotmail account, the one I'd set up for my study. The author was someone I deemed a sexual deviant, though I wasn't yet sure if he was a predator. When I asked Bennett what he was doing, he said, "You left it open, I was curious. I notice this guy always refers to himself in the third person. Is that characteristic?" I hadn't even realized this respondent did that; not only did that realization scotch my discomfort with Bennett's presumptuous behavior, it underscored the quality of his attention when it came to my research. Once again he had helped me. And this thought occurred to me: I could neither apologize nor thank him. Despair owned me again.

"When am I going to get out?"

"The involuntary admission was over three days ago," Cilla said. "Your stay at this point is voluntary."

"Do I have to leave?"

•   •   •

Odd that I had an erotic dream while I was in a psych ward. Or maybe not.

"Tell me what feels better," Bennett had said in the dream. He kissed my lips, then he pulled my hair so hard it hurt.

I surprised myself by saying, "My hair."

He stroked my inner thigh and then bit it. Again he asked me what felt better.

"The bite."

Bennett said, "Good girl," then licked my cheek like a dog.

He told me to roll over, and in the dream I felt him enter me twice at the same time. How was this possible?

"What feels better?"

"I can't choose," I said, and he continued like two men at once.

When I told Cilla about the dream during our next session, she said it was not unusual for grief to spark feelings of a sexual nature, that my body was bereft as well as my psyche. She said that sex, even in a dream, is life affirming.

The hands of other men were agile and teasing; Bennett's touch was assured. He would begin his touch at a point on my body that made the caress feel infinite. And the pressure was never timid—it was the same pressure a sculptor used to mold wet clay.

On our first date, we rented just one room at the Old Orchard Beach Inn in Old Orchard Beach, Maine.

We agreed that our first in-person meeting would be in the privacy of the room. I was surprised to find that I felt shy, having looked forward to this for a month. We also agreed that Bennett would already be in the room waiting for me. At that moment I wished we had planned instead to meet in public, somewhere we might be able to do something—a boat ride, a tour, anything but face each other in a small room with a large bed. Before Bennett I had only been with boys. It didn't matter what age they were, boys were randy, fun, fast, dangerous, selfish, and hot, but they were not confident. I had barely opened the door when Bennett firmly took my wrist and pulled me in. I saw a man who was not conventionally handsome. And I knew instantly that it didn't matter. His features were not symmetrical—one side of his mouth turned down slightly. His complexion betrayed a case of teenaged acne. His long-lashed, blue eyes were especially clear, set in the roughened skin. What would have detracted from another man's looks here contributed to the draw that the young Tommy Lee Jones exerted on women. The power was kinetic: his movements were languid.

His kiss was slow. He sensed when to break away.

And when to resume.

He was holding my face as he kissed me. I held fast to the back of his neck. Women are raised to prize the tall man, but Bennett was no more than five-eight, and I liked the way we fit. I was glad he wore no fragrance; he smelled like clean lake water.

We fell onto the bed and he pulled me closer, but not, this time, by my wrist. What annulled my shyness was his desire for me. When he told me I was more beautiful in person, I believed him. I no longer felt inhibited; it was as though his confidence had transferred to me. I helped him unbutton my blouse; there was no clasp to fumble with as I had worn a silk camisole. He lifted it over my head. He took his time. He took my hand and placed it on his erection. He lifted my hand and kissed the palm. He took

each of my fingers in his mouth for a moment. He got on his
knees, still fully dressed in jeans and a white shirt, and removed
the rest of my clothes. He brushed his chin across me and kissed
my inner thighs. I wanted him, but I took my cue from his lead.
He was in no rush and neither was I. He had me lie back on the
bed and spread my legs, and he put his tongue inside me. None of
the boys had done this, not like this. The speed with which I came
embarrassed me until I saw the pleasure it had given him. He
stood up and now I was the one to kneel. He was wearing an old
pair of button-front Levi's. I undid the buttons, feeling his erection. I leaned over and brushed my breasts against it.

"Come here," he said.

He put a finger inside me and kissed my throat when he felt
how ready for him I was. He made me wait a few seconds more.
His movements had authority. He understood that there was
power in stillness, and excitement in the pause.

"Come here," he said again.

My Bellevue roommate was a Sarah Lawrence freshman who
had tried to commit suicide by stuffing her mouth with toilet
paper. "I'd drunk all my daddy's liquor and taken all my grandmother's pills, but nothing was working," she told me. Our
room was not unlike a standard college dorm room, except the
windows were made of impact glass and the "mirror" in the bathroom was stainless steel. Closing our door didn't give us privacy;
in the porthole-shaped view of the hallway the lights never went
out. My roommate, Jody, told me that Cilla, our shared psychiatrist, had once been a backup singer for Lou Reed. Jody's life
outside, whatever it had been, had aged her beyond her eighteen

years, and the heavy kohl lining her eyes didn't help. The admitting staff had made her remove her facial studs, and a row of tiny piercings punctuated her lower lip.

By contrast, Cilla wore no makeup, but she still looked younger than I imagined she was. Her unlined face was as calming as her benevolent gaze. It must have taken a conscious effort to perfect that expression—neutral, nonjudgmental, as if she were looking at a patient, not a woman responsible for her fiancé's death. I had tried for that expression when I met weekly with the Internet scammers and public exhibitionists at Rikers as part of my training.

I sat on her sofa while she sat on a wing chair with an orthopedic cushion. I pictured her back in the day: black leather pants, platform shoes, singing behind the coolest rocker in New York.

She took out her pack of Nicorette gum. "Do you mind?"

The bare, institutional office was painted in soothing earth tones. An orange-and-sienna color-field painting hung behind her desk, the kind of abstract art once considered radical that now graced every therapist's wall. The painting was the only note of bright color.

"You look like you got some rest last night."

"If you call nightmares restful."

"I can increase your Ambien."

"There is no dosage that will bring me any peace."

"Maybe peace isn't the goal just yet."

"Then what are we doing here?"

"Tell me the last time you felt at peace."

I didn't have to coax the memory: it was late June, Bennett's and my first weekend together. We met again between Montreal and Brooklyn, at an old-fashioned B&B in Bar Harbor that Bennett had found. He drove down and I took the bus up. We were kayaking parallel to the shoreline when a moose came out of the woods. The antlers must have spanned twelve feet— half-animal, half-tree. I'd never seen a creature more majestic. Bennett and I shared a moment of awe, neither needing to say anything.

"What's making you cry?" Cilla asked.

"I was with him."

She offered the requisite box of tissue, but I chose not to take one.

"I destroyed what I loved. Can you find the right dosage for me to accept that?"

She said nothing. What was there to say?

"And here's how twisted I am. I miss my dogs."

She looked at me with that neutral, still gaze, as though challenging me to find a way to crack it.

"Sometimes I feel as guilty about Cloud as I do about Bennett. Why did I take in those fosters?"

"You were trying to be kind."

"Was I? This wasn't the first time."

"You took in fosters before?"

"Hoarders use animals to self-medicate."

"Do you consider yourself a hoarder?"

"The potential is there. I was the kid who brought home every stray cat and dog, every featherless baby bird who fell out of a nest. You know what? Those baby birds were diseased. That's why their mothers threw them out in the first place. I brought one home and it ended up killing my beloved parakeet."

"Should people stop being kind because of unforeseeable consequences?"

I reached for a Kleenex from the box on the low table between us, though I didn't need it; I wasn't crying, I just wanted to crush something with my hands.

"Was Bennett's death unforeseeable?" I asked. "What about the mother of a newborn who keeps a pet python? What about a woman who takes in her evicted boyfriend and then doesn't believe what her daughter says he does to her?"

"Is that the kind of predator you study?"

"I study victims."

I finally told her how I met Bennett. He was the control subject I'd been looking for. *Yes or no. He would rather be right than happy. He often feels challenged. He enjoys feeling protective of women. He enjoys feeling powerful with women. Women lie to him.* On all criteria, Bennett fit the type B personality, the nonaggressive male, the type of guy your mother wants you to marry. I never went for men my mother approved of. That's why his charming response to my online persona caught me off guard. The e-mail wasn't flirty. He didn't use the computer screen as a mirror to primp in. He didn't use *I* once in his first response. I count *I*'s. The average male responder uses it nineteen times in the introductory e-mail. *You* normally appears less than three times. Bennett's e-mail was in the form of a questionnaire. What book would you not take to a desert island? What's your favorite-sounding word in the English language? Do you like animals more than people? What song makes you cry but you're ashamed to admit it? Where would you not take a vacation? Do you think numbers radiate color?

"Do you think Bennett was your victim?" she asked.

Why did he have to be? I could not get past the why of it. The pitties had not threatened him, except for Chester's initial behavior protecting me. Bennett had not been afraid of them, he said, but he did make a point of telling me about the time Chester had snarled at him when he tried to remove the frozen marrow bones I had left for the dogs. Bennett wasn't an animal lover, but there was provisional acceptance. How had he treated them when I wasn't there?

"Why did you choose to study victimology?" Cilla asked.

"I think it chose me."

Victims become survivors only after the fact. How is a victim chosen?

Say five schoolgirls are leaving a playground. The predator is sitting in his car across the street. His method of selection in no way resembles a wolf pack choosing a lame elk, or does it?

He studies the gaits of each of the girls, how her dominant personality trait—shy, brazen, alert, dreamy—determines her carriage and stride. He will hold back from choosing his victim until one that meets his needs comes along. The first girl to leave skips as she walks: me as a schoolgirl. She would be an easy choice, but this particular predator doesn't want a "skipper." Skippers, it turns out, make troublesome prey. They fight back. The second girl who catches his eye is flanked by laughing friends, and although she is his type, he doesn't want to work that hard to separate her and risk failing. The third girl is yelling into her smartphone, and the fourth possibility is dressed too mannishly for his taste. The fifth girl is slightly overweight and twists a hank of her bangs as she walks. Most of her face is hidden behind her hair, a reliable sign of low self-esteem and emotional withdrawal. The "twister" never fights back. She already knows she's a victim; if not now, some other time. He won't have to bother to charm her. Does the wolf have to charm the lame elk?

The *method of approach* is a term that refers to the offender's way of getting close to his victim. It provides clues about the offender, such as his social skills, physical build, and ability to manipulate. The three general methods of approach are the con, the surprise, and the blitz. The con describes someone who deceives a victim into believing he needs help—think Ted Bundy with the cast on his arm, asking young women to help him get something from his windowless van. The surprise is someone who lies in wait, then quickly subdues that person—think slasher under the car waiting for women to finish shopping and unlock their minivan, his target the Achilles tendon so his intended victim cannot run away. The blitz requires rapid and excessive use of force to quickly overcome the victim's defenses—think home invasion in which anyone unlucky enough to be there is swiftly killed or raped and killed.

Risk assessment refers to the likelihood of a particular person's becoming a victim. Victim risk is broken into three basic levels: low risk, medium risk, high risk. These ratings are based on their personal, professional, and social lives. The prostitute is the obvious example of a person at high risk: exposed to a large number of strangers, often in contact with drug users, often alone at night, and unlikely to be missed. A low-risk victim has a steady job, lots of friends, and an unpredictable schedule.

But what if there was a different kind of risk factor, the risk of being too trusting, not because of gullibility, but because of compassion. What about the little girl who is lured into the predator's car because he asks her to help him find a lost kitten?

This is how it works for humans.

I studied under a psychiatrist who allowed his patients to bring their dogs to sessions. He told me about one patient who arrived with her well-behaved shepherd mix who remained in a down-stay at her feet even while she waved her arms to make her agitated points with considerable drama. But another patient, on antipsychotic meds, sat uncommonly still beside his Gordon setter, speaking in a calm monotone, and *his* dog got up and paced nervously in the office, even growling low and showing flattened ears. The point? That dogs can differentiate between neurotic behavior and behavior that is truly a threat.

Did Bennett threaten the dogs?

Cilla helped me compose a condolence letter to Bennett's parents. Bennett had shown me a picture of them. His old father was playing a button accordion in a farm kitchen while his mother danced in her apron. When Cilla asked me what he had told me about them, what I recalled was generic. He offered little and I wished I had asked more about them. Cilla advised me not to make the letter about *my* loss.

My brother, Steven, asked one of his law firm's investigators to ferret out an address for them since the police weren't able to find one: M. Jean-Pierre and Mme. Marie Vaux-Trudeau in Saint-Elzéar, Quebec, a town of less than three thousand.

"The parents don't exist," Steven told me when he next came to visit me in Bellevue. I was beginning my second week there and he had been coming almost every night. We sat on plastic chairs in the common room while on television *Happily Never After* was on the Investigation Discovery channel. Imagine filling an entire season with stories about spouses who killed each other . . . *on their honeymoon.* My roommate, Jody, had tagged along, knowing Steven always brought chocolate. She sported her earbuds to give us privacy, but I saw her turn off the sound.

"You mean your investigator couldn't find them," I corrected him.

"Next time, Steve," Jody interrupted, "could you get the kind with bacon bits and salt?"

"Bacon in chocolate?" Steven said.

"Maybe I spelled their last name wrong," I said.

"My guy checked every derivation. There is no one by that name in Saint-Elzéar."

"Maybe I got the town wrong."

"He checked all over."

"They have to be somewhere. Someone has to tell them their son is dead."

"I had my guy check the town's records for Bennett's birth certificate. No one by his name ever lived there."

"I didn't ask you to check on Bennett."

"I wasn't checking on Bennett, I was trying to find his parents for you."

I knew my brother better than anyone else. We'd been inseparable as kids, and fiercely protective of each other, a pattern often found in the children of a manic-depressive. When our father was depressed, he ignored Steven, and when our father was manic, he attacked him. Bipolar disease is one of the rare instances where a predator and a victim can occupy the same body at the same time. It makes for an unfair fight.

"Do you want my guy to keep looking for Bennett's parents?" Steven asked.

"Of course I do."

After Steven left, Jody worked on her chocolate. "My creative-writing teacher at Sarah Lawrence had the same thing happen to her. She met this English guy online and fell in love."

"Why would your professor tell you about her love life?" I asked, though I could barely concentrate on Jody. I was stuck back at the moment when Steven had said that Bennett wasn't born where he told me he was.

"We're required to meet privately for a half hour a week to discuss my writing. There's nothing to say. We both know it. Turns out the guy was really twelve years old."

"That must happen all the time." I reached for the bedside lamp to turn it off.

"Wait. I finally figured it out. You're the bad version of that actress, Charlotte Rampling—the sexy-lidded eyes that change from hazel to green depending on the light, the cheekbones. It's been driving me nuts."

"The *bad* version."

"Also the short version," Jody said. "My sister and I say we are the bad versions of Joan Fontaine and Olivia de Havilland. We watch a lot of old movies. Your brother, on the other hand, is sort of the *good* version of Nic Cage."

"I think he could go with that. I don't know your sister, but I don't think you're the bad version of anyone," I added, making nice. This time I turned off the light on my nightstand. "Sleep well." I even turned away from Jody to underline my intention to end any conversation. But the light from the window in our door illuminated the room, enough that I could not pretend I was the only one there.

Why would you say you were born somewhere you weren't?

Of all the lies men have told women, this one was baffling. It didn't seem to serve a purpose I could identify. Unless he had changed his name. But the reasons people change their name— short of marriage when a woman sometimes changes her last name—are to sever ties to the past and to start over. And if he had changed his name, what else might he have changed—the story of his childhood? But he talked about his parents with such love. Was that the childhood he wished he'd had? Who were the people in the photograph? Bennett looked like the man in the photo.

I rolled over until I was facing the other bed. Jody was, if not asleep, then at least lying still. I could not get her silly game out of my head. Who was Bennett the bad version of? I thought of all the actors of yesteryear that I had watched on late-night TV, and I landed on the iconic Montgomery Clift. He had been in a serious car accident—he drove into a tree—while filming *Raintree County*, and though the facial plastic surgery he had required was pretty good for the fifties, his looks had a definite before and after. Bennett, I thought, was the bad version of the *bad* version of Montgomery Clift. As soon as I landed on this, I was ashamed— why the snarky take? All he had done was lie about where he was from.

Still no sound from Jody. The roommate I wished I had was Kathy. I would not have turned off my light and turned my back to *her*. We would have dissected the possibilities of this odd situation, escalating into wilder scenarios until we were both laughing. Ultimately, she would have made a case for duality—that I needed to do recon *and* take the risk that faith presents.

Faith had served her well. An adventurous, indomitable, and wise spirit had guided her through a life many would envy—up to a point. At twenty-eight, in her third year of med school at NYU, she was diagnosed with breast cancer, and it had already gone to the bone. She continued to attend classes and do rounds during her initial chemo and appeared on the ward with her head uncovered—no wig, no wrapped scarf. Her patients saw her bravery daily, her showing up for them when another would have capitulated.

She lived for eight years after the diagnosis. For four of those years, we shared an apartment in Vinegar Hill near the on-ramp to the Brooklyn Bridge. She died just before I met Bennett.

And now I was in a loony bin with a Sarah Lawrence student.

What would Kathy have done?

I would make a plane reservation for Montreal in the morning, use the key Bennett had given me, and find out what I could.

"I'm checking myself out this afternoon," I told Cilla the following morning. We were sitting in her office drinking tea. I'd seen her daily since I'd been admitted, and she had promised to see me as an outpatient. I picked at the threads of my trendy ripped jeans.

"You don't think you should stay a few more days? At least until you have a support structure in place?"

I felt that she was my support structure, she and Steven. "Steven hired a crime-scene cleaning service for my apartment."

"You're sure you're ready to go home even if your apartment is clean?"

"Are there different cleaning products than the ones the rest of us use? I couldn't even get the blood from a bloody nose out of a washcloth," I told Cilla. "I'm not going home. I need to go to Montreal, to Bennett's apartment to find his parents' home number and address. I can't go home until I face them."

"Do you think it's your job to tell them, not the authorities?"

"No one else could find them, not even Steven's investigator."

"And you think you'll find them?"

"He was so organized. He hung his shirts and ties by color. I'm sure I can find his parents' address somewhere in his desk. It was the neatest desk I'd ever seen."

"So you've been to his apartment?"

"No, he showed me on Skype."

We used to have dinner on Skype. We would decide on Chinese, order in the same dishes, and have dinner as though sitting across from each other. Bennett's table had a tablecloth; I used a place mat.

"Are you prepared for what you might find?" Cilla asked.

It was a stock therapeutic question, one I had asked while interviewing inmates at Rikers. Everyone always says yes.

But first I had to see my dogs.

I took the express train all the way to East Harlem. I thought today might be the Puerto Rican Day Parade—the PR flag was flying from so many honking cars, and the traffic was so thick— but then I realized the parade was in June, and this was September. The smell of the city pound annex hit me a block away, a mixture of feces and fear. The front door was covered over in taped-on flyers urging the spaying and neutering of pets. Just inside, presiding over a waiting area filled with crying children and expressionless teenagers and beleaguered parents, were three women who looked no older than twenty. Two were on phones, which left only one of them to deal with the emotional crowd, some there to look for their lost dog, some there to give their dogs up. At this rate, it would be hours before someone would speak to me.

I caught the eye of a burly kennel worker that one of the women at the desk had called Enrique. I asked him quietly if he knew where the two dogs that Animal Control had brought in ten days ago were being held.

He told me they get more than a hundred dogs a week: "Do you have their kennel numbers?"

I knew nothing about kennel numbers, and said instead, "The ones in the paper, the man was killed."

"The red-nose pit and the big white one?"

"Great Pyrenees, yes."

"They're in Ward Four, but they're on DOH-HB hold." When I looked blank, he said, "Department of Health Hold for Human Bite. Though I saw in the paper they did a lot more than that."

"They're my dogs."

"I can't let you take them out or let you inside their kennels. Their kennel cards are stamped CAUTION."

"But can I at least see them? Could you take me to see them?"

I saw Enrique look to the preoccupied women at the front desk, then he motioned me to follow him. We slipped past the EMPLOYEES ONLY sign and were instantly inside a howling asylum, not unlike Bellevue. I tried to look without seeing—the dogs crazed with fear and frustration, turning in circles in their too-small cages, water bowls overturned, feces not only on the floors but on the walls. Why were there no other attendants to minister to the dogs' needs?

Cloud had never slept anywhere but my bed.

She was pressed against the rear of the cage, her head down, her ears flattened back in terror. I approached her and she looked up and whimpered. I cried out her name and reached for her.

Enrique stopped me. "You can't touch the dog."

I dropped to my knees and spoke to Cloud. "Oh, sweetie, I'm sorry you're here."

Was I looking at Bennett's killer? No one could make me believe that *this* dog had killed Bennett, which left Chester and George.

"Where's George, the pittie?"

"Next kennel over. He's right here."

I realized that the whimpering I'd been hearing was coming from George, who recognized my voice, my scent. I wished I'd never met this dog. I wished I hated this dog. If not for this dog, and for the now-dead Chester, Bennett would still be alive. Maybe George had been on death row for a reason when I took him home to foster. A reason other than an overcrowded shelter. But he had been so gentle and grateful. He was the only dog I knew who wouldn't use his teeth to eat from my hand, only his lips.

I started to cry. George was the beta dog to Chester's alpha. Did that factor into whether I could forgive him? I did not want an eye for an eye. Strange given the circumstances, but I did not want George to suffer. What about the mother whose son kills his father, her husband? Is she expected to hate her son? It's the same boy she loved an hour before. Doesn't she make a choice to forgive? And how is that ever possible?

"I got work to do," Enrique told me. "I'll send in one of the volunteers. Promise you won't touch the dogs."

I thanked him as he quickly shut the door behind us, and then I sat between the dogs' cages, on the filthy floor where I could see them both and they could see me, but not each other. I wished I knew what I was feeling. I felt responsible for Cloud's fate. She wouldn't be here if not for my—the therapist in me took over—pathological altruism, when selfless acts backfire and inadvertently do great damage to others.

"You're a brave woman to come here," said a woman who entered the ward. My first thought was how clean she looked, considering where she worked. She wore a T-shirt with the shelter's name on it. Maybe her shift had just begun? "Enrique told me you were here. I'm Billie." She squatted beside me. She reached out to George's cage, waited for George to rise and muster the courage to come closer, then reached inside with her fingers to let George lick them.

"You're not frightened? You know what my dogs did?"

"Your picture was online." She knew the whole story, yet she was now stroking George. He had pressed his flank against the metal bars so that she could touch as much of him as possible. I heard him sigh, a baritone exhalation of contentment. "He's a love bug," she said, her fingernails scratching his flank.

I couldn't believe what she was doing.

"I'm sorry for your loss," she said, withdrawing her fingers. George turned around in his tiny cage, so that she could do his other side. She took his cue and started in on his other flank. "Was he good-looking? Your fiancé."

It was the second thing about her that surprised me. Who would ask the grieving such a question? Yet I liked her. She was the first person, other than Cilla, who spoke to me as though I would survive this. I had learned from Kathy that surviving such an experience was possible. Only in my case, in the moment, I had to "act as if" I would make it. I could not pretend to the faith that was available to others, but I acted as if I could.

Back to Billie's odd question—I found myself answering no. No, Bennett had not been remarkably good-looking, and when I'd first met him, I registered that and, almost simultaneously, dismissed it. I had responded to something else in him—his confidence, a different kind of strength.

"Your dogs are stronger than you think. We'd better leave before someone finds you in here. You're supposed to have a court order to see them. Your dogs are evidence."

I said good-bye to Cloud, but did not speak to George, although his body was still pressed against the bars.

Billie and I walked out of the ward together.

"Are they safe?" I asked.

"For now. Nothing will happen to them as long as they're evidence."

I didn't ask, *And after that?* We both knew what would happen.

"I'll look out for them. Here." She gave me her card—no profession, only a name and a number. "I'm here three times a week. Call me and I'll give you updates on how they're doing."

I thanked her and asked how she came to volunteer here.

"I had my own dog in here once, a shepherd mix with some chow in him. He bit a neighbor's child. I'd have bitten the child, too, if she had been taunting me the way she taunted Cubby."

"What happened to Cubby?"

"He wasn't evidence."

"And you still choose to work here?"

"It's where I'm needed."

Steven picked me up in his car outside the shelter. He had offered to take me to the airport. He thought I was insane for visiting my dogs. "How can you look at them knowing what they did?"

I tried out the analogy of the mother with the murderous son, but Steven said, "These are dogs, not children."

The analogy worked for me. "You've known Cloud since she was eight weeks old."

"I'm talking about the other one."

I didn't plan to spend the night in Montreal. My plan was to find contact information for Bennett's parents and leave.

Steven made me promise to return to his apartment when I got back. "I went to your place yesterday to check on the cleaning service. It's spotless, but there's nowhere to sleep. They took the bed away."

"What else did they take away?"

"It looks pretty empty. But they did what they needed to do. Are you sure you want to go back there?"

This kind of concern from my brother had precedent. A lifetime of precedent. He had deflected our father's madness when it was directed at me. Our father was not a violent man except when his mania broke and he plunged into depression. In his blackest moods, he was capable of brandishing a knife at our mother. He saw me as a smaller version of her, and just as insubordinate. One summer night when I was ten and Steven was eighteen, our father came into the kitchen and saw the empty fruit bowl.

"Who ate my peaches?" he yelled. We heard him from the finished basement, where Steven and I were watching TV. We heard him turn on our mother. "Did you let them eat my peaches?"

We heard our mother say, "They were for everyone."

Steven started up the stairs to the kitchen and I followed him.

"I ate the fucking peaches," Steven said, when, in fact, I had eaten them.

He took the beating for me. Two months later, our father threw him out of the house, and Steven hitchhiked to New York City. He hired on with a construction crew in Hoboken and took night classes in criminology at John Jay. By the time I got to New York, Steven had left for Afghanistan to work as a lawyer for the State Department. He traveled to outlying villages, encouraging chieftains to follow one of the pillars of Islam—to support the poor and establish a public defense system. He found the work immensely meaningful, but the living conditions wore him down. He and his coworkers lived in a hotel-turned-bunker, which was blown up by the Taliban a few months after Steven left. When he got back to New York, he went to work with Avaaz, an NGO whose name meant "voice" in several European, Middle Eastern, and Asian languages. He felt aligned with their humanitarian mission and programs, from human trafficking to animal rights.

I landed at Dorval just before rush hour, got a cab, and gave the driver Bennett's address in the Quartier Latin, on rue

Saint-Urbain, Montreal's equivalent to Bedford Avenue, the hipster epicenter, a half mile from where I lived. Although the houses in the Quartier Latin were the same as row houses found in Williamsburg, the French had painted them pale blue and adorned them with the wrought-iron balconies you find in New Orleans; in Williamsburg, the houses were ornamented with shrines to the Virgin and high-kitsch tributes to Italy.

We started down a commercial street. It was early fall and already freezing, but people were still sitting at outdoor cafés.

Another couple of blocks and the driver slowed down to read the street numbers. There was no forty-two. "Are you sure you have the right address?"

"Is this Saint-Urbain Street? Is there a north or south?"

"It should be right here."

I paid the driver and got out. I wondered if I had reversed the number and walked back two blocks, but twenty-four was a Laundromat. Bennett had told me about this little restaurant below his apartment where the owner made him the best omelet he'd ever tasted, Deux something. I walked up and down the block but saw no restaurant at all. I typed Bennett's address into my phone's GPS and waited for directions, but the window showed there was no such address. "Oh, come on," I said aloud. I went into a shop and asked if there was a restaurant nearby called Deux something.

"This is Montreal. Everything is Deux something," said the clerk.

I retraced my steps as though the numbers would magically change and my mounting sense of unease would vanish. Had I ever written him at this address? No, we'd only e-mailed and Skyped. I tried to remember anything else he told me about his neighborhood or his friends, but all I could remember were the musicians he represented. He was a music agent for Canadian indie bands. Maybe one of them was playing in town. I bought a newspaper from a kiosk and a bag of Smarties. I found an outdoor café around the corner and took a seat despite the cold. I took a few deep breaths and opened the paper to the Arts section. There were no band names I recognized.

I noticed the café was filling up and people were ordering dinner. My plane home wasn't leaving until midnight. The streetlights went on. The waiter came over again and this time I ordered something—poutine and a small Diet Coke.

"Is Diet Pepsi okay?"

He brought over a *petite* bottle. Unlike in America, the small was actually small, and I felt cheated.

I felt I should know what to do next. I'd spent the last two years memorizing procedures and methodologies, examining crime scenes, interpreting incident reports, investigating missing persons, all manner of victims. Yet I could think of no model to follow here. I had a funny thought: Could I file a missing person's report on a dead man? Why had Bennett given me a false address? What had he been hiding? A wife? A family? Was he in trouble with the police? So this is why he always came to me. So the B&Bs with their prying hosts and too-sweet breakfasts were about secrecy, not romance. What else had he lied to me about?

Whom was I mourning?

Steven's apartment, where I was camped on his sofa bed, was walking distance from the Manhattan coroner's office on First Avenue. This was where all bodies were brought. I found myself in full-blown anticipatory anxiety. The coroner's office had called again last night; they needed me to come in. I tried to convince myself that it would not be as bad as I imagined. I thought back to the first time I had seen a cadaver in an anatomy class. I had to will myself to look, after conquering the fear that I would be sick or faint. In fact, scientific interest had carried the day. I had been fine. But I was not about to have to view an ordinary body. Bennett—or whoever he was—was no longer identifiable. They couldn't expect me to look at his body, could they?

I had expected Steven to get angry when I told him about Montreal, and he was, but he was also angry at himself for not having voiced his suspicions when Bennett kept finding excuses not to meet him. As if I would have listened if he had.

I had not been back to my apartment since leaving Bellevue, so my choice of what to wear was limited: yesterday's jeans and ankle boots, the ribbed turtleneck I had worn to Montreal.

Steven had a meeting with the Afghani consulate: Avaaz was fighting for Afghani translators to be offered asylum. He had asked me to wait until the afternoon when he could go with me, but I had assured him that I could manage this by myself. He said it was not as if I were going for a driver's license. I insisted, needing to know the form my changing view of Bennett would take when I saw his damaged body. The body I knew had been someone else's body, after all.

A mobile boiler-room trailer fronted the monolithic, gray building. I would have expected a refrigerated trailer. I walked over the flat wooden bridge covering the electrical cables and entered a lobby.

I gave the woman at the front desk my name and told her I was expected on the fourth floor. She asked me to take a seat while she confirmed my appointment. I noticed an odd assortment of magazines on a couple of tables—*Sports Illustrated*, *Parents*, *Garden & Gun*, and the weirdly existential *Self*. A few minutes later, a young man in a lab coat came out of the elevator and asked if I was Morgan Prager. He invited me to follow him to another waiting area; this one smelled of formaldehyde and had no magazines.

"Do I have to see the body?" I asked, knowing in that moment I would not be able to look.

"We normally do IDs by photo, but I'm not going to ask you to do that. I do have some questions for you. I understand you were engaged to the deceased. Did your fiancé have any tattoos, birthmarks, scars, or deformities?"

"I guess the scar on his eyebrow is moot."

"I'm sorry, but I have to ask."

"No, I'm sorry, I just can't believe I'm here. Bennett had no tattoos. But I don't even know if his name was Bennett. What's going to happen to the body if no one can identify it?"

"The body will be kept here for six months and then buried in the city's cemetery on Hart Island. It's off the Bronx."

I could not identify the body but could I claim it? Did I want to?

The detective said that the body had been brought in without any personal identification, and none had been found in my apartment.

"What about his cell phone?" I asked. "He always had it with him."

"We hoped you would know where it was. And his wallet."

"Are you saying someone took them?"

"I'm saying the police didn't find them."

I felt that he was criticizing me for not knowing the whereabouts of Bennett's phone and wallet, that this detective was exasperated with my inability to aid in the investigation.

I was surprised to find myself in tears. "Look, I don't know who he was. I thought I did, but I didn't. When you find out, please tell me, okay?"

I took the L train back to Williamsburg, to the Metropolitan pool off the Bedford stop, a 1920s public bathing house. A skylight ran the length of the pool. You could see sunlight on the tiles as you swam in the eighty-degree water. If I squinted, I could pretend I was floating in the Caribbean.

Swimming had been my routine—five days a week, summer and winter—and my passion. Actually, *swimming* wasn't the correct term. I deep-water ran. I used an AquaJogger, a simple flotation device that fits around your waist so that you are suspended in the water. Some people jog, but I ran as fast as I could. The water slowed me, stilled me; the sensation was like trying to catch a train in a dream.

The locker room, with its broken fans and hair-clogged drains, smelling of ammonia and hairspray, didn't prepare you for the beauty of the pool, a seventy-five-foot, three-lane lap pool, shimmering with light.

I used the slow lane, designated for the sidestrokers, kick-boarders, and gossips who paddled and chatted. The lane was about the width of a subway car and peopled with the same assortment of strangers.

I normally entered by the ladder, but today I plunged in—I needed the silence and compression of water, the few seconds where nothing above the surface mattered. When I came up for air, I began running with an urgency that surprised me. I ran past the blind lady doing jumping jacks in the shallow end, past the old ladies who wore shower caps instead of swim caps and kept their makeup on, past the obese boy who treaded in place. If I were on dry land, I would have been running a six-minute mile.

I ran from the body of my former lover in the coroner's office, from my own gullibility, from shame. The more I strained against the water, the better I expected to feel, but what I was up against was so large my body didn't know if it was relaxed or just tired.

When I finally got out of the pool, I felt gravity again. Deep-water running is how astronauts learn to maneuver while weightless.

I got out of the pool just as Ladies' Only Swim was starting, a two-hour period in which only women, mostly Hasidic, could use the pool. Curtains were drawn over the glass windows that looked out to the lobby, and the lifeguard was female. In the locker room, a dozen women of all ages were getting into their swimsuits, long dresses made out of bathing-suit material. I swam in a Speedo, yet I never felt contempt from them. In truth, they treated me as if I didn't exist. Except for Ethel, who was as curious about me as I was about her. She said she lived a staid

life with her husband's Satmar family in Williamsburg, except
during the summers, when she proudly sat in as a lifeguard at a
kosher girls' camp in the Catskills. She told me about Aqua Modesta, the original kosher swimwear dealer, an online shop that
sold "modest" bathing suits. In the summer, though, she wore
Aqua Modesta's latest bathing-suit fashion: "capris." "As long as
your elbows and knees are covered," she had explained.

I toweled off in the shower area and then walked into the
crowded dressing room. For a moment, it looked as if scalps were
hanging on hooks in the lockers. The ladies' wigs!

"Did you have to look at the body?" Steven asked.

"Mercifully, no."

"They tell you who he was?"

"No fingers, no fingerprints."

The flippancy did not reflect my state of mind. It was more an
attempt to level off a mounting hysteria.

I waited for Steven to call it a night and then signed on to the
National Missing and Unidentified Persons System, a database
open to both the public and the police. Everyone in my Psychological Autopsy course had to register with NamUs. I clicked on
the case number that the man at the coroner's office had given
me: ME 13-02544.

```
Minimum age: 20
Maximum age: 40
Race: white
Ethnicity:
Sex: male
```

Weight: 148

Height: 68, measured

Body parts inventory (check all that apply):

☑ All parts recovered
☐ Head or partial head not recovered
☐ Torso not recovered
☐ One or more limbs not recovered
☐ One or both hands not recovered

Notes on body parts recovered: Canine teeth marks are visible on all limbs and partial limbs, torso, and neck.

Body condition: face avulsed.

Next I entered the Missing Persons database. Someone must have contacted the police when Bennett, or whoever he was, didn't come home—a wife or his real mother, not Mme. Marie Vaux-Trudeau.

I went to their advanced-search page and entered Bennett's physical description, the date last seen, the age when last seen. Three missing-persons cases in the tristate area matched his general description and the date he went missing.

I hesitated, both wanting and fearing the results. None of the photos remotely resembled Bennett.

I went to his website, the one he had showed me, for the list of indie bands he represented. Said he represented. The bands were real, but none had a manager named Bennett Vaux-Trudeau. I made a short list of other "facts" he had told me that I could easily verify. Turned out he had not attended McGill, had not won a

scholarship to the Berklee College of Music, had not played bass
with Radiohead.

Was there something Bennett had not lied to me about?

I had been staying at Steven's for nearly a week before I asked
him to come with me to get some clothes and books from my
apartment. The yellow crime-scene tape had been taken down
by then, but that didn't keep a couple of my neighbors from coming out into the hallway when my key turned in the lock. Mrs.
Szymanski offered condolences that seemed genuine. Grace del
Forno closed her door when I looked at her.

I waited in the living room while Steven, consulting a list I
had made for him, went into the bedless bedroom to find what
I needed. As in a movie, I looked at a photo, taken in Maine, on
the coffee table, Bennett with his arm around me, Lake Androscoggin in the background. For a moment I was confused, thinking the crime-scene cleanup service would have removed that,
too. My confusion carried over to the smile on Bennett's face.
Was that a lie? I looked at him objectively. I wanted to find a
coldness that would have been a clue had I noticed it sooner, but
to my dismay I saw him as I always had.

Steven appeared in the doorway, holding up two pairs of
jeans, a question on his face. "Both," I said, feeling cowardly
for remaining outside my own bedroom. Next, he brought out
a short stack of textbooks. I asked him not to forget my laptop.
I didn't want to keep using his. I didn't want Steven to discover
what I planned to look up: Lovefraud.com, the first website Cilla
had suggested. Then again, it might interest him as he had recently been blindsided by a new girlfriend.

Cilla, whom I'd started seeing as an outpatient in her Upper West Side office, had given me the names of websites where I might find others who had similarly been deceived; Cilla had said it helped a number of her patients.

I knew about these sites. I used them for my research, looking for women who seemed to fit the definition of pathological altruist. Women posted confessions: "He loves, he proposes, he gets money, he's gone." "Why do *I* feel guilty?" "Is his goal to break me?" "The only hope I have is that karma exists." I'd never believed in pop psychology or communal "sharing." I was a near professional in this field and felt it was beneath me. But I was desperate.

I went into the kitchen to get water for the ficus. I passed the rattan hamper that I used for storing dog toys. I lifted the lid and saw that it was now empty. Steven must have okayed their removal by the cleaning service. I looked for the dogs' bowls. I was also looking for spots of blood the cleaners might have missed.

After Steven and I returned to his apartment, I pleaded exhaustion. But the moment he went to bed, I opened my laptop.

Sociopaths make up 4 percent of the population, 12 million Americans. They are not necessarily raging criminals: most of them are charming, intelligent, and know how to mimic concern, and even love. But they lack conscience, do not feel empathy, and feel neither guilt nor shame for their behavior. They are also expert manipulators. During childhood and adolescence, 9 percent of the sociopathic population tortures or kills animals.

Anyone studying victimology knows the *DSM-5*'s criteria for *antisocial personality disorder*, the clinical term for sociopaths:

Sociopaths lie constantly.

Sociopaths do not apologize.

Sociopaths think the rules do not apply to them.

Sociopaths believe that what they say becomes truth.

The only people who tolerate sociopaths for long periods are those the sociopath is able to manipulate into doing so.

Sociopaths do not treat pets well.

Sociopaths almost always have affairs.

I opened Lovefraud.com. I read about a woman whose fiancé had another woman's name tattooed on his chest. He had told her it was the name of his little sister who had died at birth. It turned out to be the name of his wife.

Around four in the morning, reading without full comprehension, I snapped to attention.

Posted in: Hooked by a sociopath

by Lovefraud Reader

June 5, 2013

20 comments

I met him on a dating site for Jewish singles. His first letter to me was so charming. Instead of talking about himself, he asked me questions about myself. What book would you not take to a desert island? What song makes you cry but you're ashamed to admit it? Do you like animals more than people? Peter L. was a literary agent; he showed me his website, and I had heard of some of the writers he represented.

I was living in Boston at the time, and he was living in Manhattan. He came to see me, never inviting me to his place. He never introduced me to any of his friends and never wanted to meet mine. He said we had so little time together he wanted to focus on me.

When we were apart we would Skype intimately. He made me comfortable where I was first self-conscious. His interest in my work, too, seemed genuine. I analyze incident reports for the Boston PD. One night I saw that one of his writers was giving a reading at the Harvard Book Store in Cambridge. I bought the book, and when I asked him to sign it, I mentioned I knew his agent. "How do you know Harriet?" he asked, reaching for a pen. "No," I said, "Peter." He looked confused. "Who's Peter?" When I confronted Peter that night on the phone, he said, "Why were you spying on me?" Spying? Still, I continued to see him, though I felt he had noticed my new wariness. We met on weekends as before; now instead of coming to my place, we went to romantic B&Bs in Maine.

Before long he asked me to marry him. I sold my apartment, gave up my job, and arrived at Penn Station where he was supposed to meet me. I got a text from him instead, apologizing for having to work late and telling me to use the key he had given me to let myself into his place. . . .

You see where this is going. There was no such address.

I got a grim pleasure out of bringing Steven up to speed. I felt enlivened by his growing outrage.

"If the guy wasn't already dead, I'd kill him," Steven said. This was the kind of loyalty I ached for. Steven was reliably on my side and had always been, whether it was the standard bloodying of the nose of a boy who had started a rumor about me in school, or taking the time to teach me to drive a stick shift after our father had given up on me.

Steven fixed a couple of dirty martinis; he sipped his while I gulped mine. He lived on the twenty-ninth floor of a sliver building on Forty-Eighth Street. The lights at the United Nations were visible from Steven's couch.

"And I'm damned if I'm going to let Cloud pay for my mistakes," I said, holding my glass up for a refill. "Can you defend her at her hearing? It's coming up soon."

"I wish I could, but this is not my territory. You'd be better off with this guy I know from law school, Laurence McKenzie. He was the editor of the *Law Review*, but when he graduated, he turned down offers any of us would have grabbed. Instead, he devoted himself to animal advocacy law. We have drinks a few times a year. And I always see him at the Avaaz benefit. Want me to call him for you?"

"Can I afford him?"

"You're my sister. He'll do it pro bono."

• • •

McKenzie's office was on a dicey block in Bushwick near the Montrose Avenue subway stop between an auto repair shop and a new overpriced cheese store. His receptionist was a young woman with a buzz cut and a paw print the size of a silver dollar tattooed on the side of her neck. She didn't make me wait but led me directly into McKenzie's office.

The man at the desk looked to be in his late thirties. He was on the phone. He motioned me to a chair and held up a finger indicating he'd be off the call in a moment. It gave me a chance to look at a bulletin board covered with thumbtacked photos of dogs, not unlike the obstetrician who posts photos of the babies he has delivered. In a framed photograph McKenzie had an elephant's trunk resting in his hand, and there was another of him surrounded by chimpanzees. He also had the brilliant Shanahan cartoon where, in the first panel, a drowning boy calls to the collie onshore, "Lassie! Get help!!"—and in the second panel we see Lassie lying on her back on a psychiatrist's couch.

McKenzie's clothes did not say *lawyer*. The man on the phone wore jeans and an ADOPT NY T-shirt with a silhouette of a pit bull's head. He had a nicely lived-in face. The length of his prematurely gray hair would not have been a distraction when he appeared in court. I heard rustling under his desk just before a greyhound emerged and stretched.

The first thing he did when he hung up was introduce me to the greyhound. Faye was a delicate brindle wearing a standard, wide martingale collar and a string of faux pearls. Instead of licking my hand, her teeth clicked as though chattering in the cold. He said it was a greyhound thing.

The second thing he did was ask me if I had brought a picture of Cloud.

I searched through the photo app on my phone. When I saw that every recent photo of Cloud included Chester and George, I was overcome with remorse. I paused on one in which Chester and George lay side by side on my bed, while Cloud lay on her massive back across the pillows. I held up my phone to show him.

"Which one was shot by the police?"

I pointed to Chester.

"And the other two are being held in East Harlem?"

"I'm not even allowed to touch them."

"Steven told me the whole story."

I began to cry. "Did he mention that I can't afford a lawyer?"

McKenzie got up to get me a cup of water from the cooler. "I'm not in it for the money. I mean, look around." He motioned to the animal photos on the wall. "Those clients didn't pay and I got judgments in their favor."

"What was the elephant accused of?"

"Jasmine attacked her circus trainer. I was able to prove that she was defending herself against the trainer's use of electrical prods."

"But she didn't kill the trainer."

"He was lucky."

McKenzie told me what he would need first: Cloud's veterinary records and an evaluation from the American Temperament Test Society.

I asked what the chances were of saving her, and he gave what I took to be a stock reply that deflected the question, but which would prove to be an understatement: "I'm good at my job."

"Steven has a lot of admiration for you." I found myself in tears again, for which I apologized.

Faye rose and came to console me.

He said to Faye, "Good girl," and then to me, "She's good at *her* job."

Daylight had folded into gloom by the time I opened my new front door (the cops had broken down the old one). It was the first time I was going to spend the night.

The bathroom and the bedroom were the only rooms I hadn't gone into when I was last there with Steven. He had had the bathroom door replaced—it would take me a while before I understood why. And who had hung the new shower curtain?—a hotel standard, white, ribbed cotton over a clear plastic sheet. The collection of sample-size shampoos from hotels had been removed—disposed of? The toilet paper was a brand I had not used before; the wrap covering the rolls featured a cartoon of a playful puppy. Though the cleanup crew had replaced what was visible, they had not removed the contents of the medicine cabinet. On Bennett's shelves I found his razor in place. I lifted it using a length of the Cottonelle toilet paper and carried it to the kitchen, meaning to put it in a Ziploc bag for DNA. Then I realized how crazy that was: his body was in the morgue. I threw it away.

In my bedroom, almost all the furniture had been removed. Rugs, too. A new mattress was on a standard-issue, metal bed frame against the wrong wall. I always slept on the right side of the bed, and I never slept next to the wall. I had told Bennett about an episode of *The Twilight Zone* I had watched as an impressionable child, in which a little girl, asleep next to a wall, fell into the fourth dimension; the wall closed behind her. At first, Bennett found my habit charming, but the last time we'd met in Maine, he had said, "If you love me, you'll sleep next to the wall." I didn't see how doing that would show him I loved him more than my telling him I did. I remember thinking that was a standard red flag for any number of controlling pathologies. I moved next to the wall, but I didn't sleep. He made love to me the next morning with a ferocity that seduced me once again. He could always seduce me even though I knew that he prided himself on being able to do so no matter what he had done.

I found clean sheets and made the bed. I ordered Chinese food from the corner place and sat at my kitchen table sorting through junk mail and bills. Nothing that couldn't wait.

I opened my laptop and watched CNN. I might have been the only thirty-year-old in Williamsburg watching news at that hour. I kept watching after the Chinese food came. Not until I finished did I notice I had not used any soy sauce. Normally I mixed it with hot mustard and drenched the food. No wonder I hadn't tasted anything.

A quick survey of the cabinet I used for liquor showed that I had only a half bottle of tequila and some old rum. So much for the Scotch I thought I wanted.

The bedroom had no reading light. I guess the professionals couldn't get the blood off the watered-silk lampshade I bought at the Meeker Avenue Flea Market. I lay down and closed my eyes. The mattress was firmer than my old one. The sheets had a higher thread count; Steven must have splurged. Yet no amount of physical comfort could go up against the images that owned that room. The memory of what I had seen conjured symptoms of shock and grief—I started shivering and crying. Why would I think I could enter the death room, much less sleep in it? Had I lived anywhere but New York, I would have had the choice to move, but in this rental market that was not an option. Still, I did not have to sleep in this room.

The kitchen was not safe either. I remembered the mornings that Bennett had scolded me for leaving the counters littered with crumbs when, the fact was, he had made himself something to eat during the night after taking Ambien and had not remembered the common side effect of sleep-eating. Sometimes he did not remember making love to me. Or so he said. At those times, he swore that the one thing he could never forget was how much he loved me. Even though it was corny, I allowed myself to be persuaded.

I carried a glass of rum into the living room. It would not be the first night I had slept on the couch. If I could sleep. And how could I? The TV was in the bedroom (wall-mounted), but I still needed company, which left books.

I wasn't up for the Immortals, nor did I give a shit about the life of Winston Churchill. I was hardly going to reread *Crime and Punishment*. I didn't want to reread anything. Scanning the shelves, I stopped at a title I didn't recognize: *Dangerous Liaisons*. I'd seen the movie years before, but I didn't remember buying the book. This paperback copy was well worn, with many pages dog-eared. I saw comments written in the margins, but couldn't tell if they were Bennett's. I realized I didn't know his handwriting. His taste in books had not been parochial. He sometimes left behind novels I was happy to discover—Doris Lessing's *The Fifth Child*, for example. It mattered to me that we liked the same books.

Here was something underlined: "They are imprudent creatures, for in their present lover they fail to perceive their future
enemy." I backed up and saw that this was a woman speaking
about other women.

In the film of this novel about decadent French aristocrats in
the 1700s, two former paramours entertain each other with stories of their sexual conquests. The Marquise and Valmont make
an art of destroying those they have seduced, those who have
come to love them. They care nothing for these discarded souls;
for them it is all about the game and their ultimate allegiance to
each other. But when this allegiance is compromised, when the
Marquise accuses Valmont of falling in love with one of his ob-
jects of desire, the game turns deadly.

Had Bennett underlined it or had he bought the book used?

Also underlined: "A man enjoys the happiness he feels, and
a woman the happiness she gives. . . . The pleasure of one is to
satisfy his desires and that of the other above all to arouse them."

I hoped that someone else had underlined this because it
made me livid. It contradicted everything I felt about the way he
had been with me.

I carried the book to the couch. Oh, the memory of the body!

But then I remembered other things. Bennett always show-
ered immediately after we made love.

Bennett made me finish any dessert I ordered, until I stopped
ordering dessert. Then he gave me an expensive leather skirt that
was a size too small. A compliment or an admonishment?

These things did not happen at once. Plenty of time passed
between these skewed acts to override my instincts and give him
the benefit of the doubt, which is, after all, the godly thing, a
virtue. This was the guy who would stop and turn me so that we

could see ourselves reflected in a store window—"Look at them," he would say. Pride, or arrogance?

Cilla may have thought nothing was to be gained by finding out who Bennett really was, but Cilla had not been in love with him, nor had she made up the blind study of predators and controls, the study that had brought him to me in the first place.

That night, I read pages of *Dangerous Liaisons* at random, looking for clues as to who Bennett might have been, or who he aspired to be, if he had indeed underlined these passages. The more I read of the Marquise, the more unsettled I felt and the more familiar she seemed. Bennett had told me about a woman he had known—he had put air quotes around the word *known*—in his late twenties. At a casino in Montreal, celebrating the sale of two paintings he had "inherited"—the quotes here are mine—he'd been approached by a beautiful woman who said, "You've got to see this."

He said she led him to where a gray-haired woman was feeding tokens into a $5 slot machine, roped off from the rest of the slots. The woman's opera-length, white gloves were filthy from handling coins. The beautiful woman showed him where, a short distance away, an old man with a bullhorn repeatedly asked his wife to step away from the machine. The casino had phoned him when his wife was down $30,000.

Bennett told me he thought the beautiful woman meant this as a cautionary tale, but she said in his ear, "It's a game. They get all this attention. They get comped a room." Bennett told me he made the obvious point, that they didn't get the $30,000 back, and the beautiful woman told him the old man had millions. He asks his wife to put on the filthy opera gloves and elicit pity to the point where he has to be called in to save her from herself. *A man enjoys the happiness he feels, and a woman the happiness she gives.*

Bennett asked how the beautiful woman knew, and she told him she had seen them the month before at another casino. The casinos don't mind, they still get their money, she told him.

This was the woman, Bennett told me, who defined the next three years of his life.

Hours later, I still hadn't slept. I slipped on my robe and took the stairs to the roof. My building was only six stories high, but taller than my neighbors' clapboard houses with their tar roofs and crooked chimneys and satellite dishes. My roof had a clear if disrupted view of Manhattan. When I first moved here a year ago, I could see the Williamsburg Bridge, but the nonstop construction along Williamsburg's waterfront had slowly closed that view corridor. I had taken Bennett up here to watch the Fourth of July fireworks, his first time spending a weekend at my place. Steven and I normally watched the fireworks together—we had since we were kids—but I had lied to him, said I was going out of town. Bennett had said he wasn't ready to meet my big brother and he didn't want to dilute our time together.

Every other year, the city switches rivers for the show. This year's extravaganza was over the Hudson. Bennett had said it looked as if New Jersey were attacking New York. Who *was* he?

Ghostly clouds raced across the sky; I feared I would never feel normal again. Bennett had hummed the Drifters' classic "Up on the Roof" as we slow-danced. He had said one of his emo bands was going to do a new rendition. And I believed him.

Someone had left a broken lawn chair near the roof's parapet and I sat down. The only time I had ever seen stars over the city was after the lights went out during Hurricane Sandy. Tonight, most of the downtown office buildings were dark, but not the new World Trade Center. It was lit up, and a crescent moon—the symbol of Islam—was positioned such that it seemed to touch the tower.

I did it. I got through the first night. Sleep wasn't a big part of it, but I got through it. The kitchen cabinet I opened to get a coffee filter also housed Bennett's granola. I would get coffee on the way to class. I'd lost a size so I put on my thin jeans and a cotton turtleneck. My concession to makeup was a swipe of concealer under each eye.

Going on Lovefraud.com, after what I'd read the night before, spotlighted the eloquence of the Marquise versus the cheeseball American duped. In reply to the letter I had read days before, I wrote:

I read about your terrible experience with great empathy and an escalating sense of familiarity. I, too, was involved with a man who asked me those identical questions, who pretended to be an agent, who never invited me to his place but instead met up with me at B&Bs in Maine. Lastly, he gave me a key to his apartment and, as in your experience, there was no such address. You can see why it is urgent that I speak with you. You can contact me at yesorno@hotmail.com.

This was the secure e-mail address I used for participants in my study.

Returning to class was not easy. I had planned to enter the lecture after the professor began and exit a few minutes early. One of my final courses after two years of graduate school was Psychology and the Law. It sounded like an entry-level course, but was, in fact, an overview of the latest intersections of mental-health and legal issues. I had already missed a quarter of the lectures. The last one I attended was the morning of the day I found Bennett dead. I dreaded the turning of my classmates' heads, and the way I would be seen: a victimologist turned victim.

John Jay's student body ranged from the beat cop getting extra credit that would speed a promotion, to a former prison guard whose goal was to become a warden, to a psychiatrist who wanted to perform psychological autopsies. The city campus was spread out over five square blocks in the West Fifties, near Roosevelt Hospital. The building always photographed, built in 1903 of marble and red brick, the one you might find on an Ivy League campus, housed the administration. All my classes were held in a generic modern annex. I slid my photo ID card through the electronic reader and headed up the stairwell to my class. The professor was consulting with one of the students about how to operate the PowerPoint system. The lights were still on, affording everyone a good look at me. I avoided eye contact as I shrugged off my backpack and took a blessedly empty seat next to my Dominican cop friend, Amabile, who was aptly named. When he and I were briefly dating, he said it meant "kindness." He reached out and put his hand over my hand and held it there for a moment. I noticed he was wearing a GO BLOODHOUNDS T-shirt—supporting the John Jay basketball team. I must have been the topic of so much talk. It was not hard to imagine that a paper on my case would someday be included in the literature of criminology.

I went into this field of study to answer one question: not the one everyone asks—Why do certain people cross the line?—but why *everyone* doesn't cross the line. I wanted to know what held me back and by how much. My interest was more than scholarly; it was personal.

Steven and I were Midwesterners with all the attendant stereotypes: our father was conservative, self-reliant, honest, and stubborn—that is, when he wasn't cycling mania. Then he was charismatic, adventurous, and seductive. During one of those phases our mother had married him. She, on the other hand, had migrated to Illinois from California, the daughter of Okies who had fled the Dust Bowl during the Depression, failed to get a toehold in California's Central Valley, and wound up working in the Chicago stockyards, living on the South Side with the newly arrived Southern blacks. Our mother was malleable, independent, reckless, vain, and a looker. She had no intention of remaining on the South Side. She was seven months pregnant with Steven when she witnessed her husband's first ascent into full-blown mania. It began with his defying the obstetrician's caution about late-term intercourse. When she refused him, he slept with my mother's sixteen-year-old niece. Women have retaliated against their husbands for less. Why didn't our mother step over the line?

I was a middling high school student dreaming about becoming an artist, an actress, a poet, in the tradition of clueless youth, without giving any consideration to whether I had talent. I took a Greyhound to New York City shortly after I graduated and arrived at Port Authority at 2:00 a.m. on a rainy summer night.

I had planned to stay at the YWCA, but I met a girl on the bus who had already done what I was planning to do. She had been visiting her mother in Cleveland and was going back to Brooklyn, where she'd been living for six months. She was waiting tables until she could get modeling work and invited me to crash at her place. She lived in a first-floor studio looking out onto the Navy Yard. The kitchen was makeshift—just a hot plate and minifridge. The walls were bare and the institutional sea-green paint was scuffed. I slept on an air mattress, while she took the sofa bed.

Around six the next morning, I heard a key in the lock. A man let himself into her apartment. I called out to my friend, Candice, and she said sleepily, "It's just my boyfriend, Doug."

Doug said, "Hey," to me, and then to Candice, "Hey, babe." He sat on the edge of the sofa bed and took off his Frye boots. He wasn't wearing socks. And for some reason, that alarmed me further.

I started to get off the already deflated air mattress. "I can head out now. Thanks for letting me stay over."

"No need to go," he said, taking off his shirt. "I've got to be at work in a couple of hours."

My duffel bag was on the other side of the room and I would have had to pass near him to get it. I'd chosen to sleep in just a T-shirt and bikini underwear.

He took off his jeans. Without taking my eyes off my duffel bag, I could see in my peripheral vision that he had also forgone underwear. He climbed onto the sofa bed beside Candice and I told myself to calm down, I was in New York and I was lucky for the place to sleep.

The air mattress was a mere six feet from the sofa bed, so of course I could hear Candice tell her boyfriend to quit it, but she wasn't angry when she said it. I hadn't yet gone all the way, but I'd been on enough double dates to know what was going on. Those were the actual words that came to mind—going all the way. I was already constructing the story for my friends back at New Trier in Winnetka, the high school famous for talented and precocious students such as Ann-Margret and Rock Hudson, though my friends were the late bloomers.

I closed my eyes, placed my pillow over my head, and pretended that this kind of thing happened to me all the time. At some point their activity died down and I fell back asleep.

I woke up coughing, and the pillow seemed to be the reason. It was still covering my face, but pressure was behind it. I couldn't get enough air, and when I tried to remove it, I felt the arms that were holding it in place.

"Oh, for God's sake, you dick, leave her alone," I heard Candice say. But the hands didn't let go. I began thrashing and kicking.

"Let her breathe at least," Candice said.

One hand let go of the pillow and I gulped in air before the free hand pinned my arms.

"Get her feet," Doug called to Candice.

"I don't want to get kicked again," Candice said, but I felt her grab my ankles anyway. By now the air mattress was only as inflated as a sleeping bag.

"I told you the air mattress had a leak," Doug said. "This is going to be hell on my bad knee."

"You were at Walgreens yesterday."

"So?"

"They sell air mattresses."

Despite what was happening, their inane bickering made me think I might still be okay.

"If you let me up, I can go get you a new air mattress." I felt the effect of my words as his grip slackened, then tightened harder.

"You think we're stupid," Doug said.

"Candice," I pleaded, "I don't understand why you're doing this to me."

"She's not doing it, I am," Doug said.

I revised my hope of getting through this okay.

"I won't say anything if you just let me go. I don't know where I am. I just want to go."

"Babe, get the duct tape from under the sink."

His body was on top of mine, pinning me down. The pillow still covered my face but I could breathe. I twisted my head and saw Candice was dressed as I was, only the T-shirt was Doug's. She was tearing off a strip of the silver tape.

"Hold her head," Candice told Doug. Then she squatted beside me and covered my mouth with it. She was so close to me that I caught the sudden scent of Doug's ejaculation. If it wouldn't have choked me, I would have retched.

"Tape her wrist to the radiator," Doug ordered.

Doug took my right wrist and held it against the metal. As Candice tore off another strip and then wound it around my wrist, Doug hummed "Crazy Little Thing Called Love." When she finished securing my other wrist, this time to the leg of a bureau, Doug slid down the length of me, removing the bikini underwear as he did. I heard myself make a sound of protest through the tape covering my mouth.

Doug said, "Babe, can you get me a beer?"

"I'm not your servant, and anyway we're out."

"What the fuck, you were supposed to get some."

"Oh, when was I supposed to do that? I just got back from fucking Cleveland."

"Then go get some now."

"Like anything is open at six a.m."

"The Walgreens is open."

"They have beer?"

"Yeah, they have beer!"

I prayed that Candice would not leave me alone with him.

She pulled on leggings, then went through Doug's pockets for some money.

"She was so eager to buy us an air mattress, let her pay for the beer," Doug said.

Candice picked up my jeans and took all my cash, $300.

"You should really get traveler's checks next time," Candice said to me, then shut the door behind her.

"It's a shame to cover such a pretty mouth," Doug said. "Tell you what, how 'bout I take off this tape and you stay quiet."

I nodded.

"This is going to hurt a little." I thought he would rip it off like a Band-Aid, but he pulled it off slowly, as though this were foreplay. "You had a lot of boyfriends?"

My eyes teared up.

"Or just one special fellow? I bet you let him go to second base." He lifted my T-shirt and pinched my nipples. "Candice outdid herself this time." As he began rubbing his erection between my breasts, his cell phone rang. He picked it up and looked at the number before he answered. "Yeah? Now what?" While he listened, he rubbed the tip of his penis against the nipple he'd pinched. "I don't care. Coors." He hung up and said, "Shit." He climbed off me and went to the window. He was no longer fully erect.

He started rubbing himself, and when nothing happened, he walked back to me, straddled my chest, and said, "Help me out with that pretty mouth."

I reflexively turned my head away, but he grabbed my jaw and opened my mouth. He forced himself inside. I gagged and tears rolled out the sides of my eyes.

This appeared to be a turn-on because he was hard again. "I usually wait for Candice, but I don't think I can wait this time."

He pulled out of my mouth, pried my legs apart with his knee, and in an instant I was no longer a virgin. He finished quickly and I was still alive. He was inside me when the door opened—Candice with the Coors.

"You fucker, you were supposed to wait."

"Well, if you hadn't dragged your ass getting back . . ."

In spite of that, she cracked open a can and handed it to him. She cracked a second can and took a long gulp. She then opened a third and put it on the floor beside me.

"What, you're a hostess now?" Doug asked.

"She's got to be thirsty, too. Right, Morgan?"

Without ceremony, she produced a Swiss Army knife and cut one hand free. I was able to sit up, and when I did, my T-shirt dropped to cover me. The thought of having a beer with them was sickening, but I could not risk provoking them. I reached for the can and made myself swallow a small amount.

Candice looked at the alarm clock on the bureau I was still taped to. "You better think about heading in to work."

"I got a clean shirt here? Don't tell me you've been in Cleveland."

Candice went to the small closet and threw a long-sleeved shirt at him.

"Are you going to have time to drop her back at the bus station?" Candice asked.

She cut my other wrist free, gave me back my duffel, and I was hustled into a white panel van. On the drive to what I hoped would be Port Authority, Doug kept the radio on to an oldies station, one power anthem after another. I was grateful I didn't have to talk to him. I was sitting in the rear of the van watching him nod his head in time to the music.

When we reached Port Authority, Doug turned off the radio. "When I let you out, don't turn around until the count of sixty. Unless you want to see me again."

I didn't turn around for the count of six hundred.

The moment the lecture ended, Amabile took my hand. "Come with me." He pulled me away from the classroom before anyone had a chance to talk to me. He said he had an extra helmet for me and offered a ride to Rikers on his Harley. He and I both had patients this time each week, and I had a lot of catching up to do. I had never intended to be a practicing psychologist, but seven hundred clinical hours were required for the degree. Rikers wasn't a prison; it was a jail, which meant that the inmates were there awaiting trial or serving less than a year. My patients were guys hoping that by seeing a shrink, the trial judge would look on them favorably. Since most of the Rikers population (fourteen thousand on an average day) was awaiting trial, everyone there was "innocent."

I held fast to Amabile's waist as we sped over the unmarked Francis Buono Bridge from Queens—the only access to the island. In the orientation session we had learned that Rikers Island had been a military training ground during the Civil War. It became a jail in 1932.

In 1957, Northeast Airlines Flight 823 crashed onto the island shortly after takeoff from LaGuardia Airport, killing twenty and injuring seventy-eight out of a total of ninety-five passengers and six crew. Shortly after the crash, department personnel and inmates alike ran to the crash site to help survivors. As a result of their actions, of the fifty-seven inmates who assisted with the rescue effort, thirty were released and sixteen received a reduction of six months by the NYC parole board.

We also learned that a drawing by Salvador Dalí, done as an apology because he was unable to attend a talk about art for the prisoners, hung in the inmate dining room from 1965 to 1981, when it was moved to the prison lobby for safekeeping. The drawing was stolen in 2003 by some guards and replaced with a fake.

The facility was something of a small town. There were schools, medical clinics, ball fields, chapels, gyms, drug-rehab programs, grocery stores, barbershops, a bakery, a Laundromat, a power plant, a track, a tailor shop, a print shop, a bus depot, and even a car wash. It was the world's largest penal colony.

I saw my patients in a small annex off an overcrowded ward where the fluorescent lights were on 24-7. A TV played from 7:00 a.m. to midnight. The men were dressed in orange jumpsuits and looked as if they had been living in a Greyhound bus terminal waiting for a bus that never came.

After Amabile and I were ID'd, searched, and cleared, we walked the maze of hallways with bars over the windows, and doors that only the guards could open.

My office, which I shared with three other degree candidates, was six feet by eight feet, smaller than a cell, and contained two identical folding chairs and a gym locker.

My first patient was a skinny white guy with a buzz cut and a cauliflower ear sentenced to nine months for exposing himself at the Metropolitan Museum, in the Greek-sculpture wing. He had stationed himself at the end of a line of marble nudes and waited for schoolgirls on a field trip. He showed no remorse and contended that he was innocent, that his fly was open without his knowledge.

He always started our sessions with a joke to try to rattle or charm me, I couldn't always tell which. It was more than that— he only responded to my questions with jokes.

"Prisoner," he began, "'Look here, Doctor! You've already removed my spleen, tonsils, adenoids, and one of my kidneys. I only came to see if you could get me out of this place!' Doctor, 'I am . . . bit by bit!'"

"Are you asking me to get you out of this place?" I asked.

"A man escapes from a prison, finds a house, and breaks into it, looking for money, but only finds a young couple in bed. He orders the guy out of bed and ties him up in a chair. While tying the girl up to the bed, he gets on top of her, kisses her on the neck, then goes to the bathroom. While he's in there, the husband tells his wife, 'Listen, this guy is an escaped prisoner, look at his clothes! He probably hasn't seen a woman in years. I saw how he kissed your neck. If he wants sex, don't resist, don't complain, just do what he tells you. If he gets angry, he'll kill us. Be strong, honey. I love you.' 'He was not kissing my neck,' the wife said. 'He was whispering in my ear. He told me he was gay, thought you were cute, and asked if we kept any Vaseline in the bathroom.'"

"Are you frightened of being raped in here?"

"A psychiatrist makes his rounds in the mental hospital one morning. 'How are you feeling today?' he asks the first patient. The patient is naked, his penis is erect, and he is dropping peanuts on it. He turns to the shrink and says, 'I am fucking nuts. I'm going to be here for a while.'"

"Are you accepting the fact that you are going to be here for a while?"

"You know, Doc, I think I'm allergic to your face."

I awaited the dreaded punch line.

"Yeah, my dick gets swollen every time I see it."

"We're stopping early today," I said, signaling through the reinforced window in the door for the guard to relieve me.

I remained on the folding chair reminding myself why I agreed to do this work. If only Bennett had been as obvious as this exhibitionist joker. How many sociopaths does it take to change a lightbulb? One. He holds the bulb while the world revolves around him.

I saw Doug and Candice one more time.

I served them omelets and home fries and Doug asked for hot sauce. They didn't recognize me—a combination of my waitress uniform and my cut and colored hair and their generally hungover condition. When Doug dropped his knife and asked for another, I brought a steak knife and considered plunging it into his chest, two inches below his clavicle, where a natural gap exists between the ribs. Maybe it was my mother's hand that stilled mine in this defining moment. Or maybe I realized that stabbing Doug would just be the form my *self*-destruction would take. Then there's the fact that vengeance requires incrementally larger acts to satisfy the avenger.

I found a share with two medical students in Vinegar Hill, one of whom was Kathy. I'd taken the waitressing job at this diner in Bushwick to finance an extension class in poetry at the New School. Poetry felt like the most natural form for me, and in fact, I had written a couple of poems about Doug and Candice.

Their breakfast cost $21.12; they left me a tip of less than a dollar.

I saw one more patient at Rikers that day—a walk in the park compared to the exhibitionist joker. After, Amabile dropped me back at my apartment and asked if I wanted him to go in with me. I said I was okay and thanked him for his kindness and concern. We had stopped seeing each other when I had met Bennett, and I was glad we had remained friends.

After he drove off, I walked to Mother's and got a veggie burger, sweet-potato fries, and a Diet Coke, aware of how pointless it was to drink Diet Coke with fries.

I opened all the apartment windows because the smell of the cleaning solvents was still pervasive. A Buddhist friend offered to come in and "smudge" the place to neutralize the horror, but could I continue to live here even after such a ceremony? I felt dizzy and found that I'd been holding my breath. I put the bag of takeout beside my computer, had a couple of fries, and checked my Hotmail account.

I'm the person you're looking for. There are others, too. You are not the first woman to comment on the familiarity of my experience. The man I knew as "Peter" is about five-feet-eight, carries a little too much weight for that height, is dark-haired with a small scar across one eyebrow—not particularly attractive but it didn't matter. He has an assurance about him that is charismatic. Did the man you were involved with fall for you very quickly? Did he bring you Bvlgari Green Tea perfume and insist you always wear it? Did he hate your pets? If you want to talk, I'd prefer to do it in person and in a public place. Are you in Boston? I can meet you at Clarke's bar right outside South Station on the Atlantic Avenue side. I'll be wearing an orange hand-knit scarf. Is this convenient for you?

The next morning I took a train to Boston.

Clarke's bar was closed. Not for the day, forever. A FOR RENT sign was in the window. I couldn't remember if she had said to meet her inside or outside, but when I saw the sign, my memory settled on outside. I stood there for thirty minutes. Why? The same reason I walked up and down the rue Saint-Urbain looking for Bennett's omelet place. I noticed a policeman on the corner and started toward him, then realized that I wouldn't know what to ask him. I had no name for her, only knew that she worked for the police department and that she had fallen for the same man.

Had she changed her mind about meeting me? I concluded that she was brave by posting the letter in the first place, and by the fact that she was an officer. Maybe an emergency came up? We hadn't exchanged phone numbers. I e-mailed her and then walked across Atlantic Avenue to a coffee shop to wait. I chose a booth with a view of the shuttered Clarke's bar. After my third cup of coffee, I decided to go to the closest precinct, where I imagined she worked. In her posting on Lovefraud, she had said she was an incident-reports analyst. How many young, female incident-reports analysts could there be at a precinct? I had brought a picture of Bennett, or half a picture, the one I had found on my coffee table, left by the cleanup crew. I had cut my likeness out.

The precinct was ten blocks away, a large brick building that might once have served as an orphanage or a library. It was statelier than the local 90, the Brooklyn precinct I passed by every day on my way to the J train. The local 90 could never have been anything but a police station.

The officer at the front desk was being harassed by an older woman who demanded to know where they'd taken her son. I waited until the officer calmed the woman enough to get her to take a seat again.

"I wonder if you could help me," I said in an authoritative voice, one I'd mastered in order to speak to police officers and criminals alike in my professional capacity. "I'm from John Jay College of Criminal Justice in New York City. I have an appointment with your incident-reports analyst. Could you tell me where I might find her?"

"Him, not her. Second floor. But I need to see some ID."

I showed my John Jay photo ID and told him I was looking for a woman.

"Gerald Marks is our new guy. You're not talking about Susan Rorke, are you?"

"I might be. I know this sounds confusing, but I don't know the name of the woman I'm meeting, just her job and that this is the closest precinct to where she suggested I meet her today. Do you know where I can find this Susan Rorke?"

"Miss, I'm sorry to tell you, but Susan died six weeks ago."

"The woman I'm looking for quit her job, moved to New York, and then came back here sometime this summer."

"Susan did leave her job, but she came back just before she was killed."

"You said she died. She was killed?"

"Miss, I can't give you the details of an ongoing investigation."

I did a quick calculation. She must have died soon after she posted that letter on Lovefraud, if it was Susan Rorke. But if Susan Rorke had been dead for six weeks, who had responded to my e-mail? I asked the desk sergeant if I might speak with one of her colleagues.

He picked up the phone and said, "Can you come to the front desk?"

A young man who looked as though he had ridden to work on a skateboard appeared in a couple of minutes and introduced himself as Detective Homes.

"She's asking about Susan Rorke," the desk sergeant said.

"I might be," I said again, and explained myself to Homes.

"What do you know about this investigation?"

"Nothing, unless Susan Rorke knew this man." I handed him the photo of Bennett.

"Where did you get this?"

I sensed the detective had seen Bennett before. I sensed I was going to learn something I didn't want to know. But I already knew it. "Was this man involved with Susan Rorke?"

"This is my investigation. Please answer my question."

"He was my fiancé."

"What's his name?"

"You tell me." I didn't know Bennett in any sense—his history, his capabilities, his motivation. I felt dizzy with ignorance, nauseous.

"Would you come upstairs and look at some photos?"

I said nothing as we climbed the stairs. I needed the handrail. I cycled between confusion and shame at having so wildly misread a man I loved.

The detective's desk was surprisingly neat. All that was on it was a short stack of folders, one of which he opened after offering me a seat. A woman's photograph was paper-clipped inside. She looked to be about my age, an attractive woman holding a one-eyed Jack Russell terrier in her lap.

"Do you recognize this woman?"

"I assume this is Susan Rorke. But, no, I don't recognize her."

He showed me another picture. This time, Susan Rorke was smiling broadly in a sunny, mountainous landscape. Her head was resting on Bennett's shoulder.

"Is this the man you claim was your fiancé?"

"How did she die?"

"Please answer my question."

I was, by turns, sick to my stomach and utterly composed. "May I have a glass of water?"

When had this photograph been taken? Was it before I met Bennett? The detective came back from the watercooler and handed me an old-fashioned cone-shaped paper cup. "When was this taken?" I asked when I finished drinking.

"When was *your* photograph of this man taken?"

"Is he a suspect?"

"Please, I need you to answer directly."

"Fine. Mine was taken in Maine about a month before he was killed."

"He's dead?"

"Maybe you read about it. He was killed by dogs. I'm the one who found the body."

"This was in New York."

"Brooklyn. September twentieth."

"I didn't know that was who we were looking for." He excused himself and picked up his phone. I assumed he was going to notify his captain. I felt weightless. Did he think Bennett was a murderer?

When the detective hung up, he gave me his card and said he would be in touch. "How can I reach you?"

I gave him my information and opened my purse. "I think you should see this." I handed him the Lovefraud letters I had printed out.

I waited until he had finished reading them, then asked him to tell me how she died.

"She fell three stories to her death at the homeless shelter where she volunteered. We believe she was pushed."

"What makes you think that?"

"There were scratches on the window frame as she struggled."

"And you think it was Bennett who pushed her?"

"We know him by another name."

"And you can't tell me, right?"

"Can I make a copy of that photograph?"

I handed him the scissored half of the photo, and when he brought it back, I couldn't look at it. I slipped it between the two pieces of cardboard I'd used to protect it in my backpack. But this time I didn't even unzip the small compartment where I kept it separate from all the crap I'd thrown in—the makeup not used, the empty pens, a half-eaten energy bar with more calories than the Milky Way I'd wanted.

Outside, I had the hackneyed feeling of surprise that the world continued as it had before what I had just learned. When everybody is in the same circumstances, say a community after a tornado has ripped through it, a careful camaraderie prevails. I was alone with my discovery and had never felt so isolated, or afraid.

Another woman might have headed for a bar. But what occurred to me was not something I indulged—I just imagined it. I pictured myself wheeling a small cart with a laundry bag filled with sheets and towels, scented dryer sheets, and detergent. I wanted to wheel my laundry cart into a small neighborhood Laundromat and ask the proprietor simple questions about when to add softener. I wanted to sit in a plastic chair and watch my laundry spin, getting clean. I wanted to fold it, warm from the dryer, and retrace my steps, wheeling home the small proof that I could function in this world and make a small thing better.

Had my dogs saved me?

Where was the man I knew as Bennett six weeks ago when Susan Rorke was killed?

I was on the train back to New York. I checked my phone calendar and saw that I was right—Bennett had met me that weekend at the Old Orchard Beach Inn, a yellow Victorian on a bluff overlooking the ocean, walking distance to the pier.

Susan was killed that Friday. Boston to Old Orchard Beach, Maine, was a two-hour drive. Could Bennett have pushed her out the window in Boston and driven his rental the hundred miles to a resort village by the sea to spend a romantic weekend with me? Yes, there had been time for him to do that. I had already checked into the inn when he pulled up. When had he bought the white roses he gave me? He kissed me as usual and asked where we could get a drink. I said the inn was serving wine by the fireplace, and he said he wanted a real drink. I remember being surprised by that. He said he wanted to shower and change first. He said he left Montreal at nine that morning; that would have meant he'd been driving for six hours straight, so there was nothing unusual about his wanting to do that first. He seemed cheery enough and was certainly attentive to me. He had an appetite; we ate lobster for dinner, and of course we made love. Did he have any scratches? How hard had Susan fought? Afterward, he insisted we walk by the ocean in the moonlight even though it was chilly. We strolled the boardwalk, which was nearly empty given the hour and temperature. I heard a few snatches of Quebecois from passersby and asked what they were saying. He told me they were looking forward to tomorrow's exhibition game between the Maple Leafs and the Montreal Canadiens. I thought back to my fruitless search for his apartment in Montreal and wondered if he even spoke French. I googled the National Hockey League schedule and found the Montreal Canadiens had not been in an exhibition game.

Later, in the room, when he took off his pants, I saw a large fresh bruise on his shin. When I asked how he got it, he said he banged it helping one of his bands move some equipment. One of those bands he didn't represent.

That night I moved to the right side of the bed as usual. The left side was against the wall, and Bennett knew my holdover childhood fear about sleeping next to a wall and slipping through it. Just as I was falling asleep in his arms, he whispered, "If you love me, you'll sleep next to the wall." What if I hadn't obliged him? What might he have done to me? The next morning—oh, I didn't want to remember our lovemaking. Seeing it through the lens of what I had learned in Boston, it was repulsive. Yet, that night it seemed he never let go of my hand. He was still holding it when I woke up.

I got back to Penn Station a little after midnight. I was exhausted but not sleepy. As soon as I got home, I looked up every article about Susan Rorke's death in the order the stories were filed.

She was described as a thirty-five-year-old police incident-reports analyst who volunteered at the South Boston homeless shelter every week. Early on, her death was reported as an accident. She had not returned from a break after trying to fix a

window shade on the third floor. Ms. Rorke's body was found
in the alley behind the shelter. Police said it appeared Ms. Rorke
had fallen from an open window and died on impact. The next
article reported that the police were investigating the death as a
possible homicide. They were looking for a homeless man who
had stayed at the shelter that night. Witnesses said he had argued
with Ms. Rorke earlier that evening. The homeless man was
found, questioned, and released. The police were still ruling the
death a homicide, pending further investigation.

I went on Facebook next. Her profile picture was the same
one the detective had showed me, the one-eyed Jack Russell on
her lap. I wondered what happened to the dog. I scrolled through
the last few months of her postings and found the following: a
picture of her left hand, fingers splayed, presenting a view of a
diamond engagement ring. The old-fashioned, marquise-cut
diamond was approximately one carat, set in either white gold
or platinum. The comments below all said pretty much the same
thing: When are we going to meet him?

I went to my top drawer and took out the tiny leather box,
lined in velvet, that housed the ring Bennett had given me,
identical. I was tempted to throw it away but I realized it was evidence. It was proof that I belonged to this sorority of the duped.
If Susan and I were sorority sisters, then so was the woman who
had written me on Lovefraud and pretended to be Susan Rorke.
Even she suspected others. If three, why not four? More?

I went to Lovefraud and left a private message for number
three.

Who are you? Why did you pretend to be Susan Rorke? Why
do you think the man you knew as "Peter" had deceived other

women? I went to meet you in good faith and discovered that
the woman you claimed to be was killed six weeks ago. I have
information about the man I knew as "Bennett" that will
interest you. I am not making anything up to try to lure you.
I am entirely serious. I don't know why you didn't meet me,
but if you are afraid of him, you need not be. I hope to hear
from you.

I was hungry, and for the first time in weeks, I wanted something healthy. I walked a few blocks to Champs. It opened at
8:00 a.m. As usual I was the only customer without tattooed
arms and legs. The staff was reliably cheerful. I got a booth to
myself and sat beneath a piece of fifties signage on the wall. I
asked for a double order of the tofu scramble with its mysterious
spices, and the sautéed plantains. I put real cane sugar in my
coffee. When I looked for the transgender server to refill my cup,
I saw the door open. It took me a moment to place him. He was
unstrapping a bike helmet. When I saw his hair, I recognized
him as McKenzie, my lawyer. He was wearing a sweat-dappled
T-shirt and black Pursuit cycling shorts that did not look like a
costume on him.

He looked at my plate. "Those better not be the last of the
plantains."

"Would you like one?" I indicated the empty seat across
from me.

He slid into the booth and, without glancing at the menu,
ordered exactly what I had. He speared a slice of plantain off my
plate. "I lived on these when I worked in Puerto Rico."

"When was that?"

"I represented a horse in Vieques. A farmer near one of the

Navy's test-bombing ranges noticed his prize horse had stopped breeding. We won a judgment for the farmer and the stud."

I raised my coffee cup in a salute.

"Have you scheduled the temperament test yet?" he asked.

"Next Friday on Staten Island."

"Excellent. I wish you good luck."

When his food came, I wanted to change the subject so that he didn't think I'd invited him to sit down with me in order to take advantage of his legal counsel. "The closest I've been to Vieques was looking at it across the water from St. Thomas."

"I love the islands. What were you there for?"

"I always took diving vacations there so I could bring back a couple of patty-cakes." When I saw the question in his face, I said, "They're island strays that survive on cornmeal cakes they find in the garbage. I work with a nonprofit that places island dogs in mainland homes."

"What was the diving like there?"

"The reefs are suffering. Every time a cruise ship dumps two thousand tourists wearing sunscreen into the ocean, the coral bleaches and dies. I feel lucky to have seen the reefs before they're gone. Did you dive off Vieques?"

"A little."

"Isn't it amazing? Swimming through those canyons of coral. The colors. Have you ever dived at night when the soft corals come out? It's like swimming through a rose garden with only a flashlight. And the fish. Have you ever been followed by those schools of blue Tang? The way they all turn at once and become iridescent."

He put his fork down though he had not finished his plantains. I felt I had somehow stepped wrong. "Let me take you to breakfast," he said, and reached inside his zippered pocket for some cash.

I thanked him and he told me he had to file some court papers downtown.

"On a bike?"

"That way the guards think I'm a messenger and I don't have to go upstairs and schmooze."

I watched him through the window as he unlocked his bike and rode off toward the Williamsburg Bridge.

I finished his plantains, thanked the server, and walked home. Even before I checked to see if I had received a reply to my last Lovefraud posting, I went on Google and looked up Laurence McKenzie. I scrolled past his professional achievements until I came to an article that made me feel awful. Five years ago, I learned, he and his wife were diving off Vieques when his wife went missing. She got separated from the rest of the diving group during an ascent through unusually strong currents. They found her a few minutes later, floating facedown and unconscious with a partially inflated BCD and an empty tank.

She could not be resuscitated.

The odds of being struck by lightning in the United States are one in six hundred thousand. You are six times more likely to be struck by lightning than you are to be killed by a dog of any breed. And four times more likely to be killed by a cow than any dog.

I stood outside what looked like a horse show ring on Staten Island. I was waiting for the handler to bring out Cloud for the first part of her temperament test when I saw Billie walking across the parking lot. I called her a couple of times to ask about my dogs.

She waved to me.

"Are you part of this?" I asked.

"I couldn't let these pups be tested without being here to root for them."

Something in me recoiled from her breezy greeting. Was she one of those people who fed on other people's dramas?

Having only seen her in the sensory-overloading shelter, I hadn't realized how attractive and athletic she was. She wore pegged jeans and toffee-colored ankle boots. Despite the first chill of fall, her linen jacket was open over a tight-fitting T-shirt that I recognized from a rescue organization; it said SHOW ME YOUR PITS. I had one just like it, but never had the nerve to wear it.

"I can't believe you came," I said.

"I've watched a lot of these. I wish they had temperament tests for men."

She led me behind a small outcropping where we could watch without being seen. She said our presence would distract Cloud.

"I have a surprise for you," she whispered, as a female handler entered the ring with Cloud on a short lead. "You'll see."

Cloud and her handler faced the four judges, three of whom were middle-aged women, and the fourth, a man who looked to be in his thirties. Cloud looked so happy to be outside, I feared the fresh air and sunlight would distract her!

Billie explained that the first part of the test would measure the dog's reaction to strangers. First we watched the "neutral" stranger approach Cloud, stop, and tell the handler to have a nice day. Cloud did not react. The "friendly" stranger approached happily and briskly, sweet-talked Cloud, and patted her head. Cloud wagged her tail and licked the stranger's hand. The third stranger careened, swinging his arms and speaking in a loud, agitated voice.

Billie leaned over. "They are going to judge her on provoked aggression, strong avoidance, or panic."

"If I were Cloud, I'd exhibit all three."

"After what you've been through, so would I."

But Cloud aced it. She didn't take the bait.

As the handler walked Cloud slowly around the ring, they passed small stations that looked like duck blinds. From behind each one came a variety of provocations: the jarring noise of coins being shaken in a metal box, the sudden opening of a large umbrella. Cloud startled and hid behind the handler.

"The umbrella test cashiers more dogs than any other. The response they're looking for is curiosity, then continuing past," Billie said.

"But she's always been afraid of umbrellas. Will they take that into consideration?"

"It's not a deal-breaker if she passes everything else. And hiding is better than showing aggression."

After Cloud passed the gunshot test—a blank was fired near her—the judges gave her the thumbs-up. Vicki Hearne, the late philosopher and dog trainer, had written about "what the illusion of viciousness is obscuring." Cloud was a huge dog with big jowls and, covered in blood, had appeared to be a vicious dog, but it was an illusion, and what it obscured was fear.

I had been told that I would not be allowed to visit Cloud after the test, so I gathered my purse and coat, and as I turned to say good-bye to Billie, I saw the same handler walk George into the ring.

I looked at Billie and she was smiling. "Surprise."

"Who gave you permission to have George tested?"

"I just don't think he's a killer."

"This wasn't your call."

In the ring, the handler put George into a sit-stay. He then aced every test that Cloud did—the normal, friendly, and crazy strangers, shaken coins, even the umbrella test. Nothing distracted him from obeying the handler. I remembered how eager he was to please. With that recollection, came another: that Bennett had pushed a woman out a window. What might he have done to this dog? George now looked ribby, the way he did when I first saw him—you are supposed to be able to feel a dog's ribs, not see them. It was part of what prompted me to foster him. It is such a pleasure simply to feed a hungry dog.

But the gunshot test terrified him.

He rushed behind the handler and tried to keep going, but the handler pulled hard on the leash and brought him back to her side.

"He heard Chester get shot," I said. "Should I tell the judges?"

"It's not that uncommon a response," Billie said. "More dogs run away during Fourth of July fireworks than any other time of year."

It took the handler a minute or two to reassure George. She finally got him into a sit and told him he was a good boy. Even from this distance, I saw him lick the handler's hand. But after walking comfortably across the sheet of crinkling plastic, he balked at walking across the metal grate. He planted himself, deadweight, and went on strike. The handler pulled on his lead, and we could hear George growl.

"Shit," I said. "His paws are tender from years in a damp cage. Don't these people understand there are contingencies?" Instantly I was in tears from the impossible situation—I was standing up for my dog, a dog that had killed. Did Bennett try to pull George over the heat grating in the floor of my apartment? I was looking for any way to account for what had happened.

Billie responded to my distress by putting an arm around my shoulder for just a moment. "It's not over till it's over."

When it *was* over, the judges announced that they would be willing to retest George at a later date. The anxiety of watching the two tests left me exhausted and despairing. Billie asked if I'd eaten anything that morning, and when I told her I had not, she said a diner with lousy coffee and great pancakes was a couple of blocks from here. She offered to drive me.

The leather seats of her Volvo were surprisingly free of dog hair given the time she spent with the shelter dogs—unlike the leather couch that Steven had given me, which I had to cover with a throw before Bennett came over.

"Thank you for bringing George," I said.

The diner was nothing like Champs. The tattoos we saw on the patrons of this diner were standard-issue armed services and MOM-in-a-heart tats. The pancakes here were not gluten-free. I ordered a stack of chocolate chip with whipped cream, and Billie had the lousy coffee.

I had not confided in a girlfriend since Kathy's death. Though I barely knew this Billie, I found myself telling her about Bennett and his deception. The more I talked, the more I talked. In a headlong rush, I told her the crazy-making story, with its blind spots and question marks, how we met online while I was conducting research on sociopaths and victims, clear on up to the fake address in Montreal and the key to it he had given me. Billie said he reminded her of a guy she used to see, a guy who had lied to her continuously and said, when she confronted him about the lying, that he was just trying to entertain her.

"'I lie to myself all the time,'" Billie quoted.

"'But I never believe me,'" I finished.

"*The Outsiders*," we said together. "S. E. Hinton."

Turned out we had both seen the film of this novel many times, about greasers in Tulsa, Johnny and Ponyboy, one of whom kills a member of a rival gang. Matt Dillon, Patrick Swayze, Rob Lowe, and Tom Cruise were in it before they were stars.

"Bennett's story also has a murder." I told her about Susan Rorke.

"Do *you* think Bennett killed her?"

"The police do."

"Why do the police think he did it?" Billie asked.

"They always suspect the husband or fiancé."

"Bennett was engaged to her, too?"

"He gave her the same ring he gave me."

"That would be the suffer-ring? I hope it was expensive."

"I thought it was." God, I had missed this. "Can I ask you something personal? You're always at the shelter, you take a day off for this—how do you support yourself?"

"I'm a trustafarian. Under close supervision. My grandmother doesn't trust me."

The waitress finally set down the pancakes in front of me.

"So what do the police do when their prime suspect is dead? They can't exactly try him," Billie said.

"I don't think Susan Rorke and I were the only women Bennett deceived. I think I've heard from a third."

"Reportyourex.com?"

"Lovefraud.com. She said she wanted to meet me in person but she didn't show up."

"There are many reasons why she might not have shown up."

"She pretended to be Susan Rorke. Maybe she didn't know Susan Rorke was dead."

"Maybe she did."

When the check came, Billie reached for it even though she had only ordered coffee.

In the car heading back to the city, I said, "He used a different name with her. He called himself Peter. But it was him. I showed the detective a picture and he confirmed it."

"So who is the third woman?"

"Maybe she's the tenth."

"Maybe the dogs did you a favor."

"Nothing I didn't already think."

"I mean, he pushed her out a window."

"He was never violent with me. But how could I not know?"

"The dogs knew."

•   •   •

I asked Billie to drop me off on Delancey Street so I could walk across the Williamsburg Bridge. I needed to do something physical and mindless. The view was of downtown Manhattan, with the two stately bridges—the Manhattan and the Brooklyn—spanning the lower East River. The Brooklyn Bridge was the first to be built—the longest suspension bridge of its time, and one of the most beautiful. The Manhattan was third, a gridwork of metal struts. In between came the Williamsburg, said to be the ugliest design on the river. But it's not what you see when you're walking across it. The view trumps the noise of trucks, cars, and subways flanking the hardy pedestrians and cyclists. Even Edward Hopper painted a view titled *From Williamsburg Bridge.* The walkway ends in the Hasidic neighborhood where women still wear wigs and the men grow side-curls and beards. Even in the heat of summer, come the Sabbath, the men wear the large fur hats known as *shtreimel.* Within the space of ten blocks, you hear conversations in Yiddish, then Spanish, then Chinese, then Italian. It's part of why I moved here.

I climbed the five flights to my apartment and found a phone message from the Boston detective. It wasn't yet five so I called him right away.

"Ms. Prager, I have a few questions for you in the investigation of Susan Rorke's murder. Is this a good time to talk?"

"As good as any."

"I'd like to ask you about the weekend she was killed when you met the man you knew as Bennett in Maine."

"What can I tell you?"

"You said he drove from Montreal to Old Orchard Beach. What time did he arrive?"

"He arrived an hour after I did, around four, but I don't know if he drove from Montreal."

"Did you notice anything unusual about his behavior or appearance?"

"He was his usual self, but later I saw a large bruise on his shin. He said he got it moving one of his bands' equipment, but that was a lie. He didn't represent any bands."

"And when did you find out that he lied about his job?"

"And everything else. A few weeks after he died. Have *you* had any luck finding out who he is?"

"We have a protocol to follow in a murder investigation. Have you been contacted again by the woman posing as Susan Rorke?"

"No, but who was *she*? That's my question for you. And how did she know about Bennett and Susan and me?"

"We're trying to find out."

"What *have* you found out? Do you know who Bennett was?"

"I'll tell you when I know."

"But you think he's guilty?"

"Only a judge and jury can find him guilty," the detective said, "and the dead can't be tried."

That night I went to the Turkey's Nest on Bedford, picked up a guy, and went home with him. This wasn't a plan, it's just what I did. The Turkey's Nest has the least hip jukebox in Williamsburg and caters to the last of the blue-collar crowd. In a moment of splendid irony I put my quarters in the jukebox and selected Patsy Cline singing "Crazy." As the song ended, a good-looking guy asked me why I'd chosen that song. I had two whiskeys in me already and said, "See who's crazy enough to ask me to dance to it."

He reached into the pocket of his tight jeans and produced several quarters, which he fed to the jukebox. "Crazy" started up again and he pulled me to him. "Are you crazy?"

"You don't want to know," I said.

"Try me." He guided me onto the dance floor, a narrow space between the bar and the pool table.

"It's hard to know where to begin."

"I always start with my ex-wife," he said.

"What about her?"

"She cut the right sleeve off all of my shirts."

"What did your right arm do?"

"Nothing my left arm didn't. Your turn."

"My fiancé was engaged to two women at the same time. He gave us each an identical ring."

"I see your fiancé and I raise you my ex-wife: she painted the word *asshole* across the firehouse doors. I'm a firefighter."

"I see your ex-wife and I raise you my fiancé: he murdered the other fiancée."

"Whoa." The guy stopped dancing. "For real?"

"Looks that way. But I came here to not think about that."

"Is he in jail?"

"He's dead."

The guy took my hand and pulled me back to the bar. "What are you drinking?"

I had two more of what I was drinking, and he kept up with me. He lived in Greenpoint near Transmitter Park with two roommates, both firefighters. Neither was home when we got there. His room was a mess and it suited me. So did his kisses. I hadn't kissed anyone since Bennett. And that thought wouldn't leave me alone.

Would I rather have been kissing Bennett?

I knew him as well as I knew this firefighter.

I was stuck in my head again and my body just went through the motions. He stopped while we were both still dressed and said, "You're not here, are you?" He wasn't angry.

"I wish I were."

"Why don't I get you a cab," he said, no trace of irritation in his voice.

He put me in the cab and gave the driver a twenty.

"Your ex-wife is wrong about you," I said.

I was back in the dreaded apartment. Maybe Cilla was right and I should consider moving, but I wasn't ready, nor could I afford to. She'd had her walk on the wild side, but what steadiness I had now I owed to her. I sat by the living-room window, which looked out onto my neighbors' backyards—the one with topiary, the one strewn with drying laundry, the one with stones arranged in a Zen garden. There was a half moon and I sat with my untouched cup of tea until dawn.

When I had told Steven that Bennett was suspected of murder, he said, "Those dogs are heroes." When I told Cilla, she asked if this knowledge helped me forgive myself for what happened. When I told McKenzie, he said, "Now *that* I can work with."

We were back at Champs. I had asked him to meet me there. I now wanted him to defend George, too.

"Who is Bennett alleged to have killed?"

I had passed beyond my initial shame at having been duped. "His other fiancée." I watched this information register with McKenzie. He was studying me to gauge how I was doing. It felt dishonest not to tell him, though I didn't want to come across as a victim. Ha!

"How did she die?"

I told him what I knew, and he said he'd send for the police report.

"You'll see in the report that he used a different name with the woman the police think he killed."

I gave him the name of the Boston detective to contact. I gave him the name of the victim. I could give him no name for my former fiancé.

When I asked if he could defend George, too, he refused to sugarcoat George's chances, but said he would do what I wanted. This interrupted my despair. I was aware of a kind of intimacy that comes from two people aligned with each other fixing their gaze on something outside themselves. We wanted the same thing.

He walked me outside, and before I headed down Lorimer Street, I offered my hand to shake. But he gave me a hug. That it lasted a couple of beats longer than expected was something that I would think back on in the months to come.

Usually I walk off bad news, and after leaving McKenzie, the feeling of his arms around me propelled me through the neighborhood. I needed to restock my kitchen; I wanted staples, even though I never cooked. I headed for C-Town on Graham and passed the diner where the old couple sat out front every afternoon. The bench was for customers only, but no one at the diner was willing to send them on their way. A fixture, they had a kind greeting for people who walked by. They were kind to each other, too—every time I saw them I had the same thought: they still love each other. They were the type of old couple meant to elicit just such feelings, and I pushed back against having the response I was meant to have.

A guy with a tattooed spiderweb covering half his face came out the diner door. The old woman said to her husband, "He certainly has made a commitment to his lifestyle."

I checked Lovefraud when I got home and found this e-mail:

I have been following your postings about the man you call "Bennett" and I am begging you to stop. Whatever information you think you have about him will not interest me. This man is the last person I would be afraid of, and your implying that he deceives women is a lie. I am engaged to him. I did not pretend to be Susan Rorke, but if you continue to seek her out, you might do better to quiz her crazy friends. I will, however, be willing to talk with you but only because I owe it to him.

I felt as though I were living on the other side of the wall, that I had slept too close to it and, during the night, had passed through into the other world.

I met Samantha the next day at one of the Pain Quotidiens on the Upper East Side. I could never read the sign with its French pronunciation; to me it signified *pain*, and thus I found it fitting that she had chosen it as our meeting place.

Because we met on a weekend morning, the small, private tables were all taken. We would have to sit at the long communal table. I scanned the patrons for a woman with an empty seat beside her. Three women fit that description. One had her purse carelessly open on the table beside her; one was on a cell phone texting, her nails painted black; one was rearranging a sweater on the back of her chair. The one with the open purse was conventionally beautiful, her features played up by carefully applied makeup. She looked to be about my age, but she also looked too high maintenance for "Bennett." The one with the black manicure was too Goth for him. That left the nervous woman who, having rearranged her sweater, was now rearranging her silverware. As the knife and fork gleamed, so did the stone in her engagement ring. I watched her until she looked up and met my eyes. She flushed and looked away for a moment—a flush of anger, not embarrassment.

I walked toward the empty chair. "Samantha?"

"I only have fifteen minutes."

When I agreed to meet Samantha, I wanted to see who else had captured his heart. I wanted to see who else had been taken in by him. I wanted to compare the damage we had suffered at his hands. I wanted to release these women from the illusion of Bennett's devotion to them. I wanted them to know they were safe. And an ugly part of me wanted to be the one to tell his other women that he was dead.

I flagged a waiter and mouthed, "Cappuccino."

Not one to bury the lead, and mindful of her fifteen minutes, I told her straight off that "Bennett" was dead.

"No, he's not," she said with certainty.

I took out the picture of Bennett I had shown the detective in Boston and asked the woman if this was her fiancé.

She said nothing.

"He died six weeks ago."

"He sent me flowers."

"I found the body."

"You don't understand. He sent me flowers three days ago. I got an e-mail from him this morning. He's in hiding thanks to those incompetent Boston detectives. And thanks to Susan Rorke's crazy friends."

Her certainty about Bennett's being alive threw me off-balance. In the moment before I righted myself, I sped through a what-if scenario. What if the body had not been Bennett's? No one could identify it. No face. No fingerprints. What if Bennett were alive? The possibility made me sick and scared, but the chance to confront him excited me.

I confronted Samantha instead. "You didn't answer my question." I held up the photo. "Is this your fiancé?"

"Why do you have a picture of him?"

"I was engaged to him, too."

She snorted. "Did one of Susan Rorke's friends send you the photo? Did one of them send you to meet me? Are you trying to flush him out for the police? I know what entrapment is."

I opened my purse and took out the tiny leather box, lined in velvet, that held the ring Bennett had given me. I slipped it onto my finger to show her that it fit. I moved my hand next to hers.

"So you've got Susan's ring. Her friends will do anything to frame him." Her voice was louder than the murmur at the communal table. I was aware of people looking and listening. "I already know about that. Susan wouldn't return his grandmother's ring so he had a copy made for me."

Shortly before Bennett died, I had driven my Zipcar into the rear of the taxi stopped in front of me. I had been looking straight ahead, yet realized at the moment of impact that I couldn't see what was right in front of me. Samantha was the driver now. I realized I could show her any amount of proof of Bennett's duplicity and she would not see it. I tried a different track.

"Who do you think killed Susan Rorke?"

"Susan Rorke killed Susan Rorke. She told him that if he didn't go through with the wedding, she would kill herself and make it look like murder. She even scratched the window frame where she jumped to make it look as though there had been a struggle. Desperate bitch." Her voice was so loud I wanted to shush her, but I didn't dare interrupt now that she was finally saying something.

"She could have taken the high road, but, no—Susan Rorke took everyone down with her. She had no shame. She couldn't bear that we were happy and planning our own wedding. Do you know what she did the morning before she killed herself? She had an announcement of her engagement published in the *Boston Globe*."

People were no longer hiding their eavesdropping. In Samantha's agitation, her exaggerated hand gestures knocked over a pepper mill. She kept on talking. I sensed those hands might be capable of pushing a body out a window.

Samantha was still on a tear, and we had been talking for well over her designated fifteen minutes. "And another thing. Susan volunteering at the homeless shelter was self-serving. She didn't care about the poor. She cared about getting promoted at work and thought it would look good on her CV."

I interrupted, "What kind of volunteer work do you do?"

"How do you know I volunteer?"

"Do you?"

"All I'll say is that it has nothing to do with my résumé!"

A waiter came over and asked if Samantha would lower her voice.

"I saw a woman change her baby's diaper on a table in here and no one scolded her!" Samantha said.

Nevertheless, she asked for the check and then delivered a bombshell. "Maybe you should talk to his ex-wife."

"He was married?" I noted the power shift between us.

"Your fiancé never told you he'd been married? Susan knew."

Collecting our things to leave gave me a moment to collect my thoughts. "How can I reach her?"

"She's in the book. Sag Harbor. Uses her maiden name. Loewi, Pat."

Samantha said a brusque good-bye. I watched her back and felt that my suspicion would be confirmed; I would tell the

Boston detective about her. How else would she have known about the fingernail scratches on the window frame?

I hadn't read Shakespeare since high school but opened a volume of the collected plays to take another look at *Othello*. In the play, Othello's embittered ensign, Iago, makes the general believe that his wife, Desdemona, has been sleeping with a lieutenant in Othello's army. Believing this lie, the enraged Othello strangles the innocent Desdemona with his bare hands. Not until graduate school did I learn of Othello syndrome, a type of morbid jealousy that ends in violence. Not all societies punish crimes of passion. For instance, if a woman in Hong Kong discovers her husband isn't being faithful, she is legally allowed to kill him, but she can use only her hands. However, the husband's lover is allowed to be killed in any manner the wife chooses. This ancient law is still on the books. According to crime statistics, jealousy is one of the top three motives for murder.

I sat at my kitchen table debating my motive for notifying the Boston detective about Samantha. Did it matter if my suspicions were tainted with jealousy? I remembered the first time Bennett and I had the age-old conversation describing our past love affairs, except in Bennett's case the love affairs weren't in the past—they were simultaneous. A memory from that same AP lit class in which I read *Othello*, courtesy of William Faulkner: "The past is never dead. It's not even past." Bennett's lie about his matriculation at McGill might have contained this much truth: a lover he called Sam. Short for Samantha? He told me she had initially pursued him, pursued him to the point of stalking. He said he had changed phone numbers and moved, but her pursuit

had not diminished. He said she frightened him. He claimed she followed home a woman he was dating and slashed her tires. That hadn't stopped him from asking this Sam to marry him. She had the ring. He was the kind of liar who levitated just above the truth.

I dialed the Boston detective. We'd spoken enough times by now not to bother with small talk.

I told him my suspicions about Samantha. "She knew about the scratches in the window frame."

"It was in the papers. This Samantha is Bennett's third fiancée?" He did not bother to tamp down the sarcasm in his voice.

"The third one that I know about." I didn't mention an ex-wife.

"Other than her knowing about the scratches in the window frame, all you are basing your accusation on is that she claims Susan Rorke killed herself?"

"She displayed morbid jealousy and irrational anger. I say this as a professional."

I knew it hardly mattered what my degree would be in—if I could find the time and concentration to finish my thesis. All this detective would hear in my voice was the jealousy of a jilted lover.

The streetlights came on as I hung up. The November twilight started at four thirty. I hadn't eaten since Pain Quotidien and I'd only had a cappuccino. The kitchen was cleaner now than ever before. I hadn't so much as fried an egg since returning. I took out the few ingredients I had—ketchup, potato chips, and a $29 sliver of Stilton I'd bought at the cheese shop. I put a smear of Stilton on an unbroken potato chip and dipped it in the ketchup: a protein, a starch, and a vegetable. I let the darkness encroach. Steven had thought I was reckless to live here after

what had happened. But if I moved, I would keep moving and never feel at home.

I walked to the window. My view was backyards. The old Italians still hung their laundry on clotheslines. I watched a woman's thick arm pull a row of sheets through an open window.

So Bennett had an ex-wife. Of all his deceptions, that one hurt the most. After all, he had told his other two fiancées about the ex-wife. A gust blew the last sheet out of my neighbor's grasp. It landed in the backyard with the topiary, shrouding a bush shaped like a mushroom.

I called Steven and asked him if he wanted to come over.

"I'm in my socks. And I'm watching *Chopped*."

"Is that on the Crime channel?"

"The Food Network. Tonight's ingredients are watermelon, canned sardines, pepper jack cheese, and half a zucchini."

"I just made a meal of chips, Stilton, and ketchup."

"If you were on *Chopped*, you would have made lasagna from that. What are you watching?"

"*Happily Never After. The Bride Wore Blood.* He was married before."

"The groom?"

"Bennett."

I heard Steven's TV mute. "He's dead, Morgan. His lies are buried with him."

"They can't bury him until someone claims his body."

"How do you know he was married before?"

I told him about Samantha.

"You think she's dangerous?"

I told him I didn't know.

"I'll call a car service and come right over."

"Samantha can't throw me out my window. I have bars."

A half hour later, Steven rang my buzzer. He arrived with a toothbrush and the next day's work clothes, a dark suit still in the dry-cleaning bag for a meeting at the UN. He slept on the sofa he had bought me five months ago to celebrate my thirtieth birthday.

Unlike accused humans, Cloud and George didn't have the right to a speedy trial, nor was there such a thing as bail for dogs. They languished behind bars while the courts took their time. To say they languished is not accurate. Every day, they deteriorated physically and spiritually in the filthy confines of the noisy and understaffed shelter.

Then McKenzie called with news that gave me hope—he had secured a hearing date, in two weeks. We met as usual at Champs. For the first time he was there before me. His face was animated; I could see he was pleased with what he had accomplished. He presented the news to me as the gift that it was: I knew that dangerous-dog cases could sit on the docket for a year or more.

It surprised me that the first thing he said was that I looked better. Better than what? I must have looked confused because he went on, "I mean, you look rested, calm."

"Really?" I said, incredulous. Apparently staying up all night tracking down your dead lover's ex-wife was rejuvenating. "Thank you. You do, too."

"I don't need any quid pro quo. I'm just glad to see you look-ing well." McKenzie flagged a waitress. When she brought over menus, he didn't look at his.

I told him I'd brought the affidavit from my vet and handed him the folder, thick with years of Cloud's medical records. As a puppy, Cloud had eaten a pair of Fogal herringbone tights. The surgery to get them out of her stomach cost $4,000, but the vet gave me the tights back. Since the tights had cost $65, I figured I was only out $3,935.

"You spent sixty-five dollars on tights," he said, leafing through the folder.

He read on. Cloud was once stung in the nose by yellow jackets, and her muzzle swelled up so much she couldn't open her eyes. One time she was snake-bit swimming in a lake in Florida.

George's folder, by contrast, contained only three months of records. The treatments he had required were standard vaccinations and checkups.

"Why are there no charges for George?"

I told him my vet had refused to charge me for any of George's or Chester's appointments—she had a soft spot for rescues.

The waitress brought McKenzie a vivid green drink made of seven vegetables. I ordered coffee, black.

"I also brought pictures." I fanned them out on the table: all three of the dogs meeting a baby in the park, and playing ball with a team of first-graders.

I handed him testimonials from neighbors who had known Cloud since she was a puppy.

"You're very thorough," he said appreciatively, slipping them into his backpack.

"Is there anything more I can do?"

"Any of these neighbors know George well enough to testify in his defense in court?"

"My neighbors watched Cloud grow up, but they were afraid of George. I was disappointed that they were prejudiced because he's a pit bull. He never did anything wrong, and still they avoided him." That's when I remembered Billie, reaching through the kennel bars to stroke George when he and Cloud were first brought in.

"One of the volunteers at the shelter knows him and might do it. She's the one I told you about, the one who arranged George's temperament test."

"That would help us."

I was struck by his use of the word *us*. It told me something about him. I was so grateful not to be alone with this. And that made me feel calm, rested. I wasn't used to feeling this with a man. I liked it. But I didn't trust it. Normally I was drawn to men who, like Bennett, seemed kind and attentive at first, but turned out to be anything but. My reaction to that discovery was counterintuitive: I was drawn further in. The more controlling and withholding a man was, the closer I felt to him. Not because he enlisted my understanding but precisely because he did not. I worked harder to deserve his trust. The harder I worked, the *less* he trusted me. I became increasingly anxious and I mistook this anxiety for passion. The more anxious I became, the more fixated on me he became, and I mistook his fixation—Where were you? Why were you late?—for love.

"How can I reach that volunteer?"

I gave him the number Billie had given me when I'd first met her in the shelter.

"I have something for you." He reached into his backpack. "This is a copy of the Boston police report on Susan Rorke's death." I took the heavy file, but before I could slip it into my tote bag, he said, "You're used to crime-scene photos, right?"

"Not a problem," I lied. The victims in the hundreds of crime-scene photos I'd studied had not been engaged to my fiancé.

"Do you want something more than coffee?"

I made my excuses. I was so eager to read the report that I couldn't get away soon enough. (There is a fine line between apprehension and excitement.)

Did I imagine a flicker of disappointment on his face as I gathered my things? If that is what I saw, then was he disappointed in my interest in Susan Rorke over the dogs, or disappointed that I did not linger with him?

I couldn't bear to read the police report in the apartment where Bennett had been killed. I walked a block to the East Williamsburg branch of the public library, a small, one-story, vine-covered brick building.

I walked past the empty children's book area, past the crowd at the video rentals, past the line of homeless waiting for a free computer, and sat down at the deserted long table meant for readers. Normally it saddens me that so few people read, but today I was fine with it.

I spread out the crime-scene photos. I hadn't realized that Susan Rorke landed on a vendor's cart. The body was upside down, the legs caught on the cart, her upper body hanging. Her shirt had ridden up and exposed her breasts. Skewed gymnast. Hanging deer. I tried to make anatomical sense of what I was seeing. The juxtaposition of the halal cart and the broken body was obscene, and my thoughts took an obscene turn—Did they retire that cart? Ashamed of myself, I thought back to the Facebook photos in which she displayed her engagement ring, which was not in any of the crime-scene photos. Had the killer taken it? As a souvenir or to hide evidence? If Bennett—it was to hide evidence. If Samantha—it was to retrieve what she believed was his grandmother's ring, and to keep what she believed was rightfully hers.

The autopsy report said she died of blunt force trauma. As I knew from my studies, blunt force trauma is the ME's go-to attribution for accidents, suicides, and homicides. Deaths from blunt force trauma occur for a range of reasons, whereas death from gunshot wounds or stabbings, for example, are confined to fewer possibilities. I read quickly, looking for the answer to a key question: Was the blunt force trauma inflicted by the collision with the cart, or did she sustain the deadly injury prior to contact? The autopsy report was clear on this—the cause of death was listed as a blow to the back of the head with an instrument the size of a silver dollar, consistent with a hammer. Yet no hammer was found at the scene or during an extensive search of the building and surrounding area.

It was one thing to push a person out a window in a rage, another thing to have brought a hammer. Death would have been instant.

I skipped past the environmental conditions at the crime scene—I had no need to know the "exterior ambient temperature."

I skipped past the reporting officers' accounts, past the location description and "injury extent," past occupation, and started to read when I got to the evidence inventory.

The tox screen showed no blood alcohol or drugs. She wasn't impaired in any way until she was attacked by the unidentified figure photographed by a security camera in a bank across the street from the shelter. The shelter's own camera was broken.

Witnesses included the shelter's security guard, who claimed he heard a woman cry out, "No, no, no, no!" when he stepped outside for a smoke, followed by the sound of Susan Rorke's landing less than a hundred feet away. Other witnesses—three shelter residents in the infirmary—say they saw a figure wearing a hoodie running down the hallway. Two kitchen volunteers preparing the day's lunch saw the same hooded figure leave the building shortly after the time of death.

I turned to the photograph of Bennett's car going through a tollbooth on I-93 north at 1:57—forty minutes after Susan Rorke's death—on his way to meet me in Old Orchard Beach.

Then the most incriminating evidence: the DNA in the semen found in Susan Rorke matched the DNA of the body of "Bennett" in the Manhattan coroner's office.

I took a deep breath. I was upset just then by the discovery that Bennett met me in Maine after inseminating another woman, rather than by the possibility that he came to me after killing her. If I was this jealous, why not Samantha? The police report had included a 911 call Susan had made the week before she was killed. Her tires had been slashed, she said. This was Samantha's MO, if she was the "Sam" Bennett had told me about. The hoodie and baggy clothes concealed the suspect's gender. Bennett may have slept with Susan Rorke the night before and been in Boston the day she was killed, but it wasn't a slam dunk that he was the killer. Knowing that 68 percent of all murders of women are committed by their husband or boyfriend, the Boston police would have looked at Bennett first. Wouldn't I, too, if I could be impartial? But I wasn't. In my experience, Bennett's anger was not annihilating, it was controlling. But what about someone else's experience of him, someone perhaps more knowledgeable than I had been? Such as his ex-wife. If he was capable of murder, she might know.

I caught the Hampton jitney at the Eighty-Sixth and Third stop in Manhattan so as to get first dibs on a good seat. Seating in autumn wasn't the problem it was in season, but it was a habit from past summers when I had a share on the East End. I had been planning to use the trip to Sag Harbor to get work done on my three-quarters-finished thesis. The trip is advertised as taking two hours, but it's always rush hour on the LIE.

I chose a window seat midway back and opened my laptop. For the nth time, I reviewed the data I had collected over two years. Matchmaking sites work on a problem-solving model, seeking a solution. It's a basic algorithm—gathering information to find patterns in raw data. Even Petfinder works like this—only better because more hookups lead to love. Usually, however, the popular dating sites ask superficial questions that are too general to define patterns: Do you like action-adventure films or romcoms? Do you prefer beaches or mountains? What kind of animal would you be? I was operating on a different plane: I had put together questions that could be phrased for both potential victims and potential predators. For example: Do you like a man to order for you in a restaurant without asking what you want? / Do you enjoy ordering for a woman in a restaurant? Are you flattered by the attention when a man checks in with you frequently? / Do you feel the need to frequently check in with the woman you are dating? Do you find jealousy in a man flattering? / Are you interested in learning about a woman's romantic past? Do you think honesty is always the best policy? / Do you think honesty is always the best policy? With enough raw data, you can suss out unexpected correlations. For instance, the statistician Amy Webb, in her search for a husband, discovered that "men who drink Scotch reference kinky sex immediately."

More chilling was the discovery made by the forensic psychologist Adrian Raine. He found that psychopaths shared one biological factor—a low pulse rate. The significance of this discovery is that increasing levels of risk are necessary to create a heightened feeling of excitement. Dr. Raine also found that successful psychopaths—the ones who elude capture—are able to increase their pulse rate enough to make them careful. Less successful are the psychopaths who do not experience a significant rise in pulse rate; their attempts to feel excitement become increasingly reckless until they are caught.

Not all sociopaths are psychopaths. It's not just a matter of degree. The predisposition to violence is high in a psychopath, whereas it varies in the sociopath. In criminal behavior the psychopath leaves clues, whereas the sociopath schemes to minimize exposure. Most pertinent to my research was that a psychopath is unable to maintain a normal relationship, while a sociopath can appear superficially normal while actually functioning as a social predator.

Clinical definitions differentiate on the basis of the ability to feel empathy—the received wisdom says that psychopaths feel none, while sociopaths experience a diminished form of empathy, but choose to ignore it. Psychopaths are fearless; sociopaths aren't. Psychopaths don't understand right from wrong;

sociopaths do, though it doesn't change their behavior. Bennett was a sociopath if he lied so comfortably and completely to me and everyone else. He was a psychopath if he killed Susan Rorke and then drove to Maine for a romantic weekend with me.

My theory was provocative: both sociopaths and psychopaths may lack empathy, but sociopaths are aware enough of other people's feelings to see what they are missing—love—and they want some of that. They seek out goodness as well as weakness in their victims (Speck killing nurses, Bundy asking for help), because where there is goodness, there is often love.

Working on my thesis had been a worthy distraction from the meeting with Pat Loewi that I had arranged the night before. I told her that I had information about her ex-husband that I needed to discuss with her. When I sensed her hesitation, I offered to go to her and she acquiesced. I recognized her before I stepped off the jitney because she said she would have her dog with her. Two women were holding on to leashed dogs, waiting. A stock figure of the equestrienne in jodhpurs and riding boots was wrangling a retriever; and then there was, I felt certain, Bennett's ex-wife. A slight woman with curly, shoulder-length red hair, gray at the roots. She wore an oversize barn jacket, jeans, and wellies. Sitting at attention beside her was a sleek and powerful-looking rottweiler.

She held the leash with both hands. "Audie needs to know a person before you can touch her."

Far from a welcome, this woman had brought backup. We walked from the jitney stop and headed slowly up Main Street away from the wharf. I chose to walk to the right of Pat since she had Audie on her left. I thanked her for agreeing to meet me. We passed three shops targeted for tourists before she said, "I thought we might take Audie over to Havens Beach. It's about a fifteen-minute walk."

We fell into an easy pace, and after a couple more blocks I said I needed a coffee and could I bring her one, too. She said she didn't drink coffee, just tea, but when I offered to bring her tea instead, she said she only drank green tea and the deli I was heading into did not have it. I was in and out in a couple of minutes with only the coffee.

We continued up Main Street until Pat turned left onto a residential street. Everything I'd thought to ask or say was too lame to utter. The news I planned to deliver was the kind of news for which the time is never right. Still, I thought I would wait to tell her until we were on the beach.

Havens Beach, off-season, was nearly empty of people. But several unaccompanied dogs ran into and out of the gentle waves of the bay. I worried that Pat would unleash her unreliable dog, and then she did. Audie sniffed at my purse—the repository of so many treats.

"Just ignore her," Pat said.

It came out in a rush. I told her that her ex-husband was dead.

"We were never married."

Did Samantha lie to me, or did she really not know?

The moment Pat said that, Audie was at her side, fixing me in her gaze. Though Pat had not spoken loudly, the dog had picked up her distress and stood ready.

I told her the circumstances of his death. I told her that I had been engaged to him at the time. I told her that I was not the only one engaged to him at the time, and that another fiancée had just been murdered, possibly by Pat's former lover.

So much for easing her into it.

"He never liked dogs and dogs never liked him." Pat seemed remarkably composed, though her dog grew agitated, reacting to what I assumed were her true feelings. I waited for her to go on. Pat picked a piece of sea glass from the sand and examined it. "So he hadn't changed. Only two fiancées?"

"This doesn't surprise you."

"He lived by his own rules." Audie ran off into the waves. "But murder is a new one."

"The police think he did it."

"And you don't?"

"I don't know what I think." I hadn't noticed Audie's return from the water until she shook off next to me.

"I know I'm not reacting the way you might have expected. But this man put me through it."

"How long were you with him?"

"Long enough for him to derail my life. You?"

"I got off easy. Relatively." I didn't want to one-up her in any way. I wanted her to tell me what he had done to her.

"I was teaching an extension studio course out here, inter-viewing students during registration, when this cocky kid in tight jeans and a white T-shirt asked the department secretary if there was still room in my class. I was busy with another student. The kid—he looked about twenty-one—couldn't or wouldn't wait until I was free. When he turned to leave, I whispered to the secretary, 'There's always room in my class for him.' I whispered, but the acoustics of the room were such that he heard me; I saw him stop. I had twelve years on him, but from then on he pur-sued me.

"I was painting then, looking for a gallery. He claimed great enthusiasm for my work and talked about opening a gallery someday. There was no biological clock ticking, but my gallery clock was ticking. You know the old joke about how the Holland Tunnel was built: they gave New Jersey artists teaspoons and said the first one to dig to Manhattan gets a gallery. It took years for me to see what he had seen in me: an opportunity.

"He didn't have money. He had charm. And he charmed me out of everything I cared about."

We were walking in step along the hard-packed sand, taking turns throwing a stick for Audie to retrieve.

"The irony was that I taught him everything he knew about art, without even knowing I was doing it. And when he knew enough to realize the value of my grandfather's paintings, he stole the only two canvases of his that I had. His going-away present to himself."

"Jesus."

"It gets better. I was hurt that he didn't steal *my* work."

"He caused a lot of us a lot of hurt."

"How many are we talking about here?"

"Including myself, four that I know about. That's concurrent, not consecutive."

That got a small laugh from her. Audie seemed to share in the mood change; she flipped onto her back in the sand and kicked her legs in the air, then righted herself and shook the sand off. We had been walking into the wind, and a further synchronicity had us turn together to head back. Pat asked if I'd like to see her studio.

We walked for another twenty minutes before she turned onto a narrow dirt drive through the woods. I feared ticks despite the low temperature. What was the cutoff point when you didn't have to worry about them? We moved through scrub oak and pine, the soil sandy. I was wishing I had not worn my good suede boots. These woods had not been cleared of storm damage, and we had to climb over broken limbs.

Pat's studio was a weathered silver-cedar barn about the size of a three-car garage, with an old sliding door bolted shut and padlocked. After turning the combination right, left, and then right again, Pat threw her weight into the push that slid the door open. She slapped the wall where a switch was, and fluorescent light filled the space. It was much larger than it looked from the outside.

I had expected generic seascapes and was surprised by the life-size nude photographs of her posed with a bloody heart held against her left breast.

"Don't worry, it's a pig's heart."

Was I worried? I was now. In the photos she looked about ten years younger than the woman standing next to me. Pat preempted whatever I might have thought to say with a single word: "Subtle. I did these right after he left; I got them out after you called last night." She pointed to another wall. "Here's what I'm up to now."

Here were the seascapes, made modern by muted patterns of graphite waves. If Vija Celmins hadn't got there first, Pat would have been onto something. Pat was adding to what was already in the world, instead of creating something new. It appeared that Bennett had also stolen her nerve.

She made us green tea and then gave Audie an enormous smoked femur to chew on. I was incredulous that Pat didn't seem to see the horror of this after what I had told her about Bennett's death. The sound of tooth on bone was unnerving.

As if on cue there was a noise outside—a sound like the

snapping of branches underfoot. Audie raced to the window and set to barking and snarling. With the lights on in the studio, and the sun gone down, neither Pat nor I could see outside. Audie lunged at the glass and I feared it would break. I did a quick survey of the studio to see where I might hide. I was standing in a brightly lit, open space. I was close to panicking, yet Pat remained oddly oblivious.

"I switched to acrylic with this series. I don't know if I like the surfaces as much, but I'm too impatient to wait for oil to dry."

"Does Audie always act like this? Should we look outside?"

"It's either a raccoon trying to get into the trash or a coyote. In either case, I'm not letting Audie out. My other dog was killed last week by coyotes."

"Oh, God, I'm so sorry."

"Well, the neighbors think it's coyotes, but I'm not so sure."

"What else could it be?"

"Audie, enough!" The dog finally retreated from the window with a low growl. Pat walked over to where the naked self-portraits hung. Staring at her younger self, she said, "I know his real name."

My mouth felt dry. "Who was he?"

"It cost me five thousand to find out."

I expected her to go on, but when she didn't, I wondered if she was expecting payment for passing along this information to me.

"I hired a PI to track down my grandfather's paintings. He discovered that they'd been auctioned in Qatar for a little over a million dollars. He said the seller was anonymous, but he was able to determine that the seller was from Maine."

"You said you know his name."

"I know the name he started out with: Jimmy Gordon. The PI never found the paintings, but he got me an address for Jimmy's mother."

"What was she like?"

"I never contacted the woman. Why would I want her in my life?"

"Would you mind if I contacted her?"

"Ask her where my grandfather's paintings are."

I carried our empty mugs over to the slop sink in one corner of the studio. Audie watched me from her dog bed. I gave her wide berth. I asked if I could use the bathroom before I left.

"The studio doesn't have one. I just go in the woods."

I thanked her for the tea and for taking the time to meet with me.

Pat asked if I had a recent photo of Bennett. I took out the worn half of the photograph that I still carried with me and handed it to her. She glanced at it and handed it right back. "Still inscrutable. That haircut—Jesus."

I had wanted to ask her one question—Did she feel he was capable of murder?—but I wouldn't have trusted her answer.

Pat slid the door open barely enough for me to squeeze through and closed it the moment I was outside. There was only a quarter moon and no other lights were in sight. Only ten steps but I had already veered from the narrow path. I felt for a Kleenex in my tote bag and squatted. I relieved myself, terrified of poison ivy, ticks, snakes, wolf spiders, and coyotes. I'd hitched up my pants. I could hear Audie going ballistic inside the studio; I hoped it was inside.

I headed for what I hoped would be the way out. A branch scratched my cheek enough to draw a little blood, I twisted my ankle, I moved through a spiderweb face-first, all in darkness. I had to talk myself down from panic. I strained to hear the sound of traffic. All I heard was barking.

A cloud cover obscured the stars, not that I could have navigated by them. I found my cell phone and tried to get a signal, but there was no service. Why hadn't I downloaded the flashlight app?

My coat was not adequate against the damp cold. Then it hit me: find the shore and I'll know where to go. I tried to detect any scent other than the pine that surrounded me. Either it was an olfactory hallucination or I really did pick up the faintest whiff of the sea.

I moved cautiously in that direction, but after a couple of minutes I lost the scent and my short-lived confidence. I heard a sound like the one I had heard in the studio, a branch snapping underfoot. The last of my composure left me. I moved as quickly as I could away from the sound, which wasn't quick enough. I heard it again and said out loud, "Really?" This was the staple of countless horror films: a woman alone flees an unknown predator in the dark woods. Who was the predator? Audie? Coyotes? Pat? Samantha? The person who pretended to be Susan Rorke? In that instant, as though reading it on the page, I recovered a quote by Helen Keller, "Avoiding danger is no safer in the long run than outright exposure. The fearful are caught as often as the bold." I mean, if walking through your life blind and deaf doesn't teach you about fear, nothing will.

My heartbeat slowed, I took a deep breath and continued in the direction of what might be the sea. On the heels of Helen Keller, something that Cilla had told me came to mind: "Curiosity conquers fear even more than bravery does." As I felt my way through the dark, I asked the question that had guided me so far. The question wasn't whether or not Bennett was capable of murder. The question was, how had I been capable of loving him?

I smelled the sea. What's more, I saw a lighter horizon and remembered that a body of water always reflects ambient light. In another moment I could hear lapping waves.

I knew exactly where I was.

I took the C train to Seventy-Second Street so I could walk the last fifteen blocks through the park to clear my head before a session with Cilla. Single-stem roses were scattered across the *Imagine* mosaic, the tribute to John Lennon in Strawberry Fields. The night before, I had looked up Jimmy Gordon online. There was nothing on the Jimmy Gordon I was looking for, but then again, he had disappeared in 1992 at the age of seventeen. I had only been able to find a Maine coon cat named Jim Gordon with his own web page, as well as the infamous rock drummer Jimmy Gordon, who had toured with John Lennon and the Beach Boys until he was imprisoned for stabbing his mother to death.

I stood in line to buy a bottle of water from a park vendor and saw him fish out a hot dog from a vat of hot water that he would probably not change until spring. I was hungry, too, but not that hungry. When he gave me the bottle of water, I handed over two singles.

"Three dollars," he said sharply.

I walked past the teeming playground filled with toddlers minded by nannies and entered the Ramble, the only part of the park that I got lost in. Even though the wooded, hilly paths sometimes ended at a rock face or a stream, I never feared nature here. In Central Park you won't be attacked by a pack of coyotes or a wolf spider; people are the threat. Think Robert Chambers, the preppy murderer, who killed a teenaged girl not too far from here, or the "wilding" gang who were accused of attacking and nearly killing the Central Park jogger. Their convictions were vacated when Matias Reyes, a convicted rapist and murderer serving a life sentence for other crimes, confessed.

Before leaving for Cilla's, I'd phoned the coroner's office to identify the body of "Bennett." I also phoned the Boston detective to give him the real name of "Bennett." He took the information dispassionately, and I felt like saying, *The case may be over for you, but it's not for me.* I reiterated my fears about Samantha. I sensed that I had not been in the woods alone last night, and the only person who knew I was visiting Pat was Samantha. But I had no proof of anything.

Cilla's office was in a brownstone on West Eighty-Seventh Street, a ground-floor office. She buzzed me in and I sat in the waiting room until she finished with the client before me. I picked up a copy of *Tricycle*, the Buddhist magazine, and read part of the article "The Art of Being Wrong." I smiled at the copy of *Rolling Stone*, a holdover from her singing with Lou Reed.

Though I had seen her only a week before, so much had happened in the interim. I took a seat on the sofa and didn't wait for Cilla to ask how I was.

I caught her up on Samantha and Pat. I asked, "Did Bennett target troubled, insecure women or did he create them?"

"Any woman can be fooled by a practiced sociopath. It's what they do. Isn't that what your thesis is trying to prove?"

"I'm not so sure about my thesis anymore."

"Do you think that Bennett has changed who you fundamentally are?"

"How could I have had a blind spot that large? Where is

the point where giving a person the benefit of the doubt invites dangerous behavior? Should I have known when he refused to show me where he lived? Or when he didn't want to meet any of my friends?" I realized I was sitting on the edge of the couch. Pat's vulnerability was wanting to succeed as an artist. What was mine? We must all be alike in some damaged way. What did we have in common? Does there have to be something in common?

"We were all duped."

"You think trust has to be replaced by suspicion?"

"It would appear so. I don't mean to sound flippant. I don't want to be a cynic; I don't want to become embittered. But I need to understand this. That's why I'm going to see his mother."

"You found out his identity?"

"Pat told me his real name was Jimmy Gordon. She told me how to find his mother."

"What is it you feel you can get from meeting his mother?"

"She may want to claim the body."

"No, no. What would *you* get from meeting her?"

"Whatever I find will be better than what I would imagine." I was hit by the weight of the situation.

"Is this a job for you or for the police?"

"The case is closed as far as they are concerned. He killed Susan Rorke. My dogs killed him."

"What about your classes? Are you keeping up with your research?"

"This is my research. You'd tell me if I was going off the deep end, right? I mean, if I was really off the mark here?"

"Your instincts are good. Trust them."

• • •

Back in Williamsburg, I was starving when I got off the subway at Lorimer Street. I bought a Godfather wrap—soppressata, provolone, roasted red peppers—at Bagelsmith on the corner. I walked slowly—there was no wind—and had eaten about half the wrap when I saw a little white dog, unleashed, running in the street. I looked for the dog's owner, but saw only a couple of young people calling after the dog. I crouched on the sidewalk and pulled a piece of salami from between the bread I was holding. I tried to get the little dog's attention, making kissing noises. A truck was coming down the street, and I ran in front of it and waved my arms for it to stop. The young people continued to call after the dog, who had not stopped running. This was not going to end well, I feared.

Then a man on a bike stopped pedaling and approached the dog slowly, while not looking at it. I remembered that this was the way to win a stray's trust—don't look at it directly. The man slapped his leg—like a tail wagging—and he knew to swing his arm against his leg from right to left, mimicking the tail wag of a friendly dog. Left to right shows aggression. It was coming back to me—the right things to do. I had been moving toward the man as he made these gestures, and then I saw that it was McKenzie.

"Hey," I called out to him, "do you know whose dog this is?"

"Give me a minute." He asked me to bring him my sandwich.

He put half of it a couple of feet in front of him on the pavement. He sat down and told me not to move. By this time, the young couple had recognized someone who knew how best to proceed and were, themselves, now spectators at what might turn out to be a rescue, after all.

The dog was hunched under a parked car. I sat down beside

McKenzie, and we waited. We didn't speak. When five minutes had passed like this, the little white dog crawled out from under the car and dispatched the sandwich in two bites.

An amateur might then have grabbed the dog, but McKenzie unzipped his backpack and retrieved a worn bungee cord, made a quick slipknot at one end, and collared the dog gently, all the time speaking to it in a low, friendly voice. The dog looked relieved, not trapped.

Finally, McKenzie turned to me. "I've got to be somewhere half an hour ago. Can you take this pup home till we can arrange a foster?" I had two dogs on a DOH hold, but no way would I not take this stray home with me.

I took the makeshift leash from McKenzie's hand.

"I'll phone you later," he said.

The little white dog pulled in his direction, wanting to go with him.

"You're stuck with me, little one." I had plenty of dog food at home, and this would be the first time a dog had been in my apartment since the day Bennett died.

I carried her to my apartment and filled one of my dog bowls with cold water and another with kibble. The little dog tucked right in. I've always loved the sound of a dog eating. Satisfied, she leaped into my lap, so lightly that I was surprised to find her there. I stroked her gently between her shoulder blades, trying to feel for a rice-grain-size microchip. I could feel vertebrae, but nothing else. She could not have weighed more than twelve pounds. I ran a bath in the kitchen sink and eased the filthy pup into the warm bath. She didn't fight me but gave herself over to the pleasant sensation of a gentle shampoo. I towel-dried her, and a name came to me. Her big, black eyes looked like olives, so that is what I called her. Later that night, I persuaded Olive to accompany me into the bedroom. When I woke sometime after midnight, I found her sleeping on my chest. I needed to turn over, and moved slowly so as not to jar her, but it wasn't necessary; Olive moved along with me, remaining on top, log-rolling.

In the morning, while I was still in bed, McKenzie called to tell me that he'd found a rescue organization willing to take the stray.

"I'm fine fostering Olive for a while."

McKenzie laughed. "Olive? You want to take this on right now? The hearing is on Monday."

"The hearing is on Monday whether I keep her or not. How worried should I be?"

"Were you able to persuade your downstairs neighbor to testify?"

"She said she didn't want that killer dog back."

"Well, that was a long shot. I guess you won't be watering her plants when she goes on vacation."

"How many cases like this do you win?"

"Not enough."

"But you keep at it."

"The individual outcome is only part of what I'm trying to do. The law is the way I can try to change the way people treat animals."

His simple eloquence reassured me, and I thanked him again for his help.

When we hung up, I went online to check FidoFinder for lost dogs. I clicked on *lost*, *white*, *small*, and my zip code. I braced my-self against the wrenching descriptions of the missing, but none of the dogs seemed to be the stray I had taken in. I printed out a *Lost* flyer. The site recommended posting the flyers within a half-mile radius of where a small dog was found. Taking Olive with me, I papered the neighborhood. On the walk home, I posted the last flyer at the McCarren dog park. One woman held her puppy on its leash over the pen and dunked it into the play group, then withdrew it, like a tea bag.

I phoned Billie when I got home to remind her about the hearing on Monday and to tell her about my visit with Pat. I liked what happened when I brought Billie up-to-date: whatever horror I was reporting on became a narrative; it was transformed in the telling into a story, and as such felt further away from me than it actually was. It was like the times Kathy and I had regaled each other with a game called He Actually Thinks. He actually thinks he can call me on Christmas Eve to meet him for a drink. That kind of thing. Turn an upset into a game or a story, and you move ahead of it, maybe even to a place of not caring.

When I told Billie that Pat had displayed the series of naked self-portraits with a pig's heart over her left breast, Billie said, "You wouldn't want to be a muse for that girl."

"And her dog. A missile when there was the slightest sound outside. Throwing herself against the glass."

I told Billie I had taken in a stray and was caught off guard when she said, "Shouldn't your focus be on your own dogs?"

"I am entirely focused on them." I was hurt by her scolding tone.

I heard the beeps that indicated I had an incoming call, but I ignored it, knowing that Billie would hear me pass up a call to stay on the line with her—a peace offering. It worked, and we were back on track. She told me she had gotten Enrique, the head kennel worker, to write a character reference for my dogs. My phone beeped again, and this time Billie suggested I take it. "I'll see you Monday at the hearing," she said.

I took the incoming call and immediately wished I had not.

"I heard you met Pat," Samantha said.

It took me a moment to formulate the obvious question. "How did you know?"

"Did she show you the naked photographs of herself? She shows them to everyone. That fucking pig's heart?"

My own heart was beating faster.

"Did she also tell you her ex stole her grandfather's paintings? She gave them to him to sell, and it's not his fault that the auction house never paid her."

Samantha was clearly trying to bait me, but her words left me exhausted. I did not want to engage with a crazy person, a possible killer. I wanted help. I wanted this crazy woman to leave me alone. But what really scared me was what we had in common. Though I was not still defending him. How to navigate a conversation like this? Better still, how to end it? I took a submissive stance, not wanting to ignite the person who must have followed me out to Sag Harbor. How else would she have known about my visit? The Pat I met would not have called Samantha.

"I saw the pig hearts," I said, as neutrally and calmly as one can say *I saw the pig hearts.*

"She blames him for ruining her career. Ha! Who would hang a pig's heart over a sofa?"

"I know I wouldn't."

"You didn't tell her I gave you her name, did you?" Before I could answer, Samantha said, "He only married her because she pretended to be pregnant."

"Women still do that?" I said, knowing they had not married. "What did Bennett do when he found out she had lied about being pregnant?"

"Same thing he did when he found out she faked a miscarriage later—he felt sorry for her."

I knew that pity was a condescending emotion. Bennett was not capable of empathy.

"He still thinks she has it in for him," Samantha said.

It unnerved me to hear her use the present tense. I refused to side with unreality. I felt only relief when Samantha banged down the phone. She was crazy or dangerous or both. And I wanted none of it.

It was Friday afternoon, and I had no plans for the weekend. Whereas this would have troubled me a year ago, I was now glad for the unclaimed days ahead of me. I needed to be a normal person, someone not facing a court hearing or worrying about my murdered fiancé's other fiancées. I lifted little Olive and, instead of asking if she wanted to go for a walk, said, "Wanna go out to lunch?" I put her in my tote bag, forgetting it held so many dog treats. No wonder she settled in right away. Thanksgiving was a few days away, so Christmas ornaments were already crowding the streets. I'd promised Steven I would bring a pie, so I set off for the Blue Stove on Graham to order one.

It was cold and clear with the white sky familiar to New Yorkers in winter. I decided to spruce up the apartment and went to Abode on Grand. I browsed the shelves: a bottle opener that was just a nail in a board ($18.99), and the cardboard end tables made to look like tiny stacked cargo crates ($59.99). I passed up the black, geometric hanging light fixture that looked as though it contained a galaxy ($12,500). A black throw pillow had what looked like a swirl of smoke on it ($270), and I knew I'd find nothing I could afford. I stopped by the vintage store Mystery Train, but they had no pillows, just clothes. Two Jakes, on Wythe, carried furniture, mostly, and I found "accent pillows" in a color called chalk. At $39 apiece, they seemed like a bargain, and I bought one. I next walked to Grand Ferry Park—a nod to Olive. I sat down on one of the benches right by the East River and lifted Olive out of the bag. She wanted to sit on the bench next to me. The Manhattan skyline lived up to its reputation. I had never heard a metaphor that made it more than what it was on its own.

I put Olive back in the tote, and we were on to the hardware store, with its five-thousand-square-foot plant section in back. The bonus here was an eighty-five-pound hog named Franklin; he lived in a good-size pen (think studio apartment in Williamsburg) among the thousands of plants for sale. I picked up several small flats of herbs for the kitchen, and a container of lavender to scent the bedroom.

I dropped off the pillow and plants, poured Olive's kibble, and left by myself. It had been a long time since I'd seen a movie. I took the L to Union Square, where half a dozen theaters are within a few blocks. The multiplexes showed the blockbuster commercial hits, none of which appealed to me. I checked out the Village East, where I found the documentary *Twenty Feet from Stardom*, about black female backup singers. One of the women who affected me most had had no interest in a solo career. She valued the harmony several voices created. Of course I thought of Cilla. She had told me during a recent session that a time had come when she no longer knew how to harmonize. Deeply rattled, she stopped singing. Eventually, she told me, she realized that this inability just meant it was time for her to make a different kind of harmony; she brought harmony to people in trouble and turned their lives around.

"Don't say no right away," I said, "but this volunteer who's coming to testify today, you might like her." Steven and I were looking for a parking spot near the courthouse on Schermerhorn Street.

"Morgan."

"You like the outdoor type."

"Not after Claire made me train for the marathon with her."

"That was the deal-breaker? You were never in better shape."

"Physically."

Steven was not resilient in this realm, or any realm. I knew he had not yet recovered from Claire's moving out after two years together. She had wanted him to enter the private sector and make money, and he wanted to continue working for Avaaz.

"What does she look like?"

It never failed to throw me, this question from a man—because it was always the first question. "Up there on the right." I pointed to a space we could squeeze into. "You'll see her in the courtroom in a few minutes."

The room designated for the hearing was spare and worn. The bench we sat on had initials carved into it. The judge took his place behind an equally marred desk.

I nudged Steven. "There she is." Fixing up my brother was a welcome throwback to normalcy, something I had fallen out of touch with, to say the least.

Billie was already seated next to McKenzie. I had not seen him dressed for a court appearance before. Suited, polished, he looked more than capable—he looked commanding. For her part, Billie had traded her motorcycle boots for sleek calfskin boots. Her hair was pulled back in a low ponytail, and she wore a simple black blazer over a white shirt, with tight-fitting, black jeans.

Steven whispered one word to me: "Wow."

After we were sworn in, McKenzie made his opening remarks to the judge. "I would first like to cite Article Seven of the New York Agriculture and Markets Law. 'A dog shall not be declared dangerous if the court determines the conduct of the dog was justified because the injured, threatened, or killed person was tormenting, abusing, assaulting, or physically threatening the dog or its offspring, or has in the past tormented, abused, assaulted, or physically threatened the dog or its offspring.'"

McKenzie reached into his briefcase and took out a thick file. "I'd like to place in evidence Exhibit A, a copy of the Boston police file on the murder of Susan Rorke. The police believe that Ms. Rorke had her skull fractured with a hammer before her body was thrown out a window. James Gordon, aka Bennett Vaux-Trudeau, was the prime suspect. The attack that took his life occurred less than a month after the murder of Susan Rorke. This man has demonstrated a history of violent behavior. Cloud, the Great Pyrenees, has lived with Morgan Prager since eight weeks of age and has no history of aggressive behavior. Ms. Prager adopted George, the pit-bull mix, five months ago, and he has not demonstrated aggression of any kind either."

McKenzie produced the veterinary records for both dogs, as well as the affidavit from the vet. He also submitted the results of the temperament test for both dogs.

"I would like to call a witness, a volunteer at the shelter where the dogs have been quarantined for the past two months."

Billie stood and introduced herself to the judge and established the frequency with which she attended the quarantined dogs. I was impressed and pleased with the way she carried herself in this setting, on this occasion. She was confident and succinct, authoritative and convincing. She conveyed a great deal of knowledgeable observation without belaboring anything. I exchanged a look with Steven, who seemed to share my impression of her testimony.

Steven spoke next. He confirmed that neither dog had ever displayed any aggression with him either. "I was with my sister when she adopted Cloud as a puppy."

"How much time did you spend with the pit-bull mix?" the judge asked.

"I see my sister every couple of weeks and I always enjoyed playing with George. He never played rough."

The judge asked McKenzie if he had anything else to introduce on behalf of the dogs before adjournment for a decision. McKenzie said that he would like to remind the court that on April 4, 2013, the New York Supreme Court cited the case of *Roupp v. Conrad* in its Memorandum: "'The condemnation of an individual dog in the context of a dangerous dog proceeding solely by virtue of its breed is without any legal basis.'"

The judge had told McKenzie he would have a decision by three o'clock that afternoon, so Billie suggested we get some lunch at a nearby place she knew. When we got there, I caught Steven's eye—the building was a Hare Krishna temple. The only nod to

Indian architecture was three stucco arches over the standard-issue red brick. Billie led us into the basement, where a cafeteria served vegetarian food from steam tables. I noticed that Steven chose only the potatoes and carrots, two vegetables he could recognize.

I've never been good at waiting. I couldn't keep from asking McKenzie if he thought the judge would rule in our favor. Immediately I apologized for putting him on the spot. Billie had taken the seat next to McKenzie and facing my brother. I had found that a fix-up had a better chance of bypassing awkwardness and pressure if one of the parties did not know it was a fix-up.

Billie offered, "I think the judge might choose this case to send a larger message to the community: zero tolerance for pit bulls."

"Or maybe," McKenzie said, "he'll surprise us. Once he reads the police report."

Over the sound of chanting coming from speakers in a corner of the dining room, I heard Steven register a guarded optimism. I noticed that even when Steven was speaking, Billie's eyes were on McKenzie. If I noticed, then Steven had noticed.

I was so anxious about the judge's decision I had to visualize the most calming thing I could think of in order to remain seated through this lunch. I imagined myself floating on my stomach in the warm Caribbean, my eyes open in shallow water so that I saw the gentle waves in the white sand on the bottom.

When I came out of my reverie and rejoined the conversation, Billie was challenging Steven on a point of law. It occurred to me that she felt herself to be his peer. Steven said simply, "Let's not precede the outcome with an outcome."

McKenzie stepped in as a kind of referee, giving the point to

Steven. Billie was quick to turn self-deprecating and excused herself for making assumptions about legal matters.

On the way back to court, Billie stepped in beside McKenzie, so I dropped back to walk with my brother, feeling usurped. Steven whispered to me, "That girl is not your friend."

"She's been nearly as devoted to my dogs as I have."

Steven reminded me that her devotion had crossed a line when she scheduled George for a temperament test without consulting me. And I reminded him that Billie's action, albeit presumptuous, meant that George now had a chance.

As we stepped off the elevator on the courthouse's fourth floor, McKenzie motioned for me to join him off to the side. "Let's do this," he said, and put his hand on the small of my back and guided me into the courtroom.

I might once have been heading into a courtroom for another reason, and it shamed me to think of it now. After serving Candice and Doug at the coffee shop where I briefly waitressed, I found the strength to go to the police. Rather, Kathy's insistence on accompanying me gave me the strength. We had only known each other a month by then, but I knew her to be a force for good. I had been unable to report the attack when it might have done some good—after Doug left me at Port Authority with the evidence still inside me. Or that is what I told myself then. I put my need for distance from the horror over any sort of civic responsibility. The thought that I might have been able to prevent their continued predation was not a priority. I needed to protect myself.

By the time Kathy and I went to the police, my actions were

more symbolic than justice-seeking. I had no physical proof left, I had entered the apartment voluntarily, I did not even have the address of the apartment, and a month had passed since the attack. A kind officer took my statement, then drove us up and down the blocks near the Navy Yard to see if anything looked familiar. But it had been night when I arrived, and I had been hidden in the van the next morning. I had apologized to the officer for wasting his time, and he had assured me that I had done no such thing. He said I was right to come in and make the report. I knew that if I had made my report in a timely fashion, I might have found myself in a courtroom testifying against that perverted couple, maybe even sending them to jail.

We were in the front row when the judge entered briskly. He read from the document he held. "Accordingly, pursuant to Agriculture and Markets Law 123 (2) the court is mandated, and under the circumstances and as is necessary for the protection of the public, it is hereby ordered that the Great Pyrenees be remanded to an animal sanctuary that specializes in the handling of dangerous dogs, which would be the best option to keep both the public and the animal from harm."

McKenzie put his hand on my arm, as though to hold me still while the judge pronounced sentence on George: death by, in the oxymoronic legalese he employed, "humane euthanasia." He gave George only twenty-four hours to live, then declared the court adjourned.

"It doesn't end here," McKenzie whispered to me. "We can appeal."

"For both of them?"

"We can ask for a stay for George first. I can argue that he go to a sanctuary, too."

"But the good ones have no space," Billie said. "They don't even take names for the waiting lists anymore."

"Then what's going to happen to Cloud if there is no room?" I asked.

"We have time to worry about Cloud later. I need to file a stay of execution for George right now," McKenzie said. "Steven, can you get everyone home, and I'll call you as soon as I hear something?"

Steven told me that we should know something later that afternoon, and the three of us—Billie leading the way out of court—headed for the subway.

"Pitties can't catch a break," Billie said.

"I took George off death row at the shelter and now he is right back where I found him," I said.

"You gave him love he would not have known," Steven said.

It was no consolation to hear that, though Steven had meant well. At the subway entrance, Steven headed toward his car to go back to Manhattan, Billie said good-bye to us both without saying where she was headed, and I took the G train to Williamsburg to wait.

I had once read a story with a scene between a man and woman in a long and turbulent relationship; the woman turns to her companion and says, "It could be so easy." That comment moved me, its resignation and still the simple wish. What is ever easy?

The news from McKenzie later that afternoon was not what I wanted to hear: the judge had rejected the appeal for a stay of execution for George. He would be killed by lethal injection the next day. McKenzie's voice was strained. He said he was about to file an appeal for Cloud to be allowed to go home, if muzzled and insured as prescribed by law. "I'm so sorry," he said.

I could not believe there was nothing more to be done.

"Would you like me to go with you to see him at the shelter?" McKenzie asked. "I can meet you there in the morning."

"That's nice of you to offer." I was already planning a visit within the hour. We agreed to meet in the filthy lobby of the shelter at 11:00 a.m.

I phoned Billie and told her I wanted to bring George a good dinner, and could she slip me in to give it to him? She told me she wouldn't officially be on duty, but that she would show up anyway, and, yes, we'd give him his special dinner.

I went to a market and bought two pounds of rare roast beef. Then I bought a pound of honey-glazed ham. And a bag of wavy Lay's potato chips. What the hell, old boy.

On the subway to the shelter, I distracted myself with music. I scrolled through my playlists until I found Jack White's "Love Interruption." It haunted me at the best of times, and now I sought it to match my state of mind. Love is always interrupted, is it not? "I want love / to . . . stick a knife inside me / . . ."

I got off at 116th Street and headed up to 119th Street and then toward the river. Gusts of wind buffeted me. Volunteers walked dogs dressed in thin jackets that had ADOPT ME printed in large block letters on them. Like the viral video of the woman dancing alone at a bus stop, an old Hispanic woman was swaying to a tune in her head, waiting for the crosstown bus. From a second-story apartment window, a hand reached through the bars to empty a Dustbuster onto the sidewalk, which was already littered with the usual mystery of chicken bones. A trio of Dominican women flirted with a couple of men who'd caught their eye; I noticed this because it was the women who had the power and knew it.

Billie was waiting for me outside the shelter annex. She gave me a warm hug and took me in the side entrance, bypassing the lobby. I avoided eye contact with kennel workers and acted as though I belonged here. Billie slipped us into the locked ward where my dogs were housed. She reminded me of a practiced hostess, keeping others' spirits up, choreographing gently, showing one where to sit, not giving in, in this terrible place, to the feelings one expected. I was grateful to her for taking over in this casual and kind way. It calmed me and had the same effect on the dogs.

Billie and I sat on the filthy ward floor, so close together that our shoulders touched. We took turns rolling up slices of meat and slipping them through the bars for both dogs. We tried to help them savor it by holding one end of the treat, forcing them to taste before swallowing. When we had emptied the bag of roast beef and ham and chips, we fed them the Scottish shortbread that Billie had brought.

Despite the heavy dinner, the dogs looked surprised that there wasn't more.

The next morning, McKenzie met me at the entrance to the shelter. He said, "I tried to reach you. They took him early."

I would be lying to myself if I didn't acknowledge how

relieved I was that my last memory of him would be joyous, him downing the greatest dinner of his life. But that didn't keep me from simultaneously stumbling backward, McKenzie's arms steadying me. He kept his arms around me and we just stood there in the cold, not talking. He knew better than to try to console me.

I was on my way to Steven's for a halfhearted nod to Thanksgiving. He had offered to pick up the basics from Citarella and said I only needed to show up with the pie. I was about a block from his apartment when Billie called on my cell.

"I know how you're feeling and I wanted you to know that you're not alone with that."

"What are you doing for Thanksgiving?" I asked, thinking that if she had no plans, I might invite her along to Steven's.

"I volunteer at a soup kitchen—St. Cecilia RC parish in Greenpoint."

I felt one-upped and tried to shake off the feeling. It was nice what she was doing; it didn't have to mean I was selfish to celebrate with my brother.

"If you finish by eight, you're welcome to stop by my brother's for some pumpkin pie."

"That's a nice invitation, but McKenzie asked me to have a drink with him when I finished."

I saw the aura that migraine victims experience before the pain kicks in. I felt helpless and blinded by fizzing light.

"Are you there?"

I realized I had said nothing in response to this news. "I'm here."

"Did I upset you? Wait—you're not interested in McKenzie, are you?"

"It's too soon for me to think about something like that," I managed.

"Of course. But you can see why I am. Humane *and* handsome."

"I'm getting on the subway," I lied.

Billie sent her best to my brother.

Steven had bought enough food for a dozen guests.

"I hope you have room in your freezer," I said.

The TV was on, a documentary we'd already seen twice, about Danny Way, the guy who jumped the Great Wall of China on a skateboard. *Waiting for Lightning* was part of Steven's collection of DVDs on extreme-sports heroes. We often watched together: Laird Hamilton and Travis Pastrana were in it, too. We found it inspiring to see the person who was the best in the world at what he did, and who had achieved this against heavy odds.

Steven had already set the table, even lighting candles. The effect would have been complete if he hadn't been wearing flannel pajama pants and a THRASHER T-shirt.

"I could watch him every day," I said.

"You want some wine?"

"I want a *drink* drink. You have any vodka?"

He took a bottle of Stoli out of the freezer. "You've earned it," he said, handing it to me.

I poured myself a double. Steven did the same. We raised our glasses.

"To George," he said.

We took our places at the table, surrounded by food pretty

enough to be photographed. I put some of everything on my plate, knowing I wouldn't be able to eat.

"I heard from Billie on my way over just now. I invited her to join us but she's meeting up with McKenzie later," I said, fishing for a reaction. Sometimes we ask for the very thing that will undo us.

"He's seeing her again?" Steven asked, then saw in my face the weight of the word *again*. "Listen, it's going to last about three minutes. In fact, the three minutes are probably up."

"Shit, he slept with her already?"

"She has one setting: high."

"Did he say that, or is that your observation?"

"You've seen her."

What had I seen? A beautiful and energetic woman whose confidence carried her past roadblocks. What man would turn her down?

"But I didn't see it coming," Steven said.

"Why not?"

"You never met McKenzie's wife, Louise. Don't think he's quite over her. She was in law school with us. Her gaze was focused outward, not on herself. I had a thing for her myself. So did every guy in the class."

"Was she that compelling?"

"She was just so comfortable in her skin. She had a kind of confidence. There was nothing coy about her. I never understood why some women think coyness is appealing to a man. It's just silly. Claire had it, too, that confidence; you can't meet it halfway."

"I know about Louise's death."

"Did he tell you? He never talks about it."

"I found it online."

Steven's plate already had room for seconds. Mine was untouched.

I could have asked more questions about my brother's former classmate. But what was I trying to find out? Why he had asked out Billie instead of me? Steven would not have the answer.

Instead of getting up to serve himself again, Steven switched his empty plate with my full one. He was kind enough to refrain from remarking on my lack of appetite. I poured myself another Stoli to keep him company for a half hour more.

My third Stoli was poured by the bartender at Isle of Skye. I had thought of calling Amabile, who lived nearby. I was not ready to go home. But I knew he'd be with his huge Dominican family, and it was just as well; familiarity was not what I wanted. I hadn't been to this bar before; usually I went to Barcade and played the vintage arcade games, such as *Tapper*. Made me feel like a kid again. Isle of Skye had a different vibe: Scottish, black leather, a pub filled with Scots not celebrating Thanksgiving. Behind the bar was a framed photo of the queen in front of a line of seated Scotsmen in kilts; the man seated to her right wore a kilt that had ridden up to reveal his naked genitals.

I looked over the crowd—more men than women, more hipster than Highlander, then took out my cell phone and checked the Tinder account I'd opened before I met Bennett. A photo of a shirtless guy in board shorts came up on my screen with a user name of Swampthing. *Want to meet him?* the pop-up asked. *Yes? No? Maybe?* I tapped *Maybe. Do you want to see how close Swampthing is?* I tapped *Yes.* He was two blocks away. The moment I tapped *Yes*, he was able to see my profile and picture. His profile said he was an actor who taught mixed martial arts. He said he liked Bollywood films, Russian vodka, and American women. I tapped *I'm two for three.*

I had nearly finished my drink when I got a message from Swampthing asking where I was. I tapped in the name of the bar. A couple of minutes later, a rangy, loose-limbed guy walked in, and even from yards away and in the dim light of the bar, I could see that he had blue eyes. With his dark hair falling in those eyes, he was a dazzler.

"You don't look like your picture," he said in an uninflected voice. Did he mean it didn't do me justice, or that I had perpetrated a fraud?

"You look exactly like yours," I said, trying to match his ambiguous tone.

"I'm glad you were looking tonight. Holidays can be slow."

A wise friend had once told me that just because a man is good-looking doesn't *necessarily* mean he is a bastard. I realized I was making excuses for him and he hadn't done anything except respond to my query.

"Can I get you another drink?" he asked, and signaled for the bartender before I answered.

"Sure," I said after the fact.

I started asking him about himself. Not because I wanted information, per se, but so that I could listen to his voice. I had always been swayed by men's voices. His was deep, and he sounded as though he were confiding in me. The trace of a Southern accent came from time to time; Louisiana? Oh, God, let him be from New Orleans.

Close enough: he said he was from Lafayette, and that his

daddy's side was Cajun. And what had he acted in? This was a dicey question, potentially embarrassing. He said he'd had a small speaking part in a Gus Van Sant film, and he was up for a part in an HBO series.

I had never wanted to be on screen or stage, but it didn't stop me from the kind of interest many people felt for those who did. How were actors able to lose themselves in front of strangers? What if you were still trying to *find* yourself? "Do you want to keep"—here he made air quotes—"'getting to know each other,' or do you want to go have some fun?" He had managed to both mock and entice me. He had issued a dare. I had a moment of magical thinking that persuaded me that nothing bad could happen on Thanksgiving.

We went to his place in Dumbo. The way in was complicated; we had to go around to the back of a renovated warehouse, where he jimmied the lock after inserting the key. Were it not for lights on in some of the building's windows, I would not have considered going in.

Inside his apartment, in front of a window facing the Brooklyn Bridge, hung a punching bag. Leather, the color of cognac, it looked as if it might have been a movie prop. "Is this where you train?"

"No." He did not offer more.

I moved to the window to look at the view, but he cut my sightseeing short. He took off my coat and threw it over an armchair. Then he took my hair and wrapped it around his fist. He stood behind me like that. I held on to his wrist. He let go first. When I turned to face him, he picked me up the way a groom picks up his bride, and he carried me into the back of the apartment, to his bed.

Within minutes, he turned on a bright bedside lamp. "I want to see you."

I saw the bank of windows in his bedroom had no curtains or shades, and that the room faced a wall of floor-to-ceiling windows in the modern building next door. In the same moment in which I felt exposed, and on exhibit, I also felt safe. I could be seen. He took off the rest of my clothes. He said he was surprised he found me so attractive, that I wasn't his type.

Would McKenzie have said such a thing, have had such a thought? I answered my own question: Trust me, he's not giving you a thought.

The flicker passed, and I was back in the moment. "Does your type do this?" I asked, touching myself. I didn't take my eyes off his face. "Does your type do this?" I put my finger inside myself. What had put me off moments before—the brightly lit room open to the eyes of neighbors—was encouraging me in an unexpected way. I thought of Billie. She startled me. I felt myself in competition with her in front of this man, and at the same time I wanted to be her.

I performed.

While still watching me, he started to undress. I told him, "No." So he left his clothes on and crouched at the foot of the mattress where he could see my body at that level—if I moved from posing on my knees to lying down. I could sense the pressure in him, the pressure of holding back. Of waiting. I went on. I took my time. I made myself come in front of him in the brightly lit room.

He stayed where he was at the foot of the bed while I got dressed. Neither of us said a thing. I noticed a light go on in the building across the way.

He made no plea for reciprocity. Was it astonishment that let him let me go?

The semester break was a week away, and I was at Rikers for a last session with a patient, a transsexual I had met with for the past year. She was being released the following week. Shalonda was able to convince anyone she was female. She had delicate features, a warm and lilting voice, and breasts she had saved up for since high school. She had taken the rap for her lover in a check-fraud scam, yet hoped they could resume their domestic life in Ozone Park.

"I know JJ is a fuckup, but I also know he loves me," Shalonda said.

"How does he show it?" I really wanted to know.

"He tells his friends, and it gets back to me."

"He never tells you?"

"He bought me a dress for when I get out. He wants me to have the final surgery."

"What do *you* want?"

"I want to make JJ happy. You think that's not a good reason."

I felt then that we had made no progress whatsoever. She still could not acknowledge her own wants and needs.

"I learned a long time ago," Shalonda said, "that you can be happy, or you can be right. I'm happy when JJ thinks he's right."

My affair with Bennett had been so complete a secret that performing the night before in the brightly lit room with a stranger had been a kind of extreme antidote; it made me feel that I set the terms.

"Say again?" I said to Shalonda.

"Where did you go?" She was grinning. "You just went some-where."

I blushed at the unprofessional lapse. I apologized for a late night and turned my attention back to my patient.

"I said I know who I am in whatever form I take. The surgery doesn't take anything away from me. Well, besides the obvious."

This felt like cheating—I was getting as much if not more from the session than Shalonda. Her solid sense of herself, her calm wisdom—I felt better the longer we talked.

I told Shalonda it had been a privilege to work with her and said I hoped she would let me know how she was doing on the outside. I gave her a business card, after adding my home number to it in ballpoint pen. We hugged each other, and Shalonda said, "It's a good feeling to surprise yourself—you'll see."

Was Shalonda a mind reader? I'd certainly surprised myself last night.

I decided to walk across the bridge to Queens even though it looked like a military zone with its razor wire and checkpoints. The wind was chafing.

I'd had all the surprise I needed, thanks to Bennett. Or so I thought. When I passed a deli with a newsstand, I stopped when I read the *Post* headline: "Heartless." The cover story was about a fifty-two-year-old woman found in her painting studio in Sag Harbor with her heart cut out of her body and placed on top of her chest.

I sat down on a milk crate and put my head between my knees. When I could, I stood up and bought the paper. The clerk called after me to give me my change.

The reporter wrote that the body had been posed in an ap-proximation of self-portraits the victim had made in which she photographed herself with a pig's heart on her chest. The coroner estimated the death had occurred a week prior. There were no leads yet as to who might have committed the grisly murder.

I was in that studio a week ago. Pat's dog had lunged at the window, at a sound outside. If I hadn't left when I did, would I have been killed, too? My hair lifted slightly from my scalp as though lightning had passed through me. Had Pat's killer seen me through the windows? Was the killer watching me now? I flagged a taxi and gave Steven's address to the driver. I'd have to ask Steven to pay the fare from Queens.

"You're staying here tonight," Steven said after I told him what had happened.

"What about Olive?"

"We'll smuggle her in." Dogs were not allowed in his building.

"Samantha was the one who told me where Pat lived. She still thinks Bennett's alive. She says he writes to her and sends her flowers."

Steven asked if I thought Samantha was capable of an act of such savagery.

"I think she followed me to Sag Harbor."

"You didn't tell me this. You've got to go to the police."

"They didn't take me seriously when I called them about Susan Rorke."

"You weren't there when she was killed." Steven handed me his cell phone.

I did what he wanted. I was connected with a detective in the Suffolk County PD and told him my suspicions in the calmest "I'm not a crazy person" manner I could summon. I said I thought this person had killed twice and told him about Susan Rorke. He scheduled an early-morning appointment for me to make a statement.

I was exhausted when I got off the phone. I slumped into a chair in Steven's living room, head in hand, the picture of defeat. Then Steven asked if I was ready to go pick up Olive. I saw that while I'd been on the phone, he had emptied out his gym bag and outfitted it with a soft fleece and towels warm from the dryer for my little dog.

The local news coverage of Pat's death seized on her being the granddaughter of the abstract expressionist Paul Loewi. Loewi was a contemporary of de Kooning and Pollock's, famous for his *Slaughterhouse* paintings, giant, black canvases with carcasslike red forms. An "artist's artist," he had not shared the wealth or international acclaim of his friends, but his paintings were valued by those in the know.

Steven and I watched the coverage on every news channel. I needed to hear every account of the gruesome murder. Yet no matter how many reporters spoke about it, I could not shake the feeling of disbelief.

Nancy Grace was on a tear: One theory about the murder put the blame on a religious cult in the area that practiced ritual animal killing as part of their worship. She said that pets had disappeared on the East End over the past six months. The deceased's dog was still missing. Another theory was a drug-fueled thrill kill, she said. But no suspects were in custody.

"Nancy Grace should meet Samantha," I said.

Her next guest was an expert on religious ritual killings. He said that removing the heart from an animal is not uncommon, that in many animist religions, the heart signifies strength; by biting into it, the person who removed it assumes that creature's strength. But to remove a human heart and place it atop the body is a desecration, unheard-of in any religion. It is an act of violence with nothing to redeem it spiritually, the expert said. Nancy Grace asked if he felt this murder was more along the lines of a cult like Charles Manson's followers.

The expert said, "The violence in this case is personal."

I asked Steven to pass me my cell phone on the table near him.

I called Amabile and asked him to come with me to the precinct. I needed a cop who would believe me, not suspect me. I knew he had a cousin who was a detective in the Suffolk County PD.

"He'll listen," Amabile said. "He's a stand-up guy. If you don't mind the motorcycle, I can drive you."

Amabile was a stand-up guy. And I told him so.

Riding a motorcycle on salted, icy streets in early winter put me in mind of the nickname donorcycle. I'd had spinouts on bikes as a teenager, and even though Amabile gave me a helmet to wear, my legs were vulnerable if we skidded out. On the other hand, holding on to a guy and leaning against his body is a sexy ride. I worried that Amabile might misread this—I was pretty sure he still wished things could have worked out with us.

I got the cycle equivalent of sea legs and wobbled when I climbed off the bike. Amabile righted me with a hand on my arm, so that I first leaned into him. His arm went around me until I got my footing. We carried our helmets as we entered the precinct house.

Amabile's cousin, Bienvenido, invited me into an empty interview room and brought me a cup of hot coffee.

"I may have been the last person to see Pat Loewi alive." I told him why I had gone to see her and that it was the only time I had met her.

"When did you get there and what time did you leave?"

This was the first question in an hour of questions designed to eliminate me or establish me as a suspect. He gave his notes to another cop to check out my story, then asked if I'd noticed anything strange about Pat's behavior that afternoon. I told him it would be easier to tell him what wasn't strange about it. I asked if Amabile had told him that Pat had once lived with my late fiancé.

"I know the history," Bienvenido said. "What else can you tell me?"

"You could look at Samantha Couper." I told him why.

When we finished, Amabile said, "Thanks, man. Appreciate this."

I thanked Bienvenido, too, and he said, "You're welcome."

"No, *you're* 'welcome,'" I said. "I know that much Spanish." *Bienvenido.*

Amabile insisted on driving me home. On the back of his bike, as the cold wind seeped through my jacket and pants, I questioned the strength of my suspicions. What did *I* know? Maybe there wasn't a connection between the two women's murders.

And then I thought of a third woman I needed to factor in.

Steven was against my going. To put it mildly. "How do you know Samantha's not right and Bennett's still alive? The police never identified the body."

"I know it was his body."

"You were in shock. What if this guy Jimmy Gordon is out there, and you're about to visit his mother? What if he's staying with his mother?"

"The Boston PD matched the DNA found on Susan Rorke with the body in my bedroom."

"Someone is sending Samantha flowers," Steven said.

"She's insane. She's probably sending them to herself."

"You can't know that."

"Can I borrow your car?"

"You don't know what you might run into. Plus, what if someone *is* sending flowers to Samantha? I don't want you to be collateral damage if someone is gaslighting Samantha. Maybe it's the same person who tricked you into going to Boston."

"I'm pretty sure that was Samantha."

"Pretty sure isn't the same as sure," Steven said. "What do you expect to learn?"

"What I need to find out is something no one but his mother can tell me: how I fell in love with him."

"Why do you think she can tell you that?"

"Because she must have loved him, too."

The nine-hour drive to Rangeley, Maine, gave me too much time to think about what I was headed into. I'd stopped alongside the Androscoggin River to walk for a bit, even in the cold, to try to summon compassion for Bennett's mother before I got to the Lake House, the bed-and-breakfast she owned.

Rangeley in winter is a quiet, snow-packed small town, nothing like it would have been in summer, with tourists filling the small lodges and covering the lake in kayaks and sailboats.

I didn't hurry to the Lake House. Bennett's mother was not expecting me until evening, and I regretted having allowed her to insist that I stay there. When I told her on the phone that I had been engaged to her son, his mother—who had only been told ten days before that her long-missing son was dead—thought that I was calling about coming to his funeral. It was scheduled for this Sunday. I swallowed my surprise at what I had blundered into. I didn't tell her the real reason I wanted to talk with her. She told me how much it would mean to her to meet me and have me at the service. I found myself relenting in the face of a mother's wishes. I would use the occasion to find out as much as I could about her son as a child. I would conduct research.

I parked Steven's used Saab a couple of blocks away and walked past the Lake House. I wanted to size it up before entering. I passed a couple of sporting-goods stores, a homemade-doughnut shop, and a pub with a couple of old men at the bar. Across the street, behind a strip of cafés and a gas station, was Rangeley Lake, iced over in patches, boathouses locked. I assumed his mother's would be similar to the B&Bs Bennett had taken me to. But instead of lace curtains and lit-candle lamps, the windows of the Lake House were covered with dark shades. While I would not expect window boxes planted with flowers in early December, I was surprised that the flagstone path to the front door was not even marked by small lanterns in the dark. Nothing covered the glass front door, so I could see into the sitting room before I rang the bell. Nothing frilly, just knotty-pine paneling and utilitarian camp furniture.

A wiry, white-haired woman opened the door. "I'm Jimmy's mother." From there on, I made myself think of Bennett as "Jimmy." Renee hugged me, whereas I had offered my hand in greeting. She put a hand to my back to urge me into the warmth of the parlor. She had a pot of water boiling for tea in the kitchen and asked if I'd eaten.

Had I?

"I'll warm up some chicken soup someone brought over last night. People have been very kind."

"Thank you." I thought nothing she could tell me about Jimmy was worth this.

"You'll have your pick of rooms tonight. I'll show you the place after dinner. It'll just be the two of us. Jimmy's sisters can't join us."

Fuck me.

Instinctively, I looked toward the door, gauging an exit. I would rather have had the sisters join us than sit with the grieving mother through dinner. But was she grieving? She moved

about the kitchen like an athlete—efficient and deft. She wore
no makeup. She was maybe sixty-five, and her white hair was
braided down her back. She wore jeans and a turtleneck, topped
with a heavy, red plaid overshirt. She must have kept the temperature on the low side to save money, I thought. It was chilly.
Her eyes were red-rimmed and her lids puffy, as though she
had been crying—over her son's death, or a lifetime of being
wounded by him?

I wandered into the parlor and looked at the framed photos
set about the room. Several were shots of what must have been
the two daughters as young girls on a rocky beach. With them—a
boy. Their brother, Jimmy. The girls are focused on something in
the plastic pails they carry, but Jimmy is looking into the camera.
I had to be careful not to project what I knew about his later behavior onto this image of a boy who looked to be no more than
eight. Even so, his gaze had an intensity that I did not associate
with a child.

Another family photo showed his sisters playing with a kitten. Beside it was a photo of the girls, looking no older, playing
with a dog. What had happened to the kitten? Jimmy was not in
either of these photos. I tried to rein in my worst-case scenarios,
but why wasn't he pictured with their pets? And where was
their father? On the mantel was a photo of Jimmy as a teenager,
maybe around seventeen. I would have had a crush on him
in high school. He wore a leather bomber jacket over a white
T-shirt and jeans—the universal bad-boy fashion he had continued to wear for years. His hair was long and he had an attitude;
he had potential. I wondered if his mother always displayed the
photo, or if she had brought it out when she learned of her son's
death.

Renee called me into the kitchen and asked if I minded eating at the small table there. She said it was warmer because of the stove. I had peeked into the main dining room for guests, and it was dark and uninviting.

Sitting inches from Jimmy's mother, I was suddenly shy. I was glad that she jumped right in with a question about her son. "Can I ask you something? What was my son like?"

I couldn't begin to answer that.

"I know, it's too big a question. But I haven't known him for twenty years. And here you are."

The burden was outsize. I had contacted her, I reminded myself. I had sought her out. I owed her an answer. But did I owe her the truth?

"He was charismatic. He was adventurous. He loved Maine."

"He was here in Maine?"

Anything I might say to her would be loaded, could bring her pain. I told her a white lie. "He only talked about it." It seemed like a good save.

"Did he talk about his family?"

"Jimmy lived in the moment."

"Didn't he."

I thought she had agreed with me awfully fast. I tried to head off another question for a moment. "What was he like as a boy?"

"He certainly was charming. He could talk his older sisters into anything. He once fixed a homemade parachute and had Vanessa test it by jumping off the roof of the garage. She was lucky she didn't break a leg, or worse."

Her tone told me it amused her to recall this event—but only because her daughter had not been hurt.

"He was the brightest of my children, but he hated school. He couldn't abide teachers telling him what to do. I sent him to military school but he ran away. His father had been in the Air Force. Jimmy never met him."

I wanted to know if the father had died or deserted the family, but I didn't feel I could ask. "What did Jimmy want to do when he grew up?"

"Last I knew, he wanted to be an artist, or a musician. But I never saw him draw, and he didn't have the patience to practice an instrument. What was he doing when you met him?"

The woman would be burying her son the next day. I told her he had had an art gallery and later represented musicians, the fiction that would give her some peace. But I wanted the truth from her.

"He was such a mystery to me," she said.

That was the truth.

We finished eating, and I must have looked tired from the drive. Renee told me to follow her upstairs, where she gave me a choice of two similarly decorated rooms. "This one gets the morning light," she said, so I chose the other, hoping to sleep in. The funeral wasn't until one. We said good night to each other—no hug this time—and when I'd closed the bedroom door, I hung up the black dress I had brought for the funeral. I had worn it before to a cocktail party, but this time I'd wear it with black tights instead of lace thigh-highs.

I woke to an argument downstairs the next morning.

"How could you let her stay here?" The woman made no attempt to keep her voice down.

I heard Renee say, "It's not *her* fault. She drove nine hours to attend his funeral. I have plenty of room here."

"So now we have to make conversation with his girlfriend all day?"

"She was his fiancée," Renee corrected.

"That's her tough luck." Which sister was it who was so angry that I was there?

"She's actually quite nice. You'll see."

I chose this moment to go downstairs. I needed coffee, and I hoped that Renee had thought to make some, even for one guest. I braced myself to meet the sister.

"Morgan, meet my daughter Vanessa."

Vanessa was the female Bennett. The female Jimmy. A few inches shorter than her brother, Vanessa had the same dark hair and blue eyes, even stood the same way, leaning on one hip. She was not yet in her funeral dress, or maybe she didn't plan to change for the service. She wore basic winter gear via an L.L. Bean outlet store. Vanessa sized me up, not even pretending otherwise. I spoke first, telling her I was sorry about her brother.

"His first time home in twenty years," she said. "I guess he can't leave this time."

I asked Renee if there was coffee in the kitchen, and when she offered to bring me a cup, I said I would get it myself. But Renee insisted, so I was left with Vanessa.

"What he put her through," Vanessa said, not needing to continue. There was nothing to say to that. Especially without coffee.

I tried another approach. "When will I meet Lisa?"

"She'll be along," Vanessa said, not making anything clear.

Even though Vanessa was being rude, I was fascinated by

how much she looked and sounded like Jimmy. I wanted to goad
her, to see the likeness fully animated.

"You look like him," I said, knowing she would refute this.

"You mean, he looks like me. Looked."

"Does your mother know how he died?"

"It was your dogs, we heard. I guess it was guilt that brought
you here."

"I wanted to know more about the man I was going to marry,"
I said, not taking the bait.

"So do we. But my mother can't take any more bad news."

Renee brought in coffee and a plate of store-bought cinnamon rolls. She apologized for not making a bigger breakfast,
and Vanessa reminded her that it was the morning of her son's
funeral, and no one expected her to be bothered with anything
else.

"Sit, sit, please," Renee said to both of us.

I took a seat at the dining table, but Vanessa remained standing.

"Are you going to go change, honey?" Renee asked her
daughter. "Have you decided to come to the service?"

I had not realized this was a possibility, that Jimmy's sister
might be a no-show at his funeral.

"Lisa will be here at noon. She can give us all a ride," Renee
said.

"If I'm here, I'm here." Vanessa wrapped a cinnamon roll in a
paper napkin to take with her.

"She's protective of me," Renee said, after Vanessa left. "I
can't be short with her for that."

"I want you to know how sorry I am. Nothing could have prepared you for this." I thought the word *this* was inclusive enough
to mean as much or as little as his mother wanted to consider.

I was not going to revisit the way he died. I would take my cue from her.

"I appreciate your coming all this way, but I'd like to be alone for a while."

I grabbed my coat and gloves and made as graceful an exit as I could; I walked along the lake to the old-fashioned doughnut shop I'd seen when I drove in. I could tell I was the object of curiosity for the girls behind the counter. Was a stranger so uncommon in this place off-season?

No need to ponder this long, as a woman about Jimmy's age offered me the empty seat at her table. "You here for Jimmy's funeral?"

"You knew Jimmy?"

"Since grade school. So you're the one who got him to settle down."

The *one?*

"I had my eye on him back then, but I dodged a bullet."

What had they all known about him that I had missed? "What are you talking about?" So far, everyone but Renee had been supremely nasty to me.

"Does it matter now?"

"It matters to me."

"Maybe you dodged a bullet, too. He stole his mother's savings before he skipped town."

I remembered a wise friend once told me that if you want to know how a man will treat you, look at the way he treats his mother.

"That, and—I don't know—he sampled every girl in town."

I was both sickened and excited to have this information. I wanted to keep this woman talking, and I wanted to hear nothing more. She made the decision for me.

"Been a pleasure," she said, rising. "Give my best to Renee."

She left me with my untouched coffee and the feeling that I had chosen the wrong profession. I knew nothing about people.

Lisa picked us up in an old, black Jeep Cherokee. She gave Renee her arm as we walked to the car. Vanessa got out of the passenger seat to let her mother sit in the front, which meant that she and I would share the backseat. She hadn't changed clothes for the funeral. Renee wore a black wool skirt and cardigan over a print turtleneck, black stockings, and flats. Lisa had made an effort. She wore a simple, fitted, black dress under a camel-hair coat, and black, knee-high boots.

Vanessa said, "Would you turn on the radio?"

Lisa sounded shocked. "Are you kidding?"

"What's wrong with a little music?"

Renee said she didn't mind if they put on a classical station.

"Then forget it," Vanessa said.

My pulse sped up when she said that—it could have been her brother speaking.

We rode in silence after that, except for the sisters contradicting each other about the better route to the church. Bennett had told me he was raised Catholic, so I was not surprised to see Lisa turn into the parking lot of Our Lady of the Lakes in Oquossoc, an elegant red-brick Catholic church ten minutes from Rangeley. Inside it reminded me of a German beer hall with its Bavarian beams crisscrossing the ceiling.

I would not have been surprised to see every pew filled, nor would I have been surprised to see them empty. If it was the former, I felt the townspeople would be there for Renee, not her errant son. I was right: the congregation included only people Renee's age, and most of them were women—and I was wrong: the pews were far from filled. An organist played "Be Not Afraid," one of the standard Catholic funeral hymns, I knew. Give me a reason, I thought, to be not afraid.

"What did you spend on that casket?" Vanessa asked her mother.

Lisa shushed her, so their mother didn't have to.

"Seriously," Vanessa said. "You need a new furnace."

Renee said, "Drop it."

Then the priest approached. Father Bernard greeted the family and nodded my way when Renee introduced me. He held Renee's hands and spoke softly to her, the time-worn words of solace. When he turned from her to walk to the pulpit, I debated whether I would kneel along with the congregants during the service or keep my seat. I wasn't Catholic, but I didn't want to draw any more attention in the small town. Even if I knelt, I would not be able to take communion. Damned if I did, damned if I didn't.

The funeral mass was in Latin—Renee told me she had asked for that—and I let the sounds wash over me without meaning. I found the rituals soothing, even though they were not my rituals.

The last funeral I had attended was Kathy's, a "green" funeral. No coffin, no headstone; we carried her shroud-wrapped body on a handcart deep into a forest in her native Virginia to a designated area where we, her friends, dug the grave. Kathy weighed practically nothing at the end. We lifted her off the cart and laid her in the ground. After we filled the grave, we scattered leaves over the freshly turned earth and brushed away our footprints with branches.

After this service, the priest summoned several young men

from the congregation to carry the coffin out of the church. It was customary for the family to follow before everyone else, but was I family?

At the graveside service the priest invited the mourners to make "a suitable gesture of farewell." Renee, crying quietly, threw a single white rose onto the lowered coffin. Lisa threw a handful of dirt into the grave. Vanessa looked down on her brother's coffin. I had the terrible feeling that she was going to spit on it. But she simply turned away without doing a thing. I wondered if she would yank me back if I stepped forward to say a farewell. I had nothing to say, and nothing to scatter on his coffin.

Vanessa helped her mother leave the graveside. Lisa stood off by herself crying.

I was not a good enough actress to convince Lisa that I shared her loss, but I tried to express something along those lines anyway. She thanked me and said she would miss him, even though she'd already been missing him all those years since he had left the family. And then she said it upset her that his death was so violent.

"Can I ask you something? Was *he* ever violent?"

"What do you mean?" Lisa seemed surprised by my question. "Was he violent with you?"

I told her that the Boston police think he murdered a woman.

"No one told us that. Who do they think he killed?"

"His fiancée."

"Then who the hell are you?"

"He had more than one."

"I don't understand. What are you saying?"

Vanessa noticed her sister's agitation and left their mother surrounded by friends. She came over to ask what was going on.

"She says Jimmy's a murderer," Lisa said. "That he killed his fiancée. His *other* fiancée. How do you like that?"

"I don't know who you are or what you want from us, but you can leave right now," Vanessa said.

She looked and sounded so much like Bennett that it felt as though he were ordering me to leave his own funeral. It was the last time I would obey him.

Before I left for Maine, I had contacted animal sanctuaries that might take Cloud, starting with the gold standard—Best Friends, in Kanab, Utah. I wanted Cloud as close to me as possible, and I thought they might be able to refer me to a suitable place in the Northeast. But every place I tried had a wait list up to a year. And since a "dangerous dog" would be kept by itself and not allowed to play with other dogs or socialize with people other than the handler who would take the dog out to eliminate, it would be a life of solitary confinement. I knew people in the rescue world who felt that there was something worse than euthanasia, and this was what they meant. Dogs went crazy in such a situation, and the manifestations of their misery were many. Could I subject my dog to this? Was choosing the lesser evil the best I could do for Cloud? What *was* the lesser evil? I wanted McKenzie's opinion.

I was still sleeping on Steven's foldout. I made myself coffee and phoned McKenzie's office.

"Laurence McKenzie's office," a familiar voice answered.

"Billie?"

"Yes, may I take a message?"

"It's me, Morgan."

"Morgan! We were wondering where you've been."

"What are you doing there?"

"Helping out. His secretary quit on him." She was making herself indispensable to him.

"When will he be back?"

"Faye, stop clicking your teeth," Billie said to McKenzie's dog. "Sorry, what did you ask me?"

"I wanted to talk to McKenzie about Cloud. Every sanctuary I contacted has a waiting list."

"So what are you going to do?"

"I'm wondering if George was the luckier one," I admitted.

"You weren't asking that two weeks ago."

"I need to talk to McKenzie. Can you ask him?"

"He's right here. I'm in the outer office. I'll get him for you."

Before I could register this, McKenzie was telling me it was good to hear my voice.

I told him why I was calling and asked if he would meet me at Crown Vic's after work. The former police-car service station on South Second Street was new, thus neutral, ground. I hoped he would not bring Billie; I wanted time with him alone. The thought was obscene under these circumstances. We were going to talk about what makes a dog's life worth living, and jealousy had no place here. But even with my dog's life at stake, I entertained petty thoughts and was hurt that he preferred Billie to me.

He was sitting at the bar when I walked in. I was glad he'd chosen a seat close to the fireplace; I was freezing. He jumped down off the stool and greeted me with an outstretched hand. Quite a change from the hug he'd given me the last time I'd seen him. He slid his glass over to me. "Try this," he said, a surprisingly intimate gesture after the handshake, I thought. "It's called Angry Orchard Keeper. Whiskey with hard cider."

Dutifully, I took a sip. I nodded yes, and he ordered one for me, too.

It was still early enough that the dinner crowd hadn't come

in. I liked sitting on a barstool next to him, warmed by a fire. I let myself relax into it for just a moment, before putting my moral dilemma on the table.

"You know your dog better than anyone," he said. "There's no clean right or wrong decision here."

"Maybe George was the luckier one," I said, testing.

"For what it's worth, I think that we owe our dogs the best life we can give them, and when that life isn't good enough, we release them with love. I don't mean to suggest that that is an easy moment to identify—when it isn't good enough."

I saw that he refused to be prescriptive, and I was grateful for that. He was just vague enough that I could make the sentiment my own, if I chose to do so. I also saw that he would not judge me for whichever choice I made. I was grateful for that, too.

"Have you had to make a choice like this?" I asked.

"I had to decide whether *I* would live. After my wife died."

"Steven told me about the diving accident."

"I'm the one who persuaded her to take up diving. She was willing to conquer her fear of deep water for me."

I wanted to be the kind of listener he was for me. No judgment. No easy consolation. I let him talk.

"I even looked for a reason in books. *A Grief Observed*, by C. S. Lewis—he wrote it after his wife died, but it was about his loss of faith in God as much as his grief at losing his wife."

I told him what I knew about C. S. Lewis when he was a boy, how when he was four, his dog, Jack, was killed by a car. The future author would only answer to the name of Jack after that, and even as an old man his closest friends and family called him Jack. I hoped McKenzie did not think I was equating a boy's loss of his pet dog to a man's losing his wife. Then I saw that I didn't have to worry about that.

McKenzie laughed. "Finally, a reason to like C. S. Lewis."

"Could you eat something? Do you have time? If I ordered macaroni and cheese, would you share it?"

"I'd love to, but I have to be somewhere at seven."

I glanced at his watch and saw that we had about fifteen more minutes. I thought he might be going to meet Billie, but I wouldn't ask. Instead I said, "So C. S. Lewis didn't help, but did you find someone who did? Either on or off the page?"

"I don't know that this helped, but soon after, I was trying a case in which an elementary school in Connecticut would not allow a ten-year-old girl with cerebral palsy to bring her helper monkey, a little capuchin, to school with her. The monkey was perfectly behaved, wore a diaper so as not to soil anything in the classroom, and was pretty much a model citizen. The girl needed this helper monkey's assistance in fundamental ways. The other parents and the school board were afraid of diseases they thought the monkey carried, though there was no evidence of this, and the monkey was up-to-date on its vaccinations.

"Turned out, the girl left me little to do in court. She gave an eloquent description of her life before she got Maddie and then told the court what she was now able to do with Maddie's essential help. One of the most moving examples was also the simplest. She told the court that before she got Maddie, no one ever talked to her at school. Since she started bringing Maddie, she had become popular. All the kids wanted to meet the little helper monkey. She said, 'I didn't feel sorry for myself after that.' And neither did I."

"You didn't feel sorry for the girl, or for yourself?"

"Both."

The irony was almost too much for me, that McKenzie was opening up to me in ways more intimate than when I thought he might be interested in me. Maybe he felt safe enough to confide in me this way now that he was with someone else. But why did it have to be Billie? And why shouldn't it be Billie?

McKenzie put on his coat and asked me to call him when I had made my decision about Cloud. In parting, he did not offer his hand. He put his arms around me, and we stood like that for too brief a time.

I stayed at Crown Vic's and, this time, had no interest in finding a man to waste a night with. I finished my drink and glanced up at the TV above the bar. The news was on, and I could barely hear the reporter over the music. But I recognized the woman whose photo appeared on-screen: Pat. The next photo was of a Hispanic man, identified as a migrant worker on the East End of Long Island. According to police, he had just been arrested for the murder of Pat Loewi. The reporter used what had entered the vernacular and referred to the murder as the "Heartless" case.

I was grateful to be in a place where no one knew me, or what I had been thinking. The anonymity obviated the need to feel embarrassed. All this time I had been sure that Samantha was responsible for Pat's murder. Now I could choose to believe the police, who, after all, were good at their job. The news felt like an invitation to drop what had become, I saw, an obsession, this certainty of Samantha's guilt. But why couldn't a migrant worker have been responsible? I thought back to the Christa Worthington murder on the Cape a few years back. The whole town thought they knew who the killer was, and there was a second suspect, too, but, no—three years later, a sanitation worker named Christopher McCowen was arrested and, a year later, convicted for the murder.

I had been a fool to press detectives to investigate a connection between the murders of Pat and Susan Rorke. I had been a fool to suspect Samantha.

The momentary feeling of relief was supplanted by a dark and damning fact I did not want to face. I had fallen for Jimmy Gordon, a small-time, small-town delinquent who grew up to be the kind of predator I studied; my insider knowledge not only failed to protect me, it had led me straight to the predator, and I fell in love with him!

Etta James was singing "At Last." I moved one barstool closer to the fireplace and ordered the macaroni and cheese.

I was three months behind on my thesis and hoping that Leland, my adviser at John Jay, would cut me some slack, given the reasons I was late. I had chosen him to work with based on his books, which were not only fascinating, but beautifully written. His were the kind of books I would like to write—if I could not write poetry, I could still write well.

The requisite cartoon taped to his office door was by Gary Larson, in which a psychiatrist facing his patient on the couch has written only one note on his pad: *Just plain nuts!*—underlined three times.

Leland's office was a throwback to the sixties—with a lava lamp and dream catchers on the walls. His parents had been hippies before finding a home in academia, he'd told me. He had eschewed their early leanings in favor of a rule-bound academic life. He said he liked to see his mother's handiwork on his walls. His partner, whom he called by his last name of Emory, had given Leland a large exercise ball, and Leland was trying to stay upright on it instead of sitting in his comfortable desk chair. It was comical and his struggle made me laugh.

"I hope this trend is short-lived," he said, giving up and returning to his chair.

I took a seat across from his desk and began by apologizing.

He cut me off, saying he was just glad to see me and was sorry about what I'd been through. He had said as much in a note right after Bennett died, but I had not answered any of the large-hearted notes people had sent, even Leland's.

His kindness set off what I had hoped to keep from him: tears. There was no point in trying to pretend that I was capable and on track; anyone could see I was utterly unglued. Leland told me to take care of myself first. When I asked how much he had heard about Bennett, he said he knew Bennett was an impostor suspected of murder. Leland would support my taking a leave if I needed it. But he made a case for work as a daily practice that could get me through this, even if I only worked an hour a day.

Could I rally for an hour a day given what my days were like? Did I believe in my thesis any longer? "This isn't end-of-thesis doubt. I've been forced to make a profound reevaluation of what I thought I knew. When I started, I thought I could identify a new victim typology. I believed that compassionate women attract a certain type of predator. I thought I had the data. But now that I have been involved with one, where is my objectivity, my credibility?"

"Who better to examine the phenomenon?"

"That's the thing. The online profile I created that attracted 'Bennett' was designed to draw a control group, not a predator."

"What would you say about a cop who's been robbed? I'd say maybe he's going to be a better cop. Look at your whole hand, not just what you thought was your strong suit. You'll find a new way to interpret the material."

I told Leland how much I appreciated his understanding and his guidance. When I closed the door behind me, I hoped he had not written in his notebook, *Just plain nuts!*

•   •   •

I had scheduled appointments that day as though I were running a relay race. I went directly from seeing my thesis adviser to Cilla's office, passing the baton, as it were. I had not spoken with her since my return from the funeral in Maine the week before. I had thought we'd be talking about that, but since talking to Leland, Maine was no longer the priority.

Cilla offered me tea, which she tended to do when I arrived looking upset, which tended to be every week.

"My thesis adviser was sympathetic, but I still think my profile sent a very different signal than what I intended. In the profile, all my favorite novels were variations on a theme: things are not as they seem. I listed my favorite song as Jack White's 'Love Interruption.'"

"I don't know that song."

I sang the first few verses.

"Holy God." Cilla's laugh shaded into a cough. "Is that why you went home with the Cajun?"

"'Swampthing.' But Swampthing wasn't in charge."

"That could have overturned itself in an instant."

"I had an audience in the other apartments. Very *Rear Window*."

"But having exposed yourself to anonymous neighbors, you then walked home alone late at night, in an industrial neighborhood."

"I did indeed."

"Honey, I have to say that that is the behavior of a potential victim."

"Is that how you see me?"

"You went home with a woman you'd just met on a Greyhound bus and got raped by her boyfriend. You've been putting yourself at risk for a long time. I don't see you as a victim—not at all—but I see a pattern of self-destructive behavior. Either you learned it from living with your tormented mother, or you have a neurological predisposition to it. The latter requires some form of external activation—such as the rape you endured."

"You're saying I was 'asking for it'?"

"No one asks for what happened to you."

"Are you saying I'm the kind of woman I study?"

"At the risk of sounding like a Freudian, do *you* think you are?"

I felt snappish, but sat quietly for a moment. Then something occurred to me. The issue was not *or*, it was *and*. I was this way *and* that way. I was a woman who studied victimology, *and* I was a woman whose actions had contributed to being victimized. Didn't this duality make us human? And wasn't it less damning to think of myself as both, instead of just the one?

On my way back from Cilla's, I passed the Delacorte Theater. I had last been there to see Meryl Streep in *Mother Courage*, a rousing performance, a first and last date. You wouldn't think you'd feel like having sex after seeing *Mother Courage*, but my date and I found ourselves groping each other as we walked past Belvedere Castle after the play. We turned into the maze that is the Ramble, and my skewed logic allowed me to follow him down a rocky, unlit path, skewed because I actually believed myself safe, given that so much homosexual coupling was likely to be nearby. That's what the Ramble was known for, after all. Yet what did I think? That if I found myself in trouble, gay men having intercourse would stop to come to my rescue? Straight men having intercourse would not.

McKenzie would not have led me into the Ramble.

Oh—hello! Here was McKenzie, back in my thoughts. Cilla and I had finished the session discussing why I had so many Swampthings and no McKenzie. If I got what I wanted—the bad ones—then how did a person change what she wanted? What she wants. But I did want McKenzie. And he chose Billie. Billie offered to help him, while I had wanted him to help me.

I continued on to the ice-skating rink. I didn't feel like skating, but it had the best hot chocolate in the city. One winter I'd skated there two or three times a week, feeling like a kid, loving the gliding across the ice, even though it was crowded. I'd finally been driven off by the music—it seemed that whatever time I skated, the sound system was playing a Lionel Richie medley.

I saw a homeless man bundled up and sitting on a bench, reading from a paperback copy of *War and Peace*. A vendor selling roasted chestnuts was warming his gloved hands under the heat lamp keeping the nuts warm. Dogs wearing coats from tony stores were walked on braided-leather leashes. A well-dressed man wearing different-colored gloves saluted me as he passed. Nice, or nuts, I couldn't tell.

The salt on the paths left a white ring on my black boots; I would have to oil them when I got home. As I approached my apartment building, I thought of the study that had been done on the moment a dog knows its owner is coming home; film had been made of dogs moving to sit by the front door when their owners started home after work, even when their schedules were irregular. I hadn't yet unlocked the downstairs door when I heard Olive begin to bark. Hysterically. I raced up the stairs to quiet her before the neighbors complained.

I took Olive for a perfunctory walk, having had such a long one myself. She didn't seem to mind. She seemed glad for it.

After, she curled up at my feet as I waited for water to boil for tea. I heard the murmur of the people in the next apartment, and I liked the vague sounds—it was company without having to have company. It was the hour when the lights inside turned the windows into mirrors, the time when you can no longer discern color in the sky. I turned off the kitchen light so that I would not see my reflection. It was the opposite of my performance in the Cajun's apartment. Standing in darkness allowed me to look inside others' apartments, though I saw nothing like what I had done, just strangers making dinner.

On my incomprehensibly bundled Internet, phone, and cable service a representative had tricked me into getting—the first two months were free—all my electronics were synced, whether or not I wanted them to be. This meant that I could be watching television and the phone number of whoever was calling me would blink in the corner of the screen, interrupting my true-crime shows, which were all I wanted to watch. I used to like them because I couldn't believe how easily people were taken in, how mundane was the trigger for the crime that followed. Now I watched as one of the taken-in; in the show that most spoke to me, women discovered whom they had really married, after they had married these bigamists, murderers, and rapists.

A late-night call showed up on the screen.

"Have you heard from the man you call Bennett? I've heard nothing for ten days." Samantha sounded urgent and scared.

"Since I just got home from his funeral, no."

"What are you talking about?"

"His mother invited me. The funeral was in Maine."

"What happened to him?" Samantha's confusion was palpable.

I could have jerked her around and fed out information slowly. I could have been sarcastic and made fun of her refusal to acknowledge what I knew to be the truth. But I also knew that this woman was unhinged and desperate, or else someone was pretending to be Bennett and tormenting her. The mature psychologist part of me took over. I told Samantha that when I located his mother, his mother had arranged for her son's remains to be flown to his hometown of Rangeley, Maine, for burial. His real name, I told her, had been Jimmy Gordon. I told her that he had been killed last September, and that I was sorry to have to deliver this news twice.

"I never heard of Jimmy Gordon, but my fiancé is in Canada and was e-mailing me up until ten days ago."

"*Somebody* has been contacting you, but not him."

"I want that woman's phone number."

"You shouldn't bother his mother right now." I tried to keep my voice steady and uninflected. It would be so easy to step wrong, I knew. What would it take to convince her that he was dead? And if I convinced her, then who would she think was pretending to be him? Didn't this make her a victim twice over?

"Is the reason you're being so cruel to me because he left you for me?" I heard Samantha reaching to make sense out of what she was hearing.

"I'm just telling you what I know. I don't know what more I can do."

"You can call me if you hear from him."

In an exercise for a psychology class at John Jay, we students were paired, and one person was instructed to say, "No, you can't," to the partner. The partner was instructed to reply, "Yes, I can." This was to go on indefinitely. I remember everyone getting ready, then the professor announced, "You may start . . . *now*."

Amabile, my partner, faced me in a chair and said, "No, you can't." I said right back, "Yes, I can." He smiled and said, "No, you can't," the inflection slightly firmer. "Yes," I corrected him, "I can." We did this back and forth a few more times, until the smiles left our faces. We were shocked at how quickly the simple phrases enraged us. I could feel my face turn red. He wasn't listening to me. Amabile's voice rose. I was aware that something similar was going on elsewhere in the classroom.

This was how I felt talking with Samantha. She didn't listen. I made no impression on her whatsoever.

I took Leland's advice and spent the next day in the library at John Jay on the MEDLINE database. I read articles by Laurence Tancredi, MD, on the ways in which brain structure and functioning are profoundly affected by hormones, drugs, genetic abnormalities, injuries, and traumatic experiences. Bad judgment, he argued, could be the result of physiological abnormalities. This was a theory I wanted to include in my thesis, his idea that we are "hardwired" to act as we do.

I was mostly looking at a phenomenon called mirror cells. The neuroscientist V. S. Ramachandran had said, "Mirror neurons will do for psychology what DNA did for biology." Mirror cells were discovered in monkeys in 1992. A team of Italian scientists noticed that the same neurons fired when a monkey reached for an object as when the monkey saw another monkey reaching for an object. Ramachandran, among other scientists, believe that mirror cells are the building blocks for a number of essential human skills—imitation, the ability to intuit what another person is thinking, and most important, empathy. Ramachandran's theory is that autism is the result of broken mirror cells. I was trying to find enough data to confirm my own theory. Sociopaths also suffer from broken mirror-neuron systems.

The sole message on my machine when I got home was from Billie, calling to say she had found an animal sanctuary with a short waiting list just outside New Milford, Connecticut. She asked if I'd like to drive up together to check it out for Cloud.

She picked me up in her old Volvo, the interior as immaculate as the day she showed up on Staten Island for the temperament test. I offered money for gas, but she said she had filled the tank, and it wasn't necessary. It was a clear day for the ninety-minute drive to Connecticut.

Billie said she'd found the place through a friend who worked with Bad Rap out in Oakland, California. The friend had gone West after years in the rescue network in the Northeast. She had started For Pitties' Sake, the place we were headed for, though they did not turn away other breeds if they needed help.

"They've never had a Great Pyrenees there," Billie said.

That was all the dog talk for a while. As though we had agreed to it, we stayed quiet until the exit for Rye, no traffic to battle.

"My mother used to take us to Playland," Billie said. "Couple minutes from here. There was a ride called the Steeple Chase, a carousel with horses that looked like they were stampeding in terror. There were four horses abreast, maybe fifty horses altogether. And the thing went, like, sixty miles an hour. Amazingly, no one was ever killed on it, but a seven-year-old boy died of blunt force trauma to the head on Ye Old Mill ride, tame and slow."

Billie tuned her Sirius radio to *Coffee House*. Easy listening with an indie vibe.

"My grandmother has a place here," Billie said, when we passed through Greenwich. "That's where I rode the real horses."

"Nice," I managed.

When we took the exit toward New Milford, the landscape, for a few miles, was more scenic—nicer trees. Where I expected to see cattle grazing, we drove past small businesses and shopping centers. Billie asked if I wanted to stop for coffee or just keep going. I was glad she had asked, and we stopped for coffee-to-go from a diner.

Back in the car, we had two cups of hot coffee, but only one drink holder. I amused myself picturing the power play of who would claim the sole cup holder, though the driver usually gets it if there is only one. As though reading my mind, Billie pulled it a little farther out, and I saw that it did, in fact, hold two.

We turned off the main drag onto a barely marked dirt road and followed it for about a quarter of a mile until Billie stopped the car in front of a red-painted, raised ranch house. No sign announced the place, but I saw that the grounds went on for acres and acres, with an agility course set up to one side of the house, and a frozen-over creek on the other. Before we could ring the doorbell, the door opened, and a young man with dark hair and a mustache greeted us.

"The director made a dog-food run, but I can show you around." He took us downstairs first, where each room held two or three wire crates the size of studio apartments. A dog was in each, with piles of fleece blankets, a bowl of water, and rawhide bones and toys.

"The dogs live inside the house?" I asked, used to the foul conditions of the shelter.

"They each have their own crate in the house, and there are large areas for socialization, where they can run free upstairs and play together. Outdoors we have the agility course, and tie-outs when the weather is better.

"The idea here is to de-stress the dogs, give them exercise, get them veterinary care if they need it, and provide obedience training if that is what they need, whatever will help them get their 'forever homes,'" Alfredo said. "Upstairs it's the same—we can have thirty dogs here at a time."

"How do you pay for this?" I asked.

"We get donations; the woman who started it is a good fundraiser. There are angels, people who don't ask for recognition for the money they give us—a *lot* of money. I came here from Guatemala to work as a landscape gardener. I was hired to maintain the yard, and one day the director asked me for help walking her six unruly dogs. When I took them all out on their leashes, they instantly stopped squabbling and walked perfectly as a group. Not one of them barked. They didn't pull to chase other dogs in the park. I didn't have to raise my voice to them."

"But what about a dog you can't find a home for? My dog would be here for life."

"Her dog, the Pyrenees, was ruled a 'dangerous dog,'" Billie said.

Alfredo led us to what was once the garage. But no cars were there, and it was heated the same as the rest of the house. An industrial washer and dryer were at one end, and shelves were filled with grooming equipment and hooks for dozens of leashes. An even larger wire crate was set up on a platform a foot or so above the garage floor, so that a crated dog could see out the window. Inside the extra-large crate—filled, as the others were, with blankets and toys—was a German shepherd, reclining comfortably.

Is this where Cloud would stay? In a garage?

"We're in and out all day," Alfredo said. "The dogs who stay here get stimulation, they get 'enrichment'—we take them outside to play, but not with the other dogs."

Another crate was against the opposite wall from the German shepherd. I didn't see the dog in it at first—she had burrowed under the blankets. But when Alfredo passed by, the dog poked her muzzle out and licked at the wire. She was some kind of hound mix, with a frosty muzzle—an old dog with cloudy eyes.

Was this the dog whose death would make room for Cloud? I hated myself for the opportunistic thought.

"How's the dog I brought in doing?" Billie asked.

"She's being walked now. Bridget has her out." Alfredo told us that Bridget was a new volunteer, who took time from her nursing job at the nearby hospital to help them out. Alfredo said that the rottie had calmed down a good deal since arriving at For Pitties' Sake.

"That's great," Billie said. "I worried about that one."

"When could you take Cloud?" I asked Alfredo.

"The vet said that Boss—the hound mix you saw—probably has a few weeks at best."

I wanted to stay to meet the director, but Billie said she needed to get back—she had tickets to see a play at St. Ann's Warehouse. She said *tickets*, plural, so of course I felt I knew whom she was going with.

Not until we entered Greenwich did Billie ask if I would mind if we stopped at her grandmother's house for a minute so she could pick up her snorkel and fins.

"I've got time," I said.

Billie left the parkway, and within minutes she turned onto Round Hill Road, then onto Clapboard Ridge Road. The driveway was so long that Billie had to slow down a couple of times. "Speed bumps in your driveway are a status symbol here," she said drily.

Her grandmother's was a farmhouse on steroids. We pulled into the immense turnaround, passed the portico, and parked behind the house.

"Looks like she has company," I said.

"Those are just the house cars," Billie said. "For guests," she added, when I didn't understand.

The "house cars" were newer models than the car Billie drove.

"We'll go in the back way. I want to say hello to Cook first."

Ah, I thought—the sign of wealth: Billie dropped the article. Not *the* cook, but Cook.

The kitchen was spacious, spectacular, but also warm. It didn't look like a place where servants worked. Copper pots—dozens of them—hung from racks above the ten-burner stove. Cook, aka Jennifer, was a middle-aged woman with an Irish accent who greeted Billie with a hug and a kiss on the cheek. She was not in uniform, but wore an apron over a simple dress.

"Your grandmother is in a mood," she confided. "Last night was the gala for Children's Hospital, and she expected to raise more."

"She's never satisfied with the money raised," Billie said. "The money she raises at a single gala would run a rescue organization for a year. Not that she'd ever offer."

"Will you two be staying for dinner?" Cook asked.

"I've got theater tickets," Billie said.

Cook asked me what we were going to see. I looked to Billie, who said, "I have a date."

"Well, I'll send you home with a peach cobbler," Cook said. "Your grandmother is in the library."

I had tons of books, but most were still in milk crates.

Billie led me through several corridors and then upstairs. The door to the library was open. I could see red lacquered walls and glass-fronted bookcases. The couches looked like feather beds in a fairy tale.

Billie's grandmother was seated at her desk, her back to us. Her long gray hair was loose and reached below her shoulders. Rebellious, I thought, that she didn't have it colored and still wore it long.

She finished signing a check before she turned around. "You smell like a kennel, darling."

"Cook said you were disappointed about last night."

"Who is your friend?" the grandmother asked, not looking at me.

"She's a client of the lawyer I'm working with. Morgan Prager."

I said it was nice to meet her. I held out my hand, but took it back before she could shake it, apologizing that I hadn't had time to clean up after we visited the dog sanctuary. Billie's grandmother seemed relieved not to have to make contact.

"Do you remember where I left my snorkel and fins?" Billie asked.

"Where are you off to now?"

"I'm going down to pick up some patty-cakes in St. Thomas."

Billie said nothing acknowledging *my* annual trip to save these dogs. She hadn't known what a patty-cake was until I had told her. Still, how could I begrudge this lapse—she was going to do something good. I could begrudge her because I figured she was going to do it with McKenzie.

"There aren't enough stray dogs for you here?" the grandmother asked.

This was an old argument, I saw.

"I thought I'd get a couple of swims in. A little R and R."

I hoped the grandmother would ask if Billie was going alone. Instead she asked Billie to look up an old friend of hers on the island. "She keeps a boat there."

"Like I'll have time."

"It doesn't cost you anything to be nice," her grandmother said, and then to me, "I'll bet *you* would make time."

"I'm not going."

Billie said to me, "You'd think my grandmother didn't like dogs."

"Winston wasn't a dog."

"Winston was an English bulldog," Billie told me. "He passed gas all the time, and at my grandmother's parties, she would follow him around in her gown, lighting matches behind him."

"But *philanthropy* means 'love of humans,'" the grandmother reminded us. "Not dogs."

Billie looked stricken and forced herself to kiss her grandmother's cheek before we went to look for her diving gear.

"It should be in my old closet." Billie led me into—not a bedroom, but a suite. Not a suite—a wing! Where were the equestrienne trophies and ribbons? Where was any sign of a headstrong girl? Nothing in these rooms said that a child had grown up in them. What was missing in addition to any childhood mementos was furniture. The floors were carpeted wall to wall in the whitest of wool. The walls were painted the same white—and the sheen told me that an expensive egg tempera had been used. On the walls were paintings that even *I* recognized: Franz Kline, Ellsworth Kelly, de Kooning, Motherwell—it was a gallery.

"The Kline was my grandfather's first purchase," Billie said. "You'll appreciate this: when Kline brought his mother to his first exhibition of large abstractions—slashes of black paint across white canvas—his mother said, 'I always knew you'd take the easy way out.'"

"What did the rooms look like when you were growing up here?"

"My grandmother had her decorator do Young Girl's Room. I had a four-poster canopy bed with linens from Frette, framed horse prints on the walls, a Princess Anne Victorian dollhouse. In the bathroom: Baccarat tumblers; the mouthwash was decanted. As Rebekah Harkness said of her family's mansion in Manhattan, 'It's not home, but it's much.'"

Billie opened one of the walk-in closets, which was as crowded as the rooms were spare: boxes of plastic horses, games of Scrabble and Parcheesi, countless stuffed animals, computer games, a large box filled with toy soldiers, a row of Slinkys, Rollerblades and badminton racquets, a pogo stick, skis, but no diving gear.

Was there anything Billie had not been given as a child?

She did not find her diving gear. "Fucking hell." Billie slammed the closet door. She did not stop for the peach cobbler.

When I was sixteen, I took a summer job at a mall, while my best friend went on the grand tour of Europe. While I sold cheap earrings to girls who had just pierced their ears, Julia sent me a chocolate bar from every country she visited. I should have been touched. But I tore into each new bar of chocolate with fury, jealous that I was stuck in the mall while Julia had everything. I hadn't thought of Julia in years, until I saw Billie in her grandmother's house. I wondered what Billie might send me from St. Thomas and felt stupid for thinking like that.

"Turn on your TV," Steven said, when I picked up the phone later that night. I had just finished four hundred-calorie chocolate bars.

"What channel?"

"CNN."

The suspect in Pat's murder, the migrant worker, had been indicted. Pat's family had put up a reward for information, which I knew only slowed down an investigation, luring nut jobs and opportunists eager for the money. The TV showed a small-boned Central American man being taken from a police car and led into the Suffolk courthouse.

"It's over. You can have your life back." Steven thought my life could be returned to me as if I had merely misplaced it. "They found Pat's credit cards on him. He claims he found them in the woods."

"Billie and I went to look at a sanctuary for Cloud."

"And?"

"I could see Cloud having a life there." This was, after all, the point, I reminded myself.

"I'd like to see *you* having a life *here*."

"How much resilience can a person have?"

"You'd be surprised."

A different reporter was covering another story so I hit the mute button. "No more surprises."

I cleared the pad thai I had had for dinner, recalling my friend Patty's saying that in New York "home cooking" was any food you bought within six blocks of your apartment. I took Olive out for a last, short walk. Back in the apartment, I found the expensive bath gel I had splurged on a while back and filled the tub with hot water. The bathroom soon held the heady scent of night-blooming jasmine. I slowed my movements in contrast to my racing thoughts. I poured a glass of prosecco and got in the tub, the tub I had hidden in on that day.

Though it was just Olive and me, I had closed the bathroom door. The window in the bathroom looked onto an air well, but if you angled yourself just so, at a certain time of night, you could see the moon. I looked at my feet at the end of the tub, sticking up above the bubbles: Frida Kahlo in her self-portrait *What I Saw in the Water*, although that painting has surrealistic images—a skyscraper shooting out of a volcano, two tiny women lying on a sponge, a tightrope walker sharing his rope with a snake— floating in the tub with her.

I lay back, my neck fitting into the small waterproof pillow for this purpose. I did the exercise in which you consciously relax each part of your body individually. Eyes closed, I was up to my shoulders when I heard Olive scratching at the door to get out. Diabolical dog.

It was the new door, the one Steven had installed because of the damage the dogs had done to the old one the morning of Bennett's death. The claw marks on the inside had reached as high as the doorknob. It reminded me of those gruesome stories about people buried in Victorian times, later coming out of a trance in their coffins. Why were my dogs so desperate to get out? Who had shut them in the bathroom?

Wait. Who had shut them in the bathroom? They were loose when I entered the apartment and found Bennett's body. They were not in the bathroom. When had they been put in there? The inside of the bathroom door had been intact when I went out that morning. I had only been gone two hours. Bennett had been asleep when I left.

I felt a chill, though steam rose from the water.

Did the police question the scratched door? The dogs had scratched the cabinet where I kept their kibble, they had scratched the front door to go out, it wasn't as if a scratched bathroom door would stand out in that apartment. But these were new scratches, and they were deep. I saw them when I shut myself in and hid in the tub. The dogs had been whimpering to be let into the bathroom with me. How had I not wondered how they could be locked in but also be the killers? Why didn't the police question this?

Would Bennett have shut the dogs in the bathroom? He might have if someone had come to the front door. They were not the calmest greeters. But he didn't know anyone in the city, or said he didn't. He must have known who it was because he had to buzz them in. While a person climbed the stairs, he would have had time to shut the dogs in the bathroom. But then what?

I let some water out of the bath and turned on the hot water tap to replace it.

No human could have done what was done to Bennett.

I wished I had brought the bottle of prosecco into the tub with me. I wasn't willing to get out of the hot water to fetch it. I could not stop my thoughts, but I wanted to slow them down. Logic—just use logic. But no—I thought back to the horror of Pat's heart being cut out of her chest. Obviously no dog could do that, and her own dog was missing. But in my apartment, I had seen my bloodied dogs and Bennett's savaged body. What was I *not* seeing?

What if Bennett was killed by a person he let into the apartment, and the person let the dogs out of the bathroom before he left? What if the dogs had attacked a dead body? The ME who examined Bennett's body should have been able to distinguish between wounds inflicted by a human and a mauling by dogs. But maybe he had missed something, since everyone assumed the dogs had done it.

But back up—who wanted Bennett dead? Susan Rorke had been killed before Bennett died. Pat had a reason, but who killed her? Samantha, recipient of months of e-mails from a dead man—was that an act to cover herself? I had been kind to her the last time we had talked, but I had refused to side with delusion—it is never a good idea to side with delusion. I had not said I believed that Bennett was alive, but I had tried to be gentle with her. But was it a delusion? Maybe she was e-mailing herself. Or maybe she was just telling me he was e-mailing her. The police would know how to trace this, if I could figure out how to persuade a detective to get a search warrant.

I climbed out of the tub and pulled the plug. I wrapped myself in a towel, watching the water drain. Steven had said I could have my life back. He was wrong.

"There's something that bothers me, and it wasn't addressed in the police report."

I heard weariness in Steven's voice when he asked what I was talking about. When I told him about the scratches on the inside of the bathroom door, he said he remembered scratches on the outside of the door, not the inside. "You just got back from the guy's funeral. Let it go."

"I think I'm right about this."

"I think I would have remembered that. And even if you're right, what's the difference? What does that prove?"

"It proves that someone else was in the apartment with Bennett."

"I'd really like you to talk to Cilla."

"This is not a psychological problem," I pointed out. "This is about evidence that was overlooked."

"Who is it you think was in the apartment with him?"

If I told him I thought it was Samantha, he would have me committed.

"Samantha. I need to hack into her e-mail."

"Do you really want to provoke an insane person?" Steven asked.

"It's not provocation if she doesn't know I did it. Do you know someone I could hire to do it?"

"I could be disbarred, but that's not why I'm not helping you with this. Promise me you'll call Cilla."

I called McKenzie instead. He answered his own phone—because I had called his cell phone. If I could trust my sense of him, he sounded happy to hear from me. But I could not trust my sense of him, so I trampled over it. In my preoccupation, I rushed into the business at hand. I told him I needed to check out something in the police report on Bennett's death: "Don't you have a copy of it?" I told him what I needed to verify.

He offered to stop by my apartment with the police report after work. I did a quick inventory of everything that needed cleaning, thought, the hell with it, and thanked him.

An hour later, I was pushing an old straw broom across the floors. I had never been able to figure out a Swiffer. I popped open a plastic container of premoistened, antibacterial cloths with bleach and went down on my knees to scrub the bathroom floor. I wished Steven had not replaced the door so quickly. But if McKenzie brought over a photo that showed no scratches on the inside of the door, I would let it go. Till then, I gave myself over to a Zen-like approach to cleaning. I slowed my movements, cleaned mindfully. You couldn't help but be thorough in that state of mind. I should do this more often, I thought. Then, naw.

I had been listening to "You Go Down Smooth" by Lake Street Dive on earbuds, my iPhone safe in my pocket, when the music stopped and the ringtone sounded. The number had a Maine area code. Renee was furious. She told me she did not appreciate my giving her number to a crazy person, that she had been harassed by the woman, who accused her of lying about the death of her own son. Renee said that the woman claimed to be engaged to him. She didn't need this, Renee assured me, and would I please respect her privacy from now on.

"I did not give that woman your number," I said. "Renee, I'm so sorry."

But the woman who spoke next was not Renee, but Vanessa, as angry as she'd been at the funeral. "This may be some big joke to you—all you gals claiming to be engaged to my dead brother—but we don't think it's funny, and you're destroying my mother."

"It's not a joke. Nothing about it is funny."

"Then tell this crackpot to leave my mother alone," Vanessa demanded.

"I don't have any say in this. She's delusional."

"You're *all* delusional." Vanessa hung up.

I needed to walk off the effects of the conversation, and the questions it raised, so I stuck a credit card in my coat pocket and headed for the expensive cheese shop. I'd need wine, too—or not. What do you serve someone who is coming over with police photos of your dismembered and mauled ex-lover? I chose pitted kalamata olives, the priciest cheese sticks on the planet, and several bottles of a local craft beer called Evil Twin.

I had just turned onto Grand Street when I saw McKenzie. He didn't see me. He wasn't on a bike this time. I hadn't spied on him before. I had been at his side while walking, but from this distance I saw him objectively. He did spring forward on the balls of his feet; would-be jocks in high school walked like that, and I hadn't liked it then either. He didn't swagger, and he didn't race-walk, as though his time were more valuable than someone else's. He walked confidently, as though he walked to a tune in his head that I would have liked to hear, too.

Though I felt dishonest about it, I kept watching him without making my presence known. I followed him, keeping half a block away, until he reached my stoop. Then I ducked behind a parked FedEx truck to the count of ten, stepped back onto the sidewalk, and called out his name, rushing forward as though running late.

I noted that his smile belied the grim contents of his briefcase. Where we might have hugged if we were meeting in a bar, at my doorstep I had a bag in one hand, keys in the other, and stairs, lots of stairs, ahead of us. I hesitated in the entry, not wanting him to watch me walk up five flights, but realized he would insist I go first. It wasn't as bad as the era of loft beds, when couples undressed before climbing the ladder, one person giving the other who followed an unfortunate view.

Steven was the only other person who had been inside my apartment since Bennett's death. I suddenly wondered if McKenzie would be creeped out by being there. Too late now. Olive appeared and barked a warning before recognizing the man who had given her a provolone sandwich. She sat at his feet, wagging her tail like crazy. He crouched to greet her and she wiggled until she was a blur. "I can't believe no one ever called to find you," he said to Olive. I offered to hang up his coat. In taking it off, he had to put down his briefcase, now a loaded centerpiece on the table.

"I admire your courage in moving back here," McKenzie said.

"If I didn't, I'd keep moving and never stop."

"Still, it's brave." He wasn't going to let me deflect the compliment.

I saw how wrongheaded I had been to buy snacks—I wasn't entertaining. I did offer him a beer.

When I returned to the living room, I saw that McKenzie

had a manila folder on his lap. "It's comfortable, isn't it? Steven bought me this couch." I wanted Steven in the room with us.

McKenzie knew I had looked at Susan Rorke's crime-scene photos, but I did not protest when he offered to edit these photos of Bennett's crime scene for me. He went through them himself. I watched him look at what I refused to see again. But I did see it again—in McKenzie's expression. Finally, he held out one photo. The bloody prints on the tile floor of the bathroom were my footprints. I must have pulled down the shower curtain when I hid in the tub because it was balled on the floor. A bra was drying on a towel rack.

A band about eighteen inches high ran the width of the door; the gouges looked to be nearly a quarter of an inch deep, overlapping where the dogs had tried to claw their way through, and lighter than the surrounding wood because they had gotten beneath the stain.

I didn't even have to point a finger at what I saw. McKenzie, I knew, was seeing the same thing.

"I think he wasn't alone," I said. "I think someone came over and the dogs were in the way. What I need to know is who let them out. Do you know someone I can hire to hack into an e-mail account?" And I told him my suspicions.

He wrote down an e-mail address, hackyou@gogo.jp.com, and slid it across the table. "I didn't give this to you."

"How much does he charge?"

"She. Less than three months of Internet."

"That means everyone can afford to hack," I said.

"Everyone does."

Olive had settled on his lap. I remembered the cheese sticks and olives in the refrigerator. I asked if he had time for another beer. Without consulting his watch, he said that would be great.

I assembled a small plate of things from the cheese store and brought it out to the living room with another beer for him. I had a memory of having done exactly this with Bennett. It threw me so much that I did not get a second beer for myself.

McKenzie had moved from the couch to the bookcase. When he turned around, he was holding a piece of brain coral the size of a fist that I had found on a beach in St. Croix and used as a bookend.

"Have you ever been night diving?" he asked.

"The one time I went, the visibility was so poor, all I saw was my flashlight."

"It's spectacular. The hard corals bloom and the reef turns phosphorescent. A whole different set of fish come out, even more beautiful than the daytime crew. At night"—he held up the bleached coral—"this is the color of a sapphire."

I couldn't ask if he was planning to go diving with Billie anytime soon, so I said, "Are you planning to go diving anytime soon?" I hated how timid and suspicious I had become.

"The night I described was off Saint John. I'd like to go back there again."

But everyone who flies into St. Thomas ferries over to St. John, and Billie had said she was going to St. Thomas. To pick up patty-cakes.

"The Stilton is really good," McKenzie said, reaching for the knife and another cracker.

He was changing the subject, but I wouldn't let go. "It must be hard for you to dive again."

"I haven't yet. But I'm ready, I think."

Now I wanted to change the subject. Now I was afraid to learn that they were going on a diving trip together. I was sorry I had brought it up in the first place. So I forced McKenzie back into being my lawyer. "If it turns out that Cloud was locked in the bathroom, is there a chance she could come home?"

"We're entitled to an appeal." He looked at his watch.

I preempted his excuse to leave by thanking him for bringing over the photographs. I did not thank him for the hacker information, as he had not wanted acknowledgment. At the door, he told me to take care of myself.

I went down Grand Street toward the BQE. I noticed, as I often did, the number of pit bulls being walked by the younger residents of the neighborhood. Nowhere else had I seen so many of them as well-cared-for pets. I had my theories about why—that they were the most misunderstood and misjudged breed, that they were, in a sense, like tattoos, like instant gangsta cred (even though most of them were mushes), that young people wanted to adopt a rescue and the breed clogging all shelters was the pit bull. I'd several times seen a poster of a pit bull in shop windows: "Born to love, taught to hate." And another one: "For every 1 pit bull that bites, there are over 10.5 million that don't. Stop bullying my breed."

Near yet another construction site, I found the address I had been given by hackyou. The storefront was filled with cheap religious figurines such as one sees in the bay windows of private homes or underfunded churches in the neighborhood. I double-checked the address, given what filled the display window, and saw that I had come to the right place. I walked in, a bell chimed, and a zaftig woman of around thirty, in a black dress that resembled a nun's habit, came from the back and asked if she could help me.

"I was given this address but I think I might have written it down wrong. Do you fix computers here?"

"You're McKenzie's friend?"

"So I am in the right place. But what's with the religious statues?"

"Have you heard the one about the mohel in the clock shop? So a guy's looking for a place to find a mohel. He finds 273 Main Street, and the whole place is filled with clocks. He says to the guy at the counter, 'I'm looking for a mohel.' And the guy says, 'That's me.' 'But what are all these clocks doing in the window?' And the guy says, 'What do you *want* me to put in the window?'"

I followed her into the back room, which was as surprising in its own way as the front. There was a single laptop, not the gadgetry they always show in the movies. I said I was surprised that she could hack with one ordinary computer.

"Breaking into an e-mail account isn't hacking. It's cracking. Hacking is an art. It's discovering and exploiting the weaknesses in technology. Without hackers, we wouldn't have a hope of privacy."

"That sounds like the opposite of privacy."

"Hacking isn't personal. It's about decentralizing information and giving it away for free. I'm talking about government and corporate information, not catching some congressman looking at pornography in his home.

"So tell me what I can do for you." The woman had not given me her name.

"I need to find out if someone sent e-mails to herself as

though from another person, or if these e-mails were, in fact, sent to her by someone else."

"I can tell if they're sent from the same IP address. It's possible to reroute a message so that it appears to originate from a different IP, but you'd have to be a pro. And I can tell if this was done."

She asked me for the server and user ID, then started typing. She said that the most popular password is *password*. The second most common password is 123456. The third-ranking password is 12345678. And one in six people use the name of a pet.

"Does Samantha have a pet?"

I told her I didn't know.

"Let's see if she has pet insurance." The woman ran Samantha's name through some kind of database. The computer was facing her, so I could not see exactly what she was doing. I looked at the religious statues—a chipped Virgin Mary, a weathered apostle, an armless St. Christopher. Did anyone ever repair them?

"Samantha Couper has pet insurance with the ASPCA for a six-year-old shepherd mix named Pal, with Cushing's disease."

So we all had sick, injured, or rescued dogs. If coincidence, it was odd for a man who didn't like dog hair on his clothes. If not, then Bennett was a predator drawn to the goodness he lacked. In that case, he was the man I could build my thesis on. My pulse picked up and, for once, not in fear.

The woman typed in something new. She typed in something else. And again. On only her sixth try, she smiled. "MyPal. What is the username you suspect she's using to write herself?"

I gave her Bennett's e-mail—themaineevent@gmail—the

only e-mail address he had used with me. The woman typed it in and turned the computer so that I could see the screen. Hundreds of messages came up. About a quarter of them after his death. Again, I nearly swooned—that old-fashioned word—at the shock of seeing the username that I had once longed for.

I asked her to open the first one dated after his death. I began reading: *Sam, did you get to the bank? Did you find your passport? I trust you. I love you. We're almost there.*

"Can you tell if she sent this to herself?"

"If she sent it to herself, she didn't use the same computer." The woman clicked on an icon I'd never before seen. "You ping an address, and this sends a signal to a URL—like sonar—and it bounces back and you can determine how long the round-trip took. You press *return* and the IP address appears, followed by how many seconds or milliseconds the ping took. I know this was sent from around here."

Either she was sending them to herself from my neighborhood and following me around, or someone I didn't know was sending them from my neighborhood. Both scenarios scared me; I could think of no reasonable way to protect myself.

"Can you do one more thing for me? Can you find me the password for themaineevent?"

The woman quickly eliminated the most popular passwords. "This guy, Jeremy Gofney, created a twenty-five-computer cluster that can make three-hundred-and-fifty-billion guesses a second. But it will take me between thirty minutes and six hours. Why don't you head out, and I'll text you when I get it."

I got a coffee to go from Gimme! Coffee and went home to walk Olive. I decided to take her to Cooper Park for a change, not as big as McCarren Park, but, pleasingly, on Olive Street.

And the chances of finding small dogs for Olive to play with were better there. But on this winter afternoon, even Olive's cable-knit sweater didn't keep her warm enough, so I put her inside my coat and we sat on a bench.

Where was Samantha planning to go that she needed a passport? Or where was she being urged to go? Would this be something she would write to herself? Only if she expected someone else to see it. And why would she stop writing to herself after this? Or why did the person who might have sent this message stop?

Olive squirmed inside my coat and brought me back to the here and now, the simple needs of a living creature. Thinking she had to pee, I put her down, but she refused to go. So I tucked her back inside my coat and walked quickly home. I mimicked the tired gestures of someone being pursued—looking first over one shoulder, then the other. I didn't have it in me to fake the confident stride that would supposedly ward off an attacker.

The hacker was going to break into Bennett's account. Maybe I was better off not knowing all that he had been capable of. It would surely be a trade-off: information versus further humiliation. Was one's capacity for it endless? But the information—if I could shut down my personal response to it—would be valuable for my thesis. I would see firsthand the mind that conjures such behavior—I would see the predator as he moved in on his prey. The sociopath and his victim: me.

I probably still had a couple of hours until I could expect to hear back from the hacker. I needed to steel myself for whatever was coming. I had only four .25 mg Xanax left, but I had one more refill on the prescription Cilla had written for me. I left for Napolitano at the corner of Graham and Metropolitan. At this

old-fashioned Italian pharmacy they knew you by name. The
owner, with her red hair and perpetually white roots, greeted
me warmly. Everyone in the neighborhood had heard what I'd
been through. When I handed her the vial of remaining Xanax,
she looked at the label and said, "You only have one more refill."
Apparently, I looked as though I needed more.

I checked my phone for texts, even though my phone hadn't
buzzed. I said I would wait for them to fill the scrip. I pictured
someone with a mortar and pestle in the back. I handled the Italian soaps that you wouldn't find at other pharmacies. I felt at
peace, relatively, knowing that I was getting tranquilizers. What
if I found out that Bennett had never loved me? That suggested,
of course, that I still thought he had once loved me. But I had
never driven past an accident on the road without looking at the
injured.

I paid for the refill. Just before I got home, hackyou texted me:
I'm in.

I could have taken one of the new pills, but decided instead
to ride the excitement of the discovery, whatever it would bring.
When I got back to the store, hackyou was with another customer, a nun. Whom was the nun hacking?

"With you in a minute," the hacker called to me.

The nun was holding a small statue of the Virgin. The hacker
told the nun to come back in a week, the repair would be completed by then. So the store wasn't a front.

"Come around the counter," the hacker said. "We can talk in
the back."

I followed her and sat in the folding chair she indicated.

"Unless Samantha is a pro, she didn't send herself the
e-mails." The hacker handed me a yellow Post-it and a pen. She

told me to write down the password that she dictated to me. Not wanting to leave evidence of her own hand, I guessed.

"How much do I owe you?" I had brought cash as instructed.

McKenzie was right: I paid more for three months of Internet.

The password was evenwhenusleep.

I thought of the wall. His making me sleep against the wall.

I felt as though I was about to be served a poisoned feast. I was starving, and I would be made to poison myself. Maybe if I ate something first—a piece of dry toast—it would line my stomach so that the poison would not kill me.

Nothing was remarkable about these e-mails other than that a dead man wrote them. Just the ordinary reassurances that Samantha was on his mind and he couldn't wait to see her (though wait he would). I had expected to linger over every word and try to suss out not just the meaning but the nuance. Instead, the messages were so banal that I grew impatient. Same thing, seven times over. But in the next one, he tells Samantha that a crazy ex-girlfriend killed herself, and for some reason the police are looking at *him* for it. If he needed her for an alibi, he wrote, could he count on her?

Samantha would not have written to herself asking to be her own alibi.

I took off my pullover sweater. The apartment wasn't warm, but I was sweating.

The next message from Bennett answered a panicked question from Samantha: *I was home alone all day, but that won't hold up as an alibi.*

The day he claimed to be alone, he was driving to meet me in Maine.

I read a dozen more. Whoever was writing to Samantha claimed to be hiding in Canada, but I already knew that—Samantha had told me. I kept on, looking for something I did not already know. And there it was. "Bennett" had asked Samantha to meet him in Toronto, and they would go from there. And as I had just learned, she would be paying for this pleasure (*Did you get to the bank?*). The first e-mail mentioning the trip—or honeymoon?—appeared the day after Pat's murder. My stomach plunged. Should I notify the police? Which police? I had illegally broken into the e-mail that contained the information. Would I tell them that a dead man was planning to meet his fiancée in Toronto after he, the dead man, killed an ex-lover?

My stomach growled, but I couldn't eat anything. Instead, I poured a double shot of Stoli.

I typed in *Susan Rorke*, searching for the last e-mail Bennett had sent her, the day before her death. Now I was reading something he had actually written; I downed the rest of my drink.

Not going to be able to meet you, babe. Have meetings all weekend. Will make it up to you.

I scrolled down to see what he was replying to. Susan Rorke had invited him to Boston for the weekend.

Just because he told her he couldn't spend the weekend didn't mean he wasn't there, I reasoned, the alcohol weirdly bringing out my rational side. Instead of slowing me down, the Stoli acted as a stimulant.

I scrolled down farther. I began reading the responses of "Bennett" with an eye toward the linguistics, the syntax. I tend to go cold and analytical when I feel most vulnerable. I noticed two hallmarks of the sociopath in written communication: he repeatedly used the words *so* and *because*, indicating his view of the causes and effects of his actions. And he frequently adverted to money, to financial concerns. Though wasn't everyone concerned with money? So maybe scratch that last. Still, it was hard to ignore a line like *Needed you to pay deposit for wedding caterer so I could afford to get the tuxedo you liked.* And this one: *Because you didn't give them the right credit card number, we just lost the honeymoon suite.* I saw that he gave her a chance to make it right by giving the correct credit card number to a more expensive hotel for their honeymoon suite.

He had offered to let me pay for the wedding cake while he ostensibly bought a tuxedo.

He continued to write to Susan Rorke for two days after her death. Not hearing back from her, he changed his tone, was solicitous, asking where she was, asking her to write him. Then his tone changed again. The last message he sent to Susan Rorke was short and to the point, but not original. He fell back on the words of countless angry, rejected lovers: *Are you happy now?*

As sick as all of this made me feel, I was also relieved to know that I had not almost married a murderer. I served myself seconds of the poisoned feast. I looked for clusters of e-mails sent to addresses I did not recognize. Looking for still more women. Still more rendezvous.

On the plus side, I had not been in love with a murderer. However, I had been taken in by a womanizing sociopath who had lumped me in with the rest of his harem.

Libertine635 came up, and came up, and kept coming up. The word would not have had the effect on me that it did had I not just read of the libertines Valmont and the Marquise. I supposed that I would now see the word everywhere. The number 635 told me how many other libertines were out there online.

I checked the date of Libertine's last message to Bennett; it was the day of his death. I scrolled back to the beginning of their correspondence. I scrolled back years, back to the night they met in the casino.

Libertine wrote first, establishing a pattern of dominance. She challenged him to shed his secrets; she had no interest in conventional courtship and shot down his early efforts in that direction. She eschewed dailiness—there would be no meeting for lunch, or dinner and a movie; she did not want to hear about his day; she wanted the heightened experience, the mysterious, the transcendent. She wanted to be entertained. For his part, he got a quality of attention he had not previously known, and from a beautiful woman who constantly surprised him. He got a willing and able sexual partner who surprised him in bed as well.

She was insistent on loyalty, though of a form foreign to Bennett at the time. Maybe most pointedly, she convinced him that his first allegiance must be to her. This became relevant when, six months in, she encouraged him to sleep with other women to show him that far from being jealous, she could use these occasions to further the intimacy they shared. He interpreted her encouragement as trust, which allowed her to escalate her manipulation.

She applauded him when he seduced the earnest, the altruistic, the virtuous. She laughed at the women's tentative declarations of love as he re-created them for her. She urged him not to hold back—and he didn't.

One year in, they had their first fight. She wanted him to drop Samantha Couper; she found the man Bennett became with her boring. When Bennett let slip that he admired Samantha's work on the suicide hotline, Libertine wrote, *She should tell those losers to buck up.* After four weeks of silence, Bennett invited Libertine to see a movie with him—and Samantha. He proposed that Libertine sit behind them. When the film ended, and he asked Samantha what she thought of it, her vapid answer was his gift to Libertine.

Two years in, he brought her Susan Rorke. Their second fight. He found her work laudable, too—not only at the precinct, but the counseling she volunteered at the homeless shelter. The deal he brokered toward a rapprochement delighted Libertine. He arranged for the three of them to meet at a gun range where Susan would teach Libertine—introduced by Bennett as a family friend—how to protect herself with a handgun. I read Libertine's praise for Bennett after the lesson; the feel of Susan Rorke's hands guiding hers on the gun had been a bonus.

The closer I came to the time I met Bennett, the more apprehensive I became.

New and interesting, or just new? Libertine wrote. And a few hours later: *Well?*

Bennett replied to this second one. *You're more excited about her than I am.*

They were talking about me. Astonishing how much pain a dead man could inflict.

He made fun of my research.

What song made her cry but she was ashamed to admit it. Ha! Libertine wrote.

I was ready to put in an emergency call to Cilla.

Libertine: *Did you get anything off her?*

Bennett: *What are you, a ten-year-old boy?*

I left the computer and looked out the living-room window. A light snow was falling, but not yet sticking to the sidewalk. I was not faint, nor was I sick to my stomach. I was not enraged, not throwing a glass to break against the wall. I felt something quieter, but no less consuming. Shame. Humiliation is what you feel in front of others; shame is what you feel alone. Shame is harder to shake.

A snowflake landed on my window in its pristine geometry, and when the heat from the room met the glass, I watched geometry melt. It took less than a second. What could happen in a second?

I was glad I had refilled my prescription; I took a whole Xanax. I knew I wouldn't wait for it to kick in before taking another. I could not read any more, so I changed into a larger pair of sweatpants and continued reading more.

I was looking for clues as to who Libertine was. She never sent Bennett a photo of herself. But I found photos of myself that Bennett had sent to this person. Nothing compromising—just invasive: me making him an omelet, me with a towel wrapped around just-washed hair, even a photo of me feeding Cloud and George and Chester. She knew where to find me; I could not say the same for her. I went into the bedroom and locked the fire-escape gate, a feeble gesture in light of the violation. I could not face more of their banter.

I'd felt this kind of annihilation once before, as an intimate couple took me apart with their trivialized torture. Her taking my $300 to pay for their beer, her not untying me when she had the chance. Candice. Doug. I read these e-mails as both of these women—myself now, myself then. It was like watching a horror movie with the sound on *and* closed captioning—the horror coming at me twice. He could not have hurt me more if I read that he told her I was bad in bed.

Libertine: *Is she still pursuing her research—the victim studying victimology?*

Bennett: *I'll give her one thing—she's avid. She's a learner.*

Libertine: *Stop sounding so smug. Does she play the victim in bed?*

Bennett: *A gentleman never tells.*

As fucking if, I thought. I tried to take a deep breath and feared I might hyperventilate. I put my head down between my knees, closed my eyes, and tried to breathe normally. I jumped when I felt Olive's cold nose on my forehead. She had come to comfort me. She whined once, and I lifted her onto my lap. Stroking her brought my pulse under control, and I could breathe again. "Paging Dr. Olive," I said to the little white dog. She would not stop licking my hands, to the point that the drama of my emotions turned to melodrama in the face of her fervid attempts to soothe me, to bring me back from where I had gone.

I climbed into bed too drained to read or watch TV. I tried to reenact the meditation practice I had done in the bath not long before, relaxing one body part at a time. My knees were locked. I tried to relax first one, then the other. I would come back to them. Arms: not a problem. Shoulders and trapezius muscles fine. I came back to the knees for a second try. There was no yielding. I remembered that the Greeks believed that life resided in the knees, which was why we fell to our knees to beg for our lives. Should I be on my knees begging for my life?

I thought of all the people who had had worse things happen

to them. People endured unspeakable cruelty. What they did was bear it. Some of them even found grace. In themselves. I suspected I could bear this, too. But that didn't make the pain any less in the moment.

I rolled onto my side and surprised myself. Where was the bitterness? By all rights I should have been swearing off men, love, romance. But I found myself wanting these things again, and soon, and soon enough that what I had read earlier in the evening would not preclude this possibility.

For a moment, I mistook a streetlight for the moon.

What consumed me in the morning was the thought that Bennett might have invited Libertine to observe me, as he had done with Susan and Samantha. Had Libertine been sitting behind us in the theater when we saw *Grizzly Man?* Had she been another guest at one of the B&Bs in Maine? Had she borrowed my notes from a lecture at school? Had I met her? I tried not to cross the line between rational query and paranoia, but the fallout from reading the poisonous e-mails the night before made me think of those people who contract the flesh-eating virus. Did I still have arms? Did I still have legs? How was it I was able to stand up at the stove and wait for a kettle of water to whistle?

When the phone rang, I jumped.

"I've got good news," Billie said. "But I feel like a ghoul, saying so. I just found out that the sick dog at For Pitties' Sake has a day at the most to live."

"How come they called *you?*"

"I'm here with Alfredo, dropping off the patty-cakes. We were able to transport four. Alfredo just got them settled in their comfy, new quarters. We already have homes for three of them."

My admiration for Billie in that moment was genuine. But I still had to rally to acknowledge the good work she had done.

I thought, if I can't protect myself, I can still protect my dog.

•   •   •

I snapped on Olive's leash and took her out for a walk. Soon, Cloud would be able to go outdoors, too. We headed toward Petopia. Olive picked up her pace as she recognized the route to her toy store. By the time we turned the final corner, Olive was flying along. Inside the store, I saw a medium-size beagle-mix, unaccompanied, walk up to a dog-height barrel of rawhide treats, nose around, and select one, then trot out the door with it. I laughed and asked the clerk if he had seen that. "Rudy runs a tab," he said. Rudy worked in the travel bureau next door. We left the store with a tub of freeze-dried liver bits for Cloud.

The simple joy of pleasing a dog strengthened me enough to return to the job ahead. Back at the computer, something was obscene about having to slog through Bennett and Libertine's flippant sniping for a chance to find out who she was.

Libertine: *Are you in her will?*

Whose will?

Bennett: *The apartment is rented, and she doesn't have a car. She didn't come from money, and she gives away most of what she makes.*

My donations to animal-welfare agencies?

Libertine: *Nothing like keeping busy without making money!*

Bennett: *Isn't that what you do?*

Libertine: *I can afford to, as you well know.*

Bennett: *I keep thinking of that documentary we liked,* Grizzly Man, *the way Timothy Treadwell's passion for grizzly bears led to his ironic death. I mean, a homeless man? In the shelter where she worked to help them?*

The relief that I felt was twofold: relief that it wasn't me they were talking about, and more powerfully, relief that Bennett was dead. I thought I knew what a sociopath was; I could profile one for you. But not until that moment did I understand viscerally what one did.

He had talked this way about a woman he had planned to marry, a woman who had been killed in compassionate service to others. I even had the time-worn thought *Is nothing sacred?* And what of *Grizzly Man?* They both liked the documentary, according to the e-mail exchange, but I had seen it, too, and remembered that Treadwell's girlfriend accompanied him and she was also killed by the grizzly that mauled him.

I read to the point where the homeless man under suspicion for the murder of Susan Rorke had been cleared and released. After that, the tone of Bennett's e-mails changed. He became concerned that the police might look at him. Rather than offering reassurance, Libertine failed to take his concerns seriously. She even changed the subject, moving on to thoughts of where they might go next on vacation. But Bennett brought her back to the subject at hand. I read on, seeing the ways in which his expression of fear affected her. At one point she wrote, *Who* are *you!* And then I landed on a sentence I reread over and again, looking for a trace of sarcasm, not finding it. It was Bennett defending me to her: *Morgan is deeply kind. She would never treat me the way you do.*

I was disappointed in myself for feeling flattered.

Libertine didn't take the bait. Or maybe she did. She issued a challenge to Bennett: *I want you to fuck me in her bed. Tomorrow morning.* Bennett wrote back, *She'll be gone by 9.*

There were no more messages from Libertine. That last one had been sent the night before Bennett's death.

•   •   •

I needed to be in motion. I could not bear another moment in the apartment. Grabbed a coat and scarf, hat and gloves, and left to walk—anywhere. I needed to pass people whose mistakes I knew nothing about. I felt safer out among others. I passed the Metropolitan pool, a rack of Citi Bikes, the Colombian food truck, and a juice bar. Who doesn't need juice? I stopped in and got a small carrot juice, a nod to nutrition.

The closer I got to the water, the more the cold wind picked up. I walked out onto the pier where men fish, but no one was fishing. My eyes watered and my face stung. I surrendered to numbness. That surrender allowed me to surrender also to what I had just learned, that Libertine had been in my apartment the morning Bennett had been killed.

Is that what had ignited the dogs? Being locked in the bathroom and hearing the sounds of Bennett and this woman in my bed? It would certainly ignite me. I found myself suffused with heat. I didn't feel the cold anymore; the blood was rushing to every cold part of me. Confusion fell away, and I felt a clear, piercing understanding move through me. Another word for this feeling was anger. Normally, anger blinded me, but this time it allowed me to see. It was bracing, and welcome. It was stronger than fear. I valued this clarity; I did not want to blur it. Libertine had been in my bedroom with Bennett.

Boss died during the night. The call came in the morning from Alfredo at For Pitties' Sake. Now there was room for Cloud. Alfredo said he'd be ready to do an intake for Cloud that afternoon.

Finally, something clean. I had been able, just barely, to protect a creature I loved until I could lead her to safety. I was filled with joy that my dog was going to a place where she would be cared for with love.

Before I reserved a Zipcar, I called Billie. We'd been working toward this moment for nearly six months. I asked her if she wanted to go with me, and she told me she would pick me up. When she arrived, she had coffee and scones for the drive. Plus a rawhide chewie for Cloud. For my part, I had packed sliced ham in my tote bag.

"We did it!" Billie said.

She was right to use the plural, *we*. I could not have gotten this far without her help, and I told her so. She raised her hand to give me a high five, and I met it with my own. I noticed then that her arm, her face, was as pale as mine. She had no tan at all though she had just come back from the Caribbean. Billie didn't strike me as one to wear a big hat and gloves in the sun, but what did I know. Even people who stay out of the direct sun get tan in the Caribbean.

"I thought you'd have some color."

"I was only there for forty-eight hours. I didn't go there to tan on the beach."

"Did they finish the new shelter? Did you meet Lesley?"

"Lesley was off island. I picked the dogs up at the old one."

But every time I had gone down to pick up these dogs, Lesley, the director of the Humane Society, had brought them, paperwork completed, to the airport.

I realized I was testing Billie and I suspected she knew it. I still wanted to know if she'd gone away with McKenzie.

I asked if she had any sugar packets in the car for the coffee.

"Look in the glove."

I found several lipsticks—though I'd never seen her wear any—but no sugar. I picked up a tube of lipstick in a shade called Tiramisu. "Why don't I just eat this?" I asked in a lame attempt to joke away the tension I felt between us.

"That's hard to come by. Been discontinued."

We had been making good time on the FDR Drive north. Joggers ran along the riverside, wearing extra gear against the cold. Few boats were out on the river in the afternoon, just a single barge being pulled along by a tug. The booze cruises were a spring and summer phenomenon. These were working boats doing their best in the icy water, navigating the famously difficult currents in the inlet known as the East River.

We took the Ninety-Sixth Street exit and passed the many discount stores with merchandise displayed on the sidewalk even in the cold, and the cut-rate grocery, the White Castle, the projects, and gas stations packed with cabs. A frosted-over community garden interrupted a row of tenements just before we turned onto 119th Street.

"Have you got her leash?" Billie asked.

We had just pulled into a parking space (no meter) just short of the iron gates in front of the nearly windowless, concrete structure. My dog had been imprisoned since September, and we were about to break her out.

"Leash and collar," I said. The nylon web collar had peace signs in a rainbow of colors printed on it. Her name tag, her license, her rabies tag. Billie must have sensed my going soft because she said, "Act as if you come here all the time."

She steered me past the intake desk after waving to a kennel worker she knew. The woman at intake had recognized Billie and buzzed us in. The noise assaulted us immediately, combined with an overpowering smell of urine and feces. I followed Billie on slippery linoleum—she moved with the purpose of a soldier. It should have inspired strength in me, but I felt disequilibrium.

The occasional wall-mounted sanitary dispensers would have held antibacterial gel had they ever been filled. We passed door after door leading into the wards. Each ward contained about two dozen dogs, the large ones housed in a row of cages, the smaller dogs inhabiting smaller cages stacked three high. Overflow made it necessary to place a wall of these stacked cages in the main hallway. I saw that frightened cats in carriers were mixed in with the dogs. Fluorescent lights in the hallway pulsed and crackled, an instant headache. The ward doors were on one side of the hallway; on the other was a door marked MEDICAL.

"Don't go in there," Billie said.

I glanced in when a vet tech opened it as we passed. I saw blood on the linoleum floor.

"Told you," Billie said.

Food storage was on the same side of the hallway down a

ways from Medical. There, a deep sink was filled with aluminum water bowls and opened cans of dog food under a leaking faucet.

"Eyes right," Billie said, noting my wandering gaze. But I looked anyway. Each ward door had a narrow panel of glass at about eye level, and I looked in at the dogs. Some were clearly depressed—they sat in the back of their cage facing the wall. Others, as soon as they made even passing eye contact with a potential rescuer, began to perform tricks that someone had once taught them—a lifted paw to shake, though no one was there to shake it. I felt as though I would disintegrate. I must have gasped because Billie turned to me and said, "This is why I come here."

Adoption hours were still in effect, and we had passed clusters of people looking at dogs behind bars. Dogs cleared for adoption were in the first two wards, with small dogs in a separate room. The small dogs always had more visitors looking for a pet. I saw children holding trembling Chihuahuas and miniature poodles, as well as big-eared mutts. I saw families walk from cage to cage in the big-dog adoption wards, debating the merits of one over the other, which dog was cuter, which would require less exercise. I paused while Billie walked ahead for a moment. I'd overheard a grungy-looking guy around twenty or so gauging the likelihood of a young male pit bull's chances in the ring. I caught up to Billie to tell her about him, and she said, "We know all about that guy. Intake knows not to release a dog to him."

But the public was not allowed in the ward we were headed for.

I would not last an hour in this place. I had known this all along, but I could only now acknowledge it fully, since I was getting my own dog out. The only thing that went in the face of this horror was the generosity shown the animals by the kennel staff and volunteers, other women like Billie, for she had told me the volunteers were nearly all women. She had also told me that most of the kennel workers, there to do a difficult and distressing job, were kind to them, called the dogs by their names, even though those names were usually assigned to them at intake.

"At the end of the hall, that door goes into a backyard," Billie said. "It's the one place where dogs can be off leash. Though *yard* isn't really accurate—it's not as if there's any grass."

We were nearly to the ward where Cloud was confined when Billie said, "If the elevator were working, you'd see all of this replicated on the second floor."

When that fact washed over me, I was stricken with guilt at not being able to take more than just Cloud out of here. But where did that lead, and where would it stop?

"I can see what you're thinking," Billie said. "You can't save them all. For me, it's a matter of translation, always translating what I spend money on into what it would pay for in this place. That pair of shoes would inoculate twenty-five dogs against bordetella. Those sunglasses would spay ten dogs."

Billie took out a key ring and unlocked the door to Ward 4A, where the Dangerous Dogs were kept. In this ward, on each kennel card affixed to the top of a cage were the red-inked words CAUTION—SEVERE. This was their temperament rating. On the concrete wall facing the row of cages were thick steel rings hanging from exposed screws—tie-outs that these strong dogs had pulled clean out of the wall. Propped against the wall in one corner was a catchpole, next to the industrial, coiled black hose.

Cloud was not where I had last seen her, the first cage near the door. Instead of Cloud, that cage held a large white dog with cropped ears and pink eyes; it sat coolly facing the front bars.

"Where is she?" I asked.

"She's been moved to the end of the row."

I felt a moment's guilt at not tending to the dogs in the cages I raced past to find my own. When I saw my girl, her white coat defiled, I cried out her name and then just cried. She moved to the front bars as Billie opened the door just enough to attach her collar and leash. Billie told me to let her walk Cloud out of the ward, Cloud to the left of her, Billie's body between Cloud and the caged dogs. When we reached the entrance to the ward, I saw the white dog with cropped ears, but it was not in the first cage by the door. It was in the second cage from the door, where George had once been next to Cloud but unable to see her. I realized that there were two white dogs with cropped ears and pink eyes, mirroring each other's stance in their respective cages. The dogs had short hair and broad, muscular chests. They were not pitties, but seemed to be Molossers, the predecessors of the bully breeds. The dogs looked to be about 130 pounds, larger even than Cloud.

"Are they Presas?" I asked Billie. Years before, when Steven had lived in San Francisco, a pair of untrained Presa Canarios had gotten out of their owner's apartment into the hallway of a tony apartment building in Pacific Heights and mauled a young woman who could not get the key to her apartment out fast enough. The woman had died from her injuries, which included nearly eighty wounds, with only her scalp and feet unharmed. The resulting trial sent the dogs' reckless owners—one of them a lawyer—to jail for fifteen years for second-degree murder.

"They're Dogos Argentinos," Billie said. "But really they're scapegoats, brought in last night."

"What's their story?"

"Same old story."

Either she was giving me credit for knowing or she was blowing me off.

As we passed their cages, the Dogos rose and circled their quarters; their movements were identical, like synchronized swimmers. Yet they could not see each other to know what the other was doing. Each dog looked at me, growling and curling its lip.

Once out of the ward, I dropped to my knees and hugged my dog. Her ears were still flattened in fear, but her tail began wagging, and she leaned into me, shoving her massive head into my chest.

"You're safe now," I said.

As happy as she was to see me, she caught a whiff of the ham awaiting and dug her nose into the tote bag.

Billie waited just long enough for Cloud to get a big mouthful, then slipped a muzzle on her and fastened it. "Let's sign her out."

In the crowded lobby, a young Hispanic boy came over and asked why my dog was wearing a cage on her nose and what I was going to name her.

"Her name is Cloud."

"Cool. Can I pet her?"

I went to the desk while Billie stood with Cloud, but I heard her tell the little boy not to pet the dog, because it was dangerous. Coming from Billie, that comment spun me around. She believed that? Or she was following the rules.

A young man with a frightened-looking chow mix stood beside me, furious at the woman behind the desk, who told him that the fee to surrender a dog was $35. "Fuck that. I'll tie the dog up outside."

Billie told him to leave the dog, that she would pay the fee.

"Not again," said the woman behind the desk. Because Billie knew her, she expedited the process, and in just minutes we were walking out the door with a freed Cloud. After the din inside, noisy East Harlem seemed welcoming. I waited for Cloud to relieve herself at the curb. Distracted by the world of normal smells, she seemed overcome with the information she received from the sidewalk, the fire hydrant, the occasional city tree. We say someone has "come to her senses" to mean that person has come around to acknowledge reality, but here a creature was literally coming to her senses, and it was deeply moving. I was in no hurry to pull her along; I took my cue from Cloud. I could see that she was torn between her interest in what was around her, and her desire to be in my arms. I crouched and Cloud simply leaned against me. Billie bent down and scratched Cloud's ears and took off the muzzle, which earned her a lick and a lean.

I realized that I was laughing. Then Billie was, too, trying to stay upright while my enormous dog toppled us.

Billie started toward the car, but I said we should give Cloud a walk first. We turned east to walk to the river. The wind had died down, and there was a feeling of the coming spring, or so I imagined in my happiness. It wasn't as if early crocuses had appeared, just that the air had a softness that had been absent before. A slight breeze off the river reached Cloud and her head lifted. I realized that my dog had not set foot on grass since the temperament test five months ago. A scabby park around the corner would do for now. It also had a long sand pit for broad-jumping. Billie found a stick and threw it, but Cloud was no retriever. She stayed in the pit and rolled on her back in the sand.

I opened my tote bag and took out her celebration dinner, the pound of Polish sliced ham. After she swallowed it in a couple of gulps, Billie offered her one of our scones. I brought out a bottle of water with a squirt top, and Cloud drank from the arc of water I squeezed for her.

A police boat was patrolling the river alongside us. Across the river was Wards Island, which housed the Manhattan Psychiatric Center and Kirby Forensic Psychiatric Center. The light brown brick buildings were forbidding, with long rows of barred windows and the look of inherent desolation. They seemed a monument to suffering and despair, but they could not take the shine off this day.

We walked to the car and put Cloud in the backseat, which Billie had covered with a clean quilt. But Cloud insinuated herself into the front by pushing between the bucket seats until I could not see Billie at the wheel. Before she started the car, she took out her phone. "I know someone else who would like to be in on this." She pointed the phone at Cloud, virtually in the front seat, and took a couple of photos. "McKenzie will appreciate these."

And she would know.

We buckled in and headed up the FDR to the Willis Avenue Bridge—the way to beat the toll—to get out of the city.

Billie turned on the radio—Lolawolf.

"You know," Billie said, "you ask yourself what you want. And you try your first choice first. If you can't get away with that, then you go to the next thing you want, and try that. But you must try the first choice first."

"I've taken risks. Just a different kind. I used to write poetry."

Billie howled with laughter. "You make me think of what that guy said, that if it weren't for poetry, eighth-grade girls in corduroy jumpers and black tights would have to make some friends."

"I wasn't that bad. I just liked to read, and I tried to write now and then. I tried it, is my point. When I saw that I wasn't getting anywhere, that's when I started the work I do now."

"You've never told me what your research is about."

"Pathological altruism." Just saying it aloud centered me. It reminded me that I was working on something worth the attention, that I had a life that included work worth doing.

"Sounds like an oxymoron. How can altruism be pathological?"

"It doesn't just do damage to others, it also damages oneself. Think: the tireless worker for others who doesn't care for herself and gets sick. I think I have found a statistical link between excessive volunteerism and victimology, the pairing of accomplished, intelligent, motivated women who are preyed upon because of the depth of their compassion. It blinds them to a type of predator who is keenly aware of that trait; it predisposes the woman to give him the benefit of the doubt. I think predators seek out women with an overabundance of exactly what they lack. Predators feed off compassion."

I looked to see how Billie had registered all that I had said. She did not say something flippant; rather, she looked as though she was thinking it over. Then she asked if I thought that *she* was a pathological altruist. Did I feel that she set herself up for being victimized in this way?

"It's hard for me to see you as anyone's victim."

"Is this what Bennett saw in you?"

Could I give her an honest answer? But what would that be? I'd been turning the question over since Bennett's death. "Maybe I'm not the best judge of that."

She veered off onto the exit ramp for Cross River and Katonah.

"Where are we going?"

"We've got time. There's a really nice spot about three miles up where we can give Cloud another walk. Off leash."

Ward Pound Ridge Reservation. We passed the reservoir right off the exit, and when we made the turn to take the walk, we saw no other cars parked at the entrance. Cloud was delirious in her discoveries of country scents; we let her drink from the stream. I thanked Billie for letting Cloud have this intermission between shelter and sanctuary.

"There's a part of me that wants to take her and keep driving," I said. "Take her to some other state and start life over, away from everything that's happened in New York." I let my guard down just that much.

"But you would never do that."

"How can you be sure?"

"Because *I* would."

I returned my attention to my dog, who was loving her freedom.

A deer stood on the path several yards ahead of us. It didn't bolt. Cloud froze, did not give chase. "Good girl," I said. We stayed silent and didn't move, until people talking on the path behind us startled the whole lot of us, and the deer took off into the woods.

"We should get going," Billie said. "Better to arrive while there's still light."

We drove the rest of the way without music or talk to New Milford. Down the dirt road to For Pitties' Sake, bouncing in ruts from melting ice, we pulled up to the raised ranch house and parked alongside other cars in front of the garage. Alfredo had heard the car and came to the door to greet us. He handed Cloud a biscuit, then another.

Alfredo asked if we could stay long enough for him to give Cloud a bath. That way, he explained, he could blow-dry Cloud with the dog's head between my legs and me holding a towel around her head to shield her from the noise of the dryer. I told him that of course we would stay.

He led us into a downstairs bathroom that had been converted into a kind of dog spa. I urged Cloud into the tub and stood back while Alfredo shampooed her. Once her fur was wet and clinging to her body, I could see how much weight she had lost. I rubbed her ears through the towel and thought again about Billie's having said that I would not run away and start over with my dog. That she would, but I would not. But I no longer believed that anyone could start over. You can continue and grow, but you can't begin anew. People who believe you can don't understand the continuum of life.

I didn't want to see Cloud put into her kennel, as spacious and clean as it was, so we left while Alfredo was brushing her out. I was grateful for this vision of my girl—clean, soft, being cared for by someone who cared. Billie walked ahead of me, out into the muddy yard. The wetlands that bounded the property on one side were the reason they'd got the place at such a good price. That's what Alfredo had told us. Dogs didn't care if one side of the seven-acre property was marshy. I was glad we were leaving while it was still light. The view from the heated garage's window, Cloud's new view, was wetlands, and she loved the water.

"I got a text from McKenzie," Billie told me as we got into the car.

"Just now?"

"When he got the photos of Cloud."

"What did he say?"

"That he can finally put your case to bed."

Finally? I reached into my tote bag for a Kleenex, just to have something to do to break the thought.

"I should tell him I can't make it tonight. Could you get my phone out of my bag?"

I reflexively reached for her phone when she asked if I would text him since she was driving. Now I was the go-between.

She dictated, *Rain check. Unless you'll be up late?*

"You hungry?" Billie asked.

"I could use a drink."

"There's a bar in Danbury, a few miles ahead. We can shoot some pool while we drink."

Billie drove to an Irish pub, Molly Darcy's. A drum set and a couple of coffin-size amplifiers were onstage, but it wasn't yet seven, too early for live music. There was even a dance floor, empty now, but the scuff marks promised it wouldn't be empty for long. Maybe a dozen customers sat on garnet-red stools facing a soundless soccer match on a flatscreen on the wall. The pool table was free. I ordered two beers while Billie racked up.

She chalked the tip of a cue stick, collected the balls from the trough under the table, and filled the rack. She walked to the far side of the table.

I wondered why Billie was taking the time to shoot pool with me when she could have been meeting up with McKenzie. A choice I would not have made.

I watched her sink two more balls. "You didn't tell me you were a hustler." It was less a game than an exhibition as she leaned over to make her shots in such a way that her black tank top gapped and showed her black lace bra.

Billie missed the next shot and handed me the cue.

"I only ever played solids and stripes," I said, paving the way to a second-rate show of skill. There would be no show of skin with me; I was more than demure in a vintage T-shirt and skinny jeans. I had pulled my hair into a ponytail to reduce interference, but the bangs I had recently cut on a whim fell in my eyes anyway.

"No excuses."

I sank two balls in corner pockets, then scratched.

Billie dispatched the next four, then reached for the bridge to make a seriously difficult shot—she had to bank off three sides before sinking it. She didn't waste a motion.

I finished my beer and watched as she cleared the table. "Next round is on me," I said, conceding defeat, "unless you want to get going."

"I earned another beer. I'll rack 'em up again."

She retrieved the rack and started to fill it. A couple of guys who had been drinking at the bar walked over to the pool table. I didn't know how long they had been watching.

These guys were just off a construction job, looked like. They wore flannel shirts tucked into loose jeans, scuffed boots, and looked like men—none of that androgynous look you found in Williamsburg. When they saw Billie looking them over, they raised their beers and suggested a bet. Billie took them up on it. When she could have been with McKenzie.

"Come meet our new boyfriends." Billie waved me over.

I did not appreciate being implicated, but I gave the men a noncommittal "Hey." I told Billie it had been a long day.

"Why are you being a wet blanket?" Billie reminded me that we were allowed to celebrate the successful transfer of Cloud to her new home.

I wasn't buying it; this had nothing to do with Cloud.

The tall one asked where she'd learned to shoot pool like that.

"My grandmother. She met my grandfather that way. Hustled him."

The tall one raised his bottle in salute.

"You want to break?" Billie asked.

"You think I need the advantage?" The tall one looked over at his pal, and I knew the look that passed between them: Was the short one okay to partner up with me, since the tall one had already chosen Billie?

"You okay with me taking this one?" Billie asked me. I didn't know if she meant the game or the guy. She must have seen me try to parse what she'd asked because she turned to rack up the balls.

Billie took the break, landed a ball, and didn't miss a single shot after that.

The game, if you could call it that, went so fast that I was spared the job of making conversation with the short one. The tall one took his loss well.

The cover band had started up just before Billie's win. The tall one put his drink down and took Billie's hand. The song the band played for their dance was Toby Keith's "How Do You Like Me Now?!" Not the easiest to dance to, but rousing. I made my excuses to the short one, citing a sudden pulled muscle, and he looked relieved. We slid into a booth and watched his pal and Billie on the dance floor instead.

A couple of couples were attempting a sort of line dance. It was just them and Billie and the tall one on the floor, so we had no trouble holding them in our sights. Everyone knows that a man who can dance walks onto a dance floor unlike a man who cannot. The way the tall one led Billie onto the floor conveyed ownership. That was something to see—Billie allowing herself to be led by a man. She had the confidence to be submissive; it cost her nothing.

To my surprise, Billie could not keep up with the tall one. He led her around the floor in a two-step, but she stepped wrong and laughed. Drawing him to her, she set the pace for the next part of the dance. Slow and suggestive, even when the band finished, and then started in on Miranda Lambert's "White Liar." Nicely timed—I sang along in my head, *The truth comes out a little at a time.*

I let the short one buy me another beer.

Billie and the tall one joined us in the booth when the song ended. The tall one kept his arm around her, until Billie shook it off. His arm went back up to her shoulder, and Billie turned on him: "What do you think you're doing?" I could see that he thought she was kidding. They had just been dry-humping on the dance floor.

The short one said, "I'm out of here." He nodded a good-bye to me, then looked expectantly at his friend. It struck me that even he sensed something was off.

The tall one, however, was another matter. He was into her and said, "Play you for another dance."

"We've got to leave. Morgan?"

I grabbed my purse and stood up to go. Billie was already heading to the door. She asked me to drive and tossed me the keys.

As I was starting the car, the tall one knocked on my window and said to Billie, "Get your ass back in there."

"My boyfriend is waiting for me," Billie called out.

"Oh, your boyfriend is waiting." The tall one's face colored. "What, you come up from the city to fuck with the locals? That your idea of a good time?"

"Remember that girl at the bar? Blonde. Drinking alone. Ask her what song makes her cry but she's ashamed to admit it." Billie looked at me when she said the words. I thought it was a look of scorn, but then I felt certain it was impatience—she had had to hand it to me.

Billie said to the tall one, "You come tell me her answer and I'll go back inside with you." He strode off. "God love him, men are so predictable."

She had thought this through. She had picked her moment. She had gotten rid of the men and gotten me into her car in an empty parking lot.

I grabbed the door handle but Billie stopped me. She was holding a gun. "Just drive."

"Where are we going?"

"Head south for now."

I considered crashing the car, but feared the gun would go off, so I did what she told me to do. Feelings of stupidity nearly trumped fear. My hands were steady on the wheel; physically, I was surprisingly calm.

"What's today, Friday?" Billie asked. "By tomorrow night, guests at the Omni King Edward in Toronto will start complaining to the front desk about the taste of the water."

I had no idea what she was talking about. I looked down at the gun. The safety was off.

"A body in water, as in a water tower, decomposes about twice as fast as a dry one. It takes about forty-eight hours for a body in water to release enough gases to be detected."

"Who's in the water tower?" I knew who was in the water tower. I knew Samantha had paid for the room at the Omni. I changed lanes so that I might sideswipe the barrier on the passenger side. But at sixty miles an hour, could I control the car when it hit?

"You tell me."

I was strategizing desperately. What was in my best interest—playing dumb, or tipping my hand? "How would I know?"

"Process of elimination."

"I can guess who, but I can't guess why."

"That *would* interest you. What interests *me* is why you think you're not in the water tower."

I held the car at a steady sixty. Billie's question was not rhetorical. "I've been asking myself the same thing."

"Causality is overrated," Billie said, seeming to reverse her stance. "I mean, shit happens."

Coming up was a split on the parkway—south to New York City or west to New Jersey. "Which lane?"

"Head into the city."

I did, and I did something else as well. I leaned on the horn. She wasn't going to shoot me at this speed. But she did—shoot, that is. She aimed at the roof and fired.

I screamed.

"If this doesn't bring help, honking sure won't. Oh, come on, let's talk. I've had no one to talk to since Bennett died."

"Was he the intended victim that morning?"

"There is no right or wrong answer to that."

But I knew that there was. I knew they had an assignation in my bed that morning.

Billie opened the glove compartment and removed a pack of gum. "Want a piece? It's sugarless."

I took one hand off the wheel and held it open. Billie used her free hand to remove the wrapper before placing the gum in my palm.

"Samantha wasn't a challenge. You told her yourself he was dead. And I came along and said, 'I'm alive.' You know who she believed. All I had to do was get her to Toronto."

"Samantha killed herself?" So Billie had gone to Toronto, not the Caribbean.

"Samantha couldn't swim. Ask me about Susan."

"Did Bennett know what you were planning?"

"Susan became tiresome. So earnest: the homeless, the homeless. I told Bennett to stop seeing her. He wouldn't, so I took over and it felt right. So you see, it was really Bennett's fault. Though isn't blame boring? Where does it get us?"

The gas gauge was nearing empty. I pointed this out to Billie and she said we were almost there.

"Interested in Pat?" she asked.

"That was you in the bushes."

"Who doesn't have a bathroom in their studio? I didn't care for her or her work, did you?" Billie didn't wait for an answer. "Though Bennett did. He kept up with it. He thought the nude self-portraits with pig hearts showed a bravery he hadn't seen before he left her. He wanted me to buy one, said it was a good investment. But when I saw the work in the studio that night, it only confirmed my opinion. It wasn't brave, I mean it wasn't a *human* heart. I think of what I did as collaboration."

I didn't dare take my eyes off the road.

"Oh, don't look like that."

Billie told me to take the 116th Street exit off the FDR, and soon we found a parking space in front of the shelter annex. Billie got out first, came around to my side, and took me by the arm. I felt the gun in my ribs.

It was just before 11:00 p.m., and Billie knew that the garage entrance would still be unlocked for about another fifteen minutes before the last of the kennel staff left for the night. Sure enough, Jose was unloading one of the industrial dryers in the garage. He said, *"Buenas noches,"* and didn't ask why we were there so late.

This was probably my last chance to enlist anyone's help, but Jose had already turned his back on us and resumed his work. There would be no imploring glance on my part; on the other hand, I had not endangered an innocent man.

We slipped past him into the wing that housed the overflow of small-dog cages. The only light came from the occasional red EXIT signs. No one was swabbing a hallway or hosing down a last kennel. Billie had timed our arrival perfectly. We walked down the hallway past ward after ward.

"I never did anything to you," I reminded Billie.

As we approached Medical, I started to shake. I thought surely she was going to euthanize me. I mean, what more fitting way to mock what mattered so much to me. But we didn't stop.

I knew that the moment we opened a ward door, the preternatural silence would explode with barking and wailing. Billie had slipped behind me. She didn't exactly tiptoe, but moved soundlessly, at the ready. As much of a performance as she'd given at the pool table, these movements were authentic. She was in her element, it seemed to me, and failure was not an option. It occurred to me that this rush was what she lived for. The moment she opened the ward door would be like the moment a skydiver jumps from the open door of a plane.

You could draw out that moment just before you jumped—or were pushed—but once you were in the air, it was out of your hands.

Billie opened the door of the ward that once held Cloud and George and motioned me inside with the gun.

I experienced the moment first as a visual. The single bulb was sparking like a strobe, so that each time Billie was illuminated, she was in a different pose. The dogs in their kennels were likewise lit like wild creatures in a lightning storm. I observed this before the wall of sound hit me. As expected, the noise was a visceral sensation; I felt my body vibrate with it. I could hear the different voices, different pitches. Some sounded baleful, others sounded frightened, still others frightening.

The next time Billie was visible, she held out a key ring. "Open these two." She waited for me to unlock the kennels. When the light next sparked, I looked to see which dogs I was freeing. For a blink, I saw two large, white dogs, ghosts in the dark that followed. Eerily, they made no sound. I recognized them as the Dogos Argentinos in the kennels that formerly housed Cloud and George. The mirrorlike stances of these dogs had spooked me the first time I saw them. I felt no more comfortable with them now that I was releasing them.

Billie knelt in front of the dogs and began singing a kind of lullaby to them, but in German. The dogs sat at attention, their eyes on Billie. Still singing to the dogs, Billie produced two slipknot leads and told me to loop them around the dogs' thick necks.

"Heidi and Gunther won't do anything without my permission."

"So these are your dogs."

"I belong to them as much as they belong to me."

"*Sitz*," Billie commanded.

The dogs sat.

"*Pass auf.*"

The dogs growled low in their throats.

She put her gun in her purse.

The dogs were attack-trained. I knew enough German from school to know that the second command meant "guard." I hoped they were not waiting for the command *Reeh veer*, "hunt." If Bennett's body were exhumed, I knew now that the bite marks would match the teeth of Billie's dogs.

I raced through the methods I had learned to disarm an attacker. I was outnumbered, so I had only two options: try to humanize myself in Billie's eyes, or run for safety if I could reach a safer place within five seconds. I had already failed at the first option. Before I could try the second, Billie ordered me to unlock a third kennel. I glanced at the kennel card above it and saw in the fractured light the red-inked word CAUTION—SEVERE.

"Morgan, meet Gotti," Billie said conversationally. "He is three years old and on hold for biting. Gotti, Morgan is a thirty-year-old female who is here for not seeing what was right in front of her."

A low growl came from Gotti. I was about to credit him for picking up on Billie's vibe, but then the two Dogos moved into view. Billie had not issued a verbal command for them to approach, and she yelled, "*Sitz*." One dog sat immediately, one walked behind Billie to assume the position on her other side. Gotti barked at the trio just outside his kennel door.

Billie told me to get inside. With a last rush of adrenaline, and everything to lose, I moved to the door of the cage, and just before slamming it behind me, I yanked Billie's purse off her shoulder, breaking the leather strap.

I had the gun. I also had the key ring. I locked myself inside.

There was an odd lull—the other dogs in the ward stopped barking as though they sensed a shift in command.

The dog beside me was standing, taller than I was in my crouch. I had enough room to stand up and move a couple of feet back from the door. I said, "Good dog," over and over, a mantra. Gotti was a large brindle pit bull. His ears had been cropped too close to his head and had a yeasty smell, evidence of infection.

I slipped my hand into Billie's purse and closed it around the handle of the gun. But the dog did not attack. I reached for my cell phone and pressed 911.

"What is your emergency?" a woman's voice asked.

"I need help. I'm at the animal shelter annex on 119th near the river."

The phone went dead, but I didn't know when—before or after I had given my location. But Billie didn't know that.

"I'm in Ward Four," I said to the dead phone. "A woman with attack dogs is holding me hostage."

I had kept my eyes on Billie while I spoke. At this last, she rolled her eyes and said, "You locked yourself in."

"Please hurry," I said to the dead phone.

"I'm disappointed in you, Gotti. You didn't keep up your end." Billie acted as if I did not have a gun pointed at her.

"The police will be here any minute," I bluffed.

"There's no signal here. Nobody's plan works in here."

She sat down cross-legged in front of the cage, just as she had done when visiting my dogs. "We never had a chance to compare notes about Bennett," she said brightly. "You'd been studying men who manipulate women, but the real fun starts when a woman manipulates a man to manipulate women."

"What did you get out of it?" I asked, genuinely curious.

"What *didn't* I get out of it? He entertained me. With all of you. You can't imagine how thrilling that kind of intimacy is. It is allegiance of the first order, a singular exchange. We held nothing back. We did not judge each other. Well, until he went soft."

The Dogos were spooking the pit bull. His hackles stood. He started snarling, though nobody had moved.

"I bet sleeping next to the wall isn't looking so scary right now. Don't blame Bennett for making you do that; it was my idea. That was getting to be his problem: no ideas. He was wasting his energy on you. When he stopped making fun of you and began to defend you, the fun went out of it. Sure, you take in foster dogs. But you get them killed."

She had gotten my fosters killed. Not the time to point that out.

"Still, he was drawn to virtue. He may not have felt compassion, but he began to seek it out. And the boy went overboard— he called it 'love' and proposed to all of you."

I still held the gun on Billie but my hand was tired. Billie noticed. I leaned against my side of the cage, and Gotti remained standing inches away.

"You want to know what happened that morning. Fair enough. He wasn't so far gone on you that he didn't welcome my visit to your bed. He was less welcoming to Heidi and Gunther. But as I told him, they had a vet appointment later that morning. I told him to put your dogs in the bathroom, and it wouldn't be a problem. But there was a problem: he couldn't get it up. That was a first. And he blamed it on me. I did this, I did that, and I brought the fucking dogs. The fucking dogs.

"I had left them outside the bedroom door in a down-stay. I got out of bed, pulled on my clothes, and Bennett failed to apologize."

The dog whose kennel I shared sniffed the gun and lost interest in it.

Billie had answered my questions, except for one—was I going to have to kill her?

"You going to write me up for your thesis? I'm more interesting than Bennett."

She was interrupted by the dogs in the ward, all of them, barking. Then I heard what had set them off. I thought I did—I thought I heard a man's voice call out from somewhere inside the shelter. I strained to hear, and I heard it again. Billie did, too. A man's voice, a little closer this time, called out so that we could hear the words: "Police! Is anyone there?"

Billie put a finger to her lips and looked out the wired-glass window in the ward door. Her dogs turned their heads in unison, keeping her in sight.

Billie ducked as the beam of a flashlight shone through the window.

I screamed, "I'm in here!"

"This next is on you." Billie opened the ward door and said to her dogs, "*Reeh veer!*"

They tore out into the hall, synchronized specters, their full attention on their prey.

Billie followed her dogs.

It sounded as though every dog in the place was barking. The noise disoriented me so that I couldn't pick out Billie's dogs from the rest, if Billie's dogs were even making a sound during their attack. But I could hear one of the cops yelling. Then he screamed. Why hadn't he used his gun? But I hadn't used my gun.

"Good boy," I said to my cellmate as I unlocked the kennel door.

The cop was on the ground, but he was no longer screaming. I couldn't tell if he was still alive, but the white dogs on top of him—I saw them in the dimly lit hall—were covered in blood.

I crept up behind Billie, intending to clock her with the gun I could not make myself fire. I would have to hit hard enough to keep her down. But if I whacked her, what would her dogs do? I had never hurt anyone, nor did I have the skill to hit a moving target. The thought made me sick to my stomach. Then I saw, to the left of me, the door into the fenced exercise yard. When I got out into the yard without Billie's seeming to see me, I had a thought I almost couldn't bear in case it didn't work: maybe I could get a signal on my phone.

In the dark yard, cluttered with balls and a coiled hose that tripped me, I held up the phone, waving it to try to catch a signal. But what I heard first was a gunshot from inside the shelter. One shot. Whom had the second cop fired on? One dog? That wouldn't stop the other. I waited for a second shot.

Instead I got a signal.

"What is your emergency?"

"A cop is being killed. We're on East 119th Street, the animal shelter. Please hurry."

The door into the backyard pushed open. Billie. And one of the Dogos at her side.

Billie made a show of looking around. "Can you imagine this is the only exercise yard they have?"

"Your dogs killed that cop."

"That cop killed one of my dogs."

I saw movement behind Billie. And so did the dog. The door

opened, and I saw the second cop with his gun drawn. Before the cop was all the way through, the Dogo lunged. The cop got off a shot, but the dog's attack on his firing arm caused the bullet to hit Billie. She went down, but was not unconscious. She swore and clutched her leg. The Dogo had knocked the cop's gun out of his hand with such force that it had skittered across the pavement, stopping closer to Billie than to me.

I kicked it past Billie's reach and turned my attention to the Dogo and the cop. The cop was on his back, twisting and fending off the dog with his arms. I took aim but didn't trust myself to hit the dog and not the cop.

"Make him stop!" I yelled at Billie.

"It's the female. That's Heidi."

I turned the gun on Billie. "Make her stop," I said evenly.

"Like you're going to shoot me."

As much as I wanted to, she was right.

I shot at the dog and dropped her.

I heard sirens over the chaotic barking, meaning a full-on response—a cop was down. I turned the gun on Billie and waited for the police to find us.

"You can't say it hasn't been an education," Billie said.

"Out here," I yelled, not knowing if the cops could hear me yet.

"Always looking to a man to save you."

Then the door to the exercise yard opened. A stream of cops, guns drawn, pushed through.

"Drop your weapon," one of them yelled. For an odd moment I didn't realize he was addressing me. "Put down the gun."

I set the gun down.

One of the cops kicked it away from me and said, "Down on

the ground." He kicked my legs apart, frisked me, grabbed my arms, and twisted them behind my back to handcuff me.

"She shot me," Billie called out. "My leg. I can't walk."

"Get the EMTs out here," one of the cops yelled to another.

"Is the other officer okay?" Billie asked.

"I'm not the one you should be worried about," I said to the cop holding me down. He said nothing, just yanked me to my feet.

"You hurt anywhere else?" one of the cops asked Billie.

"She came out of nowhere. I'm just a volunteer."

The EMTs arrived and began working on the mauled cop. Seconds later, another pair moved quickly into the yard and knelt beside Billie.

"Were you shot anywhere besides your leg?" an EMT asked.

"I can't feel my leg."

I finally found my voice. "Those white dogs are hers. They're attack dogs. She commanded them to attack the officers."

"I don't think I'm hit anywhere else," Billie said.

A cop came into the yard and said to his partner, the one who was holding me, "We lost Scott. Fucking dogs ripped his throat open." The cop grabbed me by the throat. "I should rip your fucking throat out."

"Not here," said the cop holding me.

After the EMTs got an IV going for Billie, they lifted her onto a stretcher, but waited for the unconscious cop to be evacuated first.

Despite the activity all around me, I sensed things as being done in slow motion. I looked up at the run-down apartment buildings that flanked the open backyard. Lights were on, windows were open, and people on every floor were watching and taking pictures with their phones.

A dozen or so cops moved to surround me—the guilty one—
and pushed me back inside. When they marched me past the
body of the dead cop, they stopped and forced me to look. I threw
up. Billie was right—this one was on me.

Out front, the scene was militaristic; helicopters shone search-
lights on the shelter. As I was being shoved into a squad car, one
of the cops Mirandized me.

A convoy of squad cars escorted me to a precinct, the 25th. I
was taken straight to an interrogation room and handcuffed to
the table.

I had the good citizen's certainty that I would be cleared. But
I felt the soul-honing fear that I would not.

There would be no witness if the second cop died. Even if he
lived, he didn't know who was responsible. It would be Billie's
word against mine, and she had the bullet in her body.

They thought I was a cop killer. Maybe, by default, I was. I'd had a chance to kill Billie and her dogs and I hadn't taken it. I started itching all over. I felt welts rising on my back, on my chest. It made me short of breath. Anxiety could produce any number of somatic symptoms, I knew. I both wanted someone to come into the room and feared it. I was twisting in the chair, trying to scratch my back. And I had to urinate.

I gave up looking at my watch after the first hour. With no idea who might be watching me through the one-sided glass, I struggled with my free hand to pull down my jeans enough to go right there on the floor of the interrogation room. Give them a show, if that's what they were determined to wait for.

I angled my body as much as I could away from the glass and squatted. But after waiting so long, I wasn't able to release my bladder right away. I prayed that no one would enter the room now. Though maybe some of the officers were having a good laugh just outside.

The puddle covered a large area under the table I was handcuffed to and leaked out beyond the chair I had occupied. Easier to pull pants down with one hand, I discovered, than to get them back up. There was no getting the zipper up. It did not escape me that soiling their own space was what caged dogs were left to do.

Two plainclothes detectives came in, one holding a folder, the other holding his nose. "The fuck did you do in here?"

"When do I get my call?"

The disgusted one banged on the door. "Get us some paper towels." When a roll of paper towels was delivered, he tossed it to me and told me to clean up the floor.

"I'm handcuffed."

"You managed to pull down your pants."

I made no motion toward doing what he said. "I want my phone call."

The one with the folder said, "Do you know a Jimmy Gordon?"

I repeated what I wanted.

He tried again, this time showing me a photograph of the crime scene—my bedroom.

"Phone call."

"You just got a cop killed. If I were you, I'd start cooperating," said the detective who'd called for paper towels.

"I want my lawyer." I sensed the detectives were trying to employ the outdated Reid technique of interrogation—I'd learned about it in first-year psychology. A cop looks for signs of anxiety during questioning: folded arms, shifty gaze, jiggling leg, touching one's hair. They try to play down moral consequences—"Hey, everybody fights with her boyfriend." The irony is that the case policeman John Reid made his name on turned out to be a false confession.

One of the detectives signaled at the window for a phone, and in a moment he opened the door and was handed a desk phone. He plugged the line into a jack in the wall and set it down in front of me. "Local only."

I phoned Steven.

"I've been waiting up for you." His relief was palpable.

"They might be listening."

"Is Billie with you?"

"I'm at the precinct in East Harlem. Billie's in the hospital."

"Tell me you're okay."

"I'm handcuffed to a table in an interrogation room."

"Make sense."

"I understand more right now than I have in the last six months. They haven't charged me yet, but I think I'm being held as a cop killer."

"Don't say anything until I get there."

Before hanging up, I asked Steven to let McKenzie know, too.

The detectives took the phone with them when they left me in the interrogation room. They left the roll of paper towels, and knowing my brother would be coming for me, I tore off a large wad and started cleaning up the floor, in case he was brought to this room.

By the time I'd left a mound of wet paper towels under the table, the detectives were back, announcing that they were taking me to Central Booking.

"But my brother is coming here."

"Tell him to call you a lawyer."

"He *is* a lawyer."

"He'll have to go downtown to see you" is all the detective offered.

I rode in a squad car with the two detectives who'd questioned me. I remembered the day at John Jay that the professor had brought in a Yelp one-star review of Central Booking. I loved that such a thing existed, and when the professor read it aloud, the class went nuts: "Let me start off by saying . . . *Yo myyyy niggggggaaaaa!!!!!* I came out that fucker speaking Ebonics. I am college educated, yeah, that don't mean shit. I manage a pharmaceutical company. I deal with hundreds of professional people in health care who have MDs, PhDs, and degrees in shit I can't even pronounce. The word nigga this, nigga that, nigga who, nigga what. That's all I fucking heard."

Yes, I had memorized it, it was that vivid. Maybe I'd be writing my own.

We cut across Chinatown to the two gray, windowless buildings on White Street—the courthouse and the Tombs, connected by a three-story-high, windowless walkway. Richard Haas's mural *Immigration on the Lower East Side* runs across the facade of the detention center. The irony is that its placement seems to send the immigrants straight to jail.

I was processed in the manner known to anyone who watches TV crime shows. But it was one thing to have watched from the comfort of one's couch, eating chocolate, and another to be stripsearched in Central Booking. I was escorted to a cell where, to my relief, I was the only occupant. So far. I could hear trash-talking female prisoners nearby, but I couldn't see them. And then a chorus of "Yo—CO!" that went unheeded. The place was freezing. Had I heard that the Tombs was kept at forty degrees?

I should be able to prove that Billie brought the two Dogos Argentinos into the shelter. I should be able to prove that she was in my house the morning Bennett was killed—it was there in Libertine's e-mails, the e-mails that also proved she killed Susan Rorke and Samantha. But do e-mails constitute proof?

I figured I had a few hours until morning. I had been made to voucher my watch, but it must have been at least 3:00 a.m. The metal bench I sat on was so slippery that I nearly slid off it. Sleeping was out of the question. This was the poet's "dark night of the soul." The first thought to slay me was that I was responsible for a man's death, and the serious injury of another. The blame game did no one any good, as Billie said, but there it was. I read some of the graffiti on the cell walls. *Never pick up a dead man's gun. Forgive me, but I have little choice in these matters. Do whatever you think is in your best interests.*

I was treated to an argument from one of the bull pens. Two women fighting about who would get the phone next.

My thoughts went from logical and practical concerns to images and feelings I never wanted to confront again. I actually felt the moment I "snapped to" and found that I was sitting on the floor of the cell, hunched up in the position I took in my bathtub after finding Bennett's body. I knew what was happening to me: a version of post-traumatic stress. I had just seen a man killed by dogs for the second time. I made myself take deep breaths to try to avoid hyperventilating and to slow my pulse. I made myself envision peaceful scenes of the sea—white-sand beaches, floating in aquamarine water the same temperature as my skin. But even my go-to vision failed—the warm water felt like blood.

I stood and paced the cell. I remembered a story that Steven had told me when he came home from Afghanistan. While visiting a prison, he noticed an isolated cell at the end of a dank hallway. He looked through the tiny hole in the door and saw a young girl, maybe thirteen years old, lying in a heap facing the door with a blank stare, nothing else in the cell but a cot. No sink or toilet. He asked his interpreter to ask the warden what she was in jail for. The warden explained that her father had brought her there because she'd run away with her boyfriend and their families caught them, and then they ran away again. Steven asked why she had no water and why she was kept so isolated—wasn't that cruel? The warden said yes, he felt bad for her, but he had no female prison guards to take care of her. The girl was going crazy from this, Steven could see; he reported it to the US embassy, and they eventually negotiated her release.

It was quiet now; the women's argument about the phone had stopped. No COs were present. I was in the Tombs—buried alive.

This night would either dismantle me or show me what I was made of. Another person might find herself galvanized by the extremity of the situation, find herself searching for what she might have missed that led to one cop's death and another's mauling. Go over every opportunity to have stopped Billie, to have prevented the carnage. But that would not change what had happened.

I sat on the floor, leaning against a wall, and the first lines of an Emily Dickinson poem came to me: "After great pain, a formal feeling comes— / The Nerves sit ceremonious, like Tombs—" Of course that was why it came to me there.

That was the last thought I had until I was awakened by the sound of keys, and a CO saying, "When I call your name, step out, shut up. You're going into court. Don't say a word. Don't motion to anyone in the court. Just sit, look straight ahead, until they call your name."

Half a dozen names were called, but not mine.

Two cops came for me about ten minutes later. My wrists were handcuffed and secured to a belt around my waist. I was driven to the Criminal Courthouse, less than a hundred yards away, for the traditional "perp walk" up the granite steps.

Once the squad car pulled up, a swarm of reporters with cameras and microphones were waiting for me. I was led past the press into the courthouse. I was taken on an elevator up to the fourth floor, to a small booth off a holding cell where Steven was waiting. The cops left me alone with my brother.

"Fucking unbelievable." Steven hugged me and kissed my forehead.

At his touch, I started to cry. "What happens now?"

"They're going to charge you with murder. Of a cop."

"But the dogs were Billie's. I was the target, not the cop."

"Listen, we only have a few minutes. I'm going to ask for bail, but we can't count on it."

"What about the second cop? Is he going to be okay?"

"He's in ICU at Columbia Presbyterian. He's expected to survive."

"Not to sound self-serving, but will he be able to talk soon? Maybe he saw what really happened."

"You'll know when I know."

"Is that where Billie is?"

"She was released this morning. It was just a flesh wound. Her grandmother took her home."

"But her dogs killed a cop."

"She told the police that you let the dogs loose from their cages. What do you know about those dogs?"

"Billie gave them commands in German. They were attack-trained."

"Jesus."

I told him I knew how suspected cop killers were treated. I'd read Mumia Abu-Jamal's book, *Live from Death Row*. I had seen the infamous video of Esteban Carpio, beaten un-recognizable and made to wear a Hannibal Lecter–like mask, escorted to his arraignment for killing a cop. I told Steven that if convicted, I would spend twenty-three hours a day in complete isolation.

An officer unlocked the holding cell and told Steven to wrap it up. Steven told me he'd see me in the courtroom in a couple of minutes.

The courtroom was right next door. The officer led me in and sat me at the defense table. To my right, a door opened, and a group of women wearing orange jumpsuits and handcuffs were directed into the jury box. Talk about a jury of your peers.

Steven entered the courtroom through the public entrance and joined me at the table.

The judge read the charges. Steven indicated the moment when I was to declare myself "not guilty." It was over in less than half an hour. Bail denied.

The only way I could tell the time was by the arrival of meals, not that I could eat. The smell of urine and feces was constant. I didn't want to lie down on the bench; I tried to touch as few surfaces as possible. My breath was sour from vomiting the night before. My clothes were rank. The itching had subsided, but the welts remained. Anxiety had mutated to dread—of the next ten minutes, and the rest of my life.

Shortly after lunch—a bologna sandwich and a small carton of milk—which I didn't touch, a CO collected me, again in handcuffs, and walked me around the corner to a tiny office where McKenzie was waiting.

"You can take the cuffs off her," McKenzie said, standing.

"You sure?" the CO said.

McKenzie waved him off and waited while the CO unlocked me. When we were alone, McKenzie pulled me into a hug and held me for a long time. Of all the things I should have been worrying about, I worried about the way I looked and smelled.

"You know Billie did this, right?"

"I've already been to the shelter and checked the intake records. They show that the Dogos were surrendered by 'Morgan Prager.'" He watched for my reaction.

"Of course."

"Steven told me they were attack-trained. I checked with all the training schools in the tristate, and no one has worked with

Dogos in the last couple of years. Which means that she had them trained somewhere else, or she trained them herself. Do you have any idea where she might have kept them?"

"I never went to her home."

"Neither did I." My gratitude for what he had just told me must have been evident, because he repeated what he had just said. "And the address she gave when she worked for me was fake."

"Her grandmother has a horse farm in Connecticut."

"The family's lawyer told me I'll need a court order to search the property."

"Wherever she kept them, she's had them for six months at least." I asked what the press was doing with the story.

"They'll be on to something else tomorrow."

"I hope it's the murders of Susan Rorke, Pat Loewi, and Samantha Couper."

"I got it all from Steven."

"She wouldn't be the first person to get away with murder," I said.

"People slip up, even someone like Billie."

"Unless they don't."

"Steven's lining up a criminal defense attorney right now. Carol Anders will be here in the morning. She's first-rate; she was in practice with my wife.

"And now that that's out of the way, I can tell you I met with Billie before she was released from the hospital. Her grandmother was in the room—this was early this morning. With no reason to believe she would, I went there to try to get her to cooperate, to tell the truth. I asked where she had kept the Dogos. Her grandmother told me not to bother her, and Billie suggested her grandmother go down to the cafeteria for coffee while we talked.

"She became furious, but in this quiet, icy way. She couldn't risk drawing the attention of medical staff, so she kept her voice down, but the rage in her eyes was absolute. She knew I believed you and not her. And she saw she couldn't control me."

"You met Libertine." I told McKenzie the whole story.

"I knew there was something off from the start."

"But you kept seeing her."

"It's a cliché, I know, but she was like a drug. I didn't come down until she came to work in my office. I saw the way she treated people she didn't need anything from." He raised his hand to signal the impatient guard standing outside that he needed five more minutes. "She never asked about the second cop, if he was going to make it. I think she feels she's getting away with everything. And I think she's enjoying it."

"That's why she's so dangerous. I just found the silver lining to my incarceration. Billie can't get to me in here."

"I've got an investigator continuing the Dogos search. And we're hoping the injured cop will be able to give a statement soon."

I asked him to contact the Boston detective, to tell him about the e-mails I had read in which Billie as Libertine had confessed to killing Susan Rorke.

I asked him the question that had occurred to me before: "Are e-mails admissible as evidence?"

"If you can verify who sent them." McKenzie apologized for having to leave me here. He said he could do more for me outside.

No way I could argue with that. I could do nothing.

• • •

I could do nothing, that is, except conjure the single act that might exonerate me.

After McKenzie left, I was told I had to wait in my cell until there were enough "bodies"—that's what they called us—to bring upstairs. There, we were handcuffed behind our backs to another prisoner and marched down the stairs to street level, where a bus to Rikers Island was idling. It was awkward to sit while shackled to someone else, and the bus's shocks were all but gone; since we were traveling on some of the city's worst surface roads, the ride was painful. I had only ever entered Rikers as a grad student, there to get the required credit hours for clinical training. I had the absurd impulse to pull rank, immediately squelched by the woman I was shackled to, who didn't stop coughing. Shalonda, the transsexual I was fond of, had told me that the incidence of tuberculosis at Rikers is three times higher than in the city, and mostly drug-resistant.

We women were separated from the men and led to the Rose M. Singer Center, the women's prison. I was freed from my partner, taken to a small ward with only eight doors, and put in a cell. I didn't know where the rest of the women were taken.

My cell had a platform with a mattress, a metal sink, an exposed toilet, and a desk of sorts, attached to a wall. I sat on the bed on full alert. All those sessions I had conducted with inmates—was the guy who couldn't stop telling jokes still here? The guy who had exposed himself in the Metropolitan Museum? I remembered Shalonda's last words to me: "It's a good feeling to surprise yourself—you'll see."

I lay down, folding my arms behind my head since no pillow was provided. Nothing was on the filthy, long-ago-whitewashed cinder-block walls to snag my attention. No graffiti. I willed myself to envision a bedroom that was the opposite of where I was.

Whose bedroom came to mind? Billie's, the one at her grand-mother's estate. Not a bedroom so much as a wing, a gallery, I recalled. Those white-carpeted floors, the paintings displayed, blue-chip art by Motherwell and de Kooning. And in the adjoining room, the electrifying black canvas with the red shape like the letter *H* filled with blood. This last by Loewi. Pat's grandfather.

My breathing changed.

I was back in Pat's studio, her showing me the naked photos of herself, and that dog of hers, the rottweiler, throwing herself against the window. She had not been found when Pat's body was discovered.

How had I missed this? Billie had brought a rottweiler to For Pitties' Sake. When she and I drove up there, she had asked Alfredo how the dog she'd brought in was doing. I remembered what Billie had said to him: "I worried about that one."

I asked a guard if I could make a phone call.

It took McKenzie no time to find out that the rottweiler was microchipped. The information the vet scanned showed Pat Loewi as the dog's owner. Alfredo said that Billie had told him the owner had died, so he had not scanned the chip. He said he would be willing to testify that Billie brought the rottweiler in. He said it freaked him out that the dog he had been caring for was evidence in a murder investigation.

McKenzie updated Amabile's detective cousin, Bienvenido, at the Suffolk County PD, since Pat's case was in his jurisdiction.

Steven had already picked up my computer and turned it over to the police, whose forensic computer expert traced Libertine's IP address to Billie.

Once the police suspected Billie, they impounded her car, and even though she'd had it detailed since that trip, they found fur that matched the Dogos.

Billie was taken into custody at her grandmother's house. I like to think that she was put in the cell I had vacated. Carol Anders, the criminal attorney Steven and McKenzie had retained for me, got the charges against me dropped once Billie was picked up. She was charged with the murder of a police officer and the attempted murder of a second, and the murder of Pat Loewi. After another couple of days the Boston police found the hammer that had killed Susan Rorke. Billie had hidden it in the same closet at her grandmother's house where she had kept her toys. The Tiramisu lipstick found in Billie's glove compartment had been used by Samantha Couper—DNA proved it. The New York police turned this evidence over to the Toronto police, and the murder of Samantha Couper was added to the list of charges. Which left Bennett. Or Jimmy Gordon. The DA told me that in order to charge Billie with this murder, Jimmy's body would need to be exhumed. I thought of what that would do to his mother. New York had eliminated the death penalty in 2007; Billie would not be getting out of prison even without a conviction for his murder.

I knew some people looked for—believed in—closure. How I loathed that false notion, that one could tie up the loose ends of mystery and grief. Did that mean one stopped being haunted day and night? Did it mean one could get on with one's life, such as it was? I thought it was a cruel term, a grail that could never be found. But maybe some people did find it. Or convinced themselves that they did.

Whatever works.

As someone who had been deeply conned by not one person, but two, and not just conned, but exposed to a multiple murderer, I found myself examining both my suitability for the work I had chosen and the definition of the people I had been studying. Neither the term *sociopath* nor *psychopath* appears in the *DSM-5*. The closest term to *sociopath* is *antisocial personality disorder*. The criteria for diagnosis include impairments in self-esteem, self-direction, empathy, intimacy, plus the use of manipulation and deceit, and the presence of hostility, callousness, irresponsibility, impulsivity, and a lack of concern for one's limitations: risk-taking.

The most widely used test for psychopathy is the PCL–R—Psychopathy Checklist–Revised—also known as Hare's Checklist. The Canadian psychologist Robert Hare has pointed out that sociologists are more likely to focus on environmental or socially modifiable facets, whereas psychologists and psychiatrists include the genetic, cognitive, and emotional factors when making a diagnosis.

I did use Billie as the case study for the final chapter of my thesis. I ended with the question *Should these people be forgiven?*

I could not forgive myself.

Forgive yourself for what? my brother and McKenzie asked.

For thinking the best of people? For having a trusting heart? But I needed to find another way to think about forgiveness—some people think the ability to forgive will just come to them at a certain point, but others recognize that it can be a choice. That it can manifest as another form of empathy, a gift to oneself.

Billie's grandmother's money bought a team of attorneys who are fighting to get Billie committed to a private psychiatric hospital rather than prison. This despite the fact that psychopaths are believed not to benefit at all from psychiatric intervention. She is being held for now in the Kirby Forensic Psychiatric Center, a maximum-security hospital of the New York State Office of Mental Health, where she is being evaluated by a state psychiatrist for the prosecution and by eminent expert witnesses for the defense. It is the large, grim-looking structure that Billie and I saw across the Harlem River the day we got Cloud out of the shelter and walked her along the water, letting her taste and sniff her freedom.

When you meet someone during a crisis, you have immediate history, Cilla had told me. You skip over the petty revelations and embarrassments. You bypass the quotidian and go right to the core.

McKenzie had seen me in jail. He'd seen me gullible, afraid, and jealous. He'd seen me miss what was right in front of me. Yet he had seen me.

And wanted to see me again. We all have a fantasy that collides with reality. I would not have pictured a first kiss when I was just released from Rikers with dirty hair, unbathed, feeling less desirable than I ever had. But that is when McKenzie pulled me into him and held my face—that gesture that is both tender and possessive—and kissed me. I thought of the old song Betty Everett sang, "If you want to know if he loves you so, it's in his kiss." The reality was better than the fantasy. Better because desire was fused with ease, not the anxiety that accompanies obsession. Better because he had been courtly—I noted the pun even as the word occurred to me—and because I knew who this man was.

McKenzie filed a petition to get Cloud released a week after my own release.

He had offered to drive me to the sanctuary to pick her up, but I wanted to go by myself. I passed the Kirby Forensic Psychiatric Center as I drove along the FDR north and out of the city. Billie was behind one of those thousand barred windows.

The day was clear with a few clouds that, according to weather reports, would gather in the late afternoon, possibly bringing showers. There was little traffic, and I was content to drive at the posted speed limit, even though I was headed to get my dog back. I did not turn on the radio or put in a CD. I reveled in the clarity I had in the aftermath of finding myself alive. I was proud to know that I had fought for my life. It seems obvious— that a person would fight for her life—but it wasn't at the time. This is not to overlook luck, that I was lucky, too. It was humbling to acknowledge how much luck was involved.

It would be another forty minutes or so until I would reach the exit for the bar where Billie had revealed herself as Libertine.

The transformation still unnerved me. Over a couple of drinks, she had exhibited five of the seven hallmarks of a psychopath.

I pulled Steven's car into a gas station. I used to feel that I was not put on this earth to pump my own gas, but I had come to enjoy it. Something about simply knowing how to do it, and the instant gratification of filling the tank. I paid cash and got the lower price for doing so.

I was coming up on the turnoff to Greenwich, where Billie's grandmother lived. I had seen her again when I testified before the grand jury. She was sitting by herself on a bench just outside the courtroom. There's a saying: a young woman dresses to please, an old woman dresses not to *dis*please. Billie's grandmother was impeccable in a timeless Chanel suit with the accompanying strands of pearls. She had mastered the art of looking through a person and gave a demonstration when I tried to catch her eye. When my name was called and I entered the courtroom, I saw that Billie, who was sitting at a table with her defense team, looked as though she'd been dressed by her grandmother. I had never seen her in a suit before, or in stockings and low-heeled pumps. Her long hair was caught and tied in a high ponytail. She wore no makeup and looked benign. Unlike her grandmother, Billie made eye contact with me, not that I could read her expression. I might have been a docent in a museum, pointing out the brush technique of an old master. Mild interest, that was all she seemed to register, her indictment as something to pass the time.

It was just before noon when I pulled up the driveway to For Pitties' Sake. Alfredo was down by the agility course, walking two dogs. One was my Cloud, and the other was a blue-nose pittie. The dogs were in step with each other, I could see, and

when Alfredo saw me, he waved and steered the dogs in my direction. He handed off the pit bull to an assistant who had come
from the house. Then he released Cloud's leash and I called her
name. From about a hundred yards away, Cloud lifted her head.
I called her name again. This time she lowered her head and ran
toward me. When she got about ten feet away, she slowed her
pace so she didn't knock me over. Just in front of me, she threw
herself onto her back and kicked her legs in the air. I lay down in
the grass beside her and let her roll onto me. We held each other
that way, until Cloud pressed her forehead into mine; we used to
do this—press our foreheads together and close our eyes. Well,
I closed *my* eyes—when I would open mine, Cloud would be
gazing at me.

"You're going home, girl," Alfredo said to Cloud, then to me,
"She fooled everyone, that Billie. But she never fooled the dogs.
That rottie she brought in. I thought she was frightened of Billie
the same way she was frightened of everyone." Alfredo dropped
down beside us on the grass. "When Billie brought her in, I
should have known this dog had seen something that scared it.
The dog was healthy, but something spooked her bad."

"The dog witnessed her owner's murder."

"She said that Audie had belonged to an old man who died.
She said that Audie had been in the house with the body for a
couple of days before someone found them."

"How is the dog doing?" I remembered thinking that the dog
was behaving weirdly that day in Pat's studio, but Audie was in
fact behaving appropriately, given that Billie was in the woods
just outside. I wondered how Billie had subdued Audie. Did Pat
open the door to Billie's knock, thinking it was me coming back?
Did Billie bring meat laced with drugs?

"Turns out she's the sweetest thing. She protects the smaller dogs here, and I trust her with all of them," Alfredo said. "There's a term you've heard? The *blossom*? A dog finds herself out of a bad situation and can trust that she is safe?"

She blossoms.

ACKNOWLEDGMENTS

The authors wish to thank the following people for different kinds of help with this book: Rebecca Ascher-Walsh, Scott Ciment, Yolanda Crous, Martha Gallahue, Chiu-yin Hempel, Susanne Kirk, Jeff Latzer, Pearson Marx, Arnold Mesches, Barbara Oakley and her book *Cold-Blooded Kindness*, and, as coeditor, *Pathological Altruism*, our superb agents, Liz Darhansoff and Gail Hochman, and, at Scribner: Dan Cuddy, Daniel Loedel, Paul O'Halloran, and, especially, our impeccable editor, Nan Graham, whose enthusiasm, precision, and wisdom saw us through this collaboration.